Shattered Illusions

by

Neive Denis

Book six in the Sonoma Whittington series

Copyright

Cataloguing-in-publication data
Creator: Denis, Neive, author

Cataloguing-in-Publication details are available from the
National Library of Australia
www.trove.nla.gov.au

ISBN: 978-0-6483950-1-0 (paperback)
ISBN: 978-0-6483950-2-7 (digital edition)

Cover design: T A Marshall, Mackay QLD Australia

Table of Contents

Map of Regents Bay Area

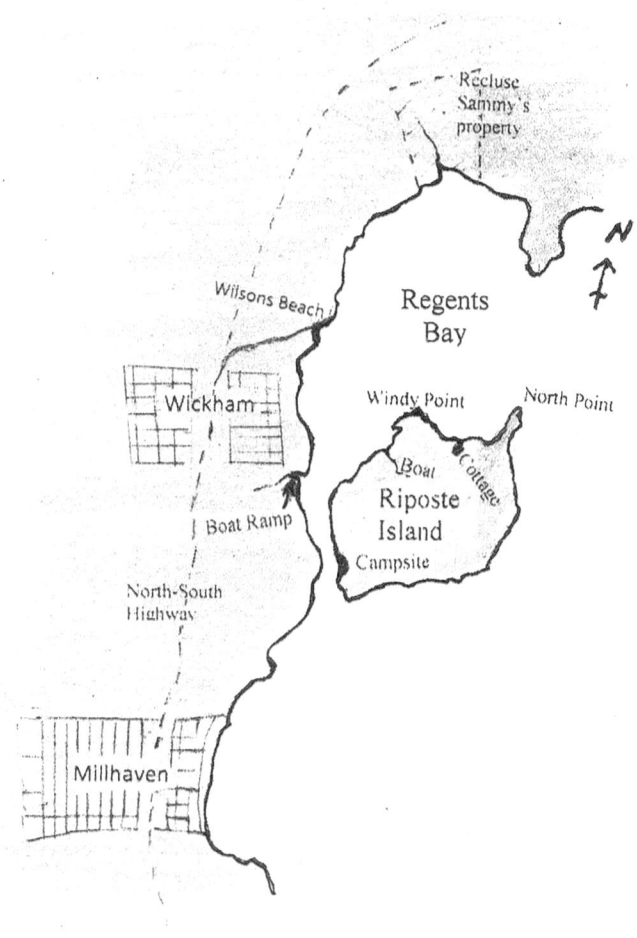

Chapter 1

"Hello. Yes, this is Whittington Investigations. How can I help? …I'm sorry. I didn't catch your name. … Hensley... Hensley… Your name is familiar but I … Oh yes, now I remember. It is a while since you called. I seem to remember your call then was about your business. Something to do with suspicions about your patrols, but nothing came of your enquiry on that occasion … Okay … Good, I'm glad my memory didn't let me down. So, what's the reason for this call?"

Emily Inneston heard me talking and eased my office door open a crack to check I wasn't with a client. We met a few years ago through a case at Ralston. Her mother, Sandra Inneston, and I became friends way back in my Public Service days. Emily helped investigate that Ralston case, and has helped out any number of times since. A chemical engineer who decided to added forensic science to her qualifications, she is now my occasional unofficial sidekick. She helps out with surveillance and research. Her enquiring analytical mind makes her an ideal sounding board to help with sorting out some of my trickier investigations. Apart from that, she looks after my office in her spare time while away, and probably spends as much time at my house as she does at her own. The only downside to Emily, if I can call it that, is her tendency to fuss over me.

I motioned Emily to come in. She flashed her watch at me as a reminder about the time. The man on the phone continued talking. When he stopped for a breath, I ended the call. "I understand, Mr Hensley, but an appointment tomorrow morning is the best I can offer … say, ten o'clock?" While unhappy about the delay, he accepted.

As she collapsed onto a chair opposite me, Emily asked, "Why are you shaking your head? Surely a potential client is a good thing. I hope you look more enthusiastic when he arrives for his appointment tomorrow. Why all the negative reaction?"

After thinking about for a moment, she also thought Hensley's name familiar but didn't know why. I prompted her. "Hensley Security Services… He saw me soon after I was released from hospital after being attacked behind the *Indulgence* coffee shop." Emily's face lit up as she remembered his visit.

"It went nowhere; just wasted your time. You sent him to fetch some documentation for you and he never returned."

"You might also remember, after he left, we both agreed there would be no need for a decision about the case. We both knew it wasn't going anywhere."

"Hmm, yeah… So, what problem brings him here now?"

"Who knows? Maybe it's the same problem. I'll find out tomorrow. Let's not waste time on it tonight. We are supposed to meet Sam for dinner to help her celebrate her birthday."

Millhaven's top cop, Ben Richards, joined us for dinner at a new Lebanese restaurant by the marina. It was a pleasant evening with good food … until the call came in. The birthday girl, Sam Keller, is a detective I have known for some years and who helped with a couple of my cases in the past. A while back, she stayed in my home for a few weeks until her permanent transfer from Ralston Division to Millhaven came through.

"Duty calls," Sam grumbled as she retrieved her bag from beside her chair. "Thanks for the birthday dinner. Stay and enjoy yourselves." As she left, Ben made a quick call.

Sam was barely out the door before Ben was on his feet. "I should check on what's happening. It might turn into something big. Best I know about it before it happens." With that, Ben was striding to the door.

Emily giggled. "I don't think Sam will appreciate her boss peering over her shoulder. I think the 'stay and enjoy yourselves' comment was aimed at Ben. Maybe Ben's excuse about keeping an eye on things was just a ruse to avoid paying his share of the bill."

We didn't hang around long. After settling the bill and dropping off Emily, I drove home with the memory of my previous encounter with Mr Hensley occupying my mind. It continued to do so while I sat sipping a coffee on my deck.

My memory of that encounter with Hensley remained clear. It happened while I was in hospital and Emily held the fort for me. On my release, I came back to a heap of messages on my desk. One call intrigued me. I rang the caller the moment I read Emily's note of the message. From a local security firm, the caller, who appeared to be the owner, had a growing suspicion something was amiss with some of their night-time patrols. He wanted me to investigate what was going on. The question that bothered me before came back to me: why did a security firm need a private investigator to look into its operations?

When told about it, Emily's reaction mirrored my own. In spite of harbouring a suspicion something was fishy about this case, I couldn't resist digging a little deeper. I rang to set up a meeting. About half an hour later, the firm's director, Frank Hensley, was sipping coffee across the desk from me. Twenty minutes of questioning later, all I gleaned from him was he held concerns about how some of his security teams conducted their patrols.

Emily shot me a look whenever an answer provided bore no relevance to the question I asked. The meeting proved farcical from the outset. Unless he provides the information I require, I'm not taking this contract. "In order to assess the scope of the work involved, here is a list of your operation's details I need. Please read it and clarify anything that is unclear or presents any likely difficulties."

"No, nothing needs clarification. How soon do you need this information?"

"You have a business to run and are busy but, the sooner you provide the information, the sooner I can decide about the case. Are you reluctant to, or uncomfortable about supplying any of the information on that list?" He shook his head. I doubted that was the truth. His naturally ruddy complexion was now a deeper red. The line of perspiration along his top lip and his increased agitation suggested the requisite information was unlikely to arrive.

As she closed the door behind the man, Emily asked, "Will it be difficult deciding whether to take on this investigation or not?"

"I suspect I won't need to make a decision." Emily laughed and agreed with my assessment of the man as not being too familiar with the truth.

That was the end of my first encounter with Mr Hensley. He did not return with the requested information and never contacted me again … until today.

His call – and the appointment I gave him – had me in a quandary. As I was wrapping up a case, I wasn't sure I wanted to start another investigation right now. Troy Donaldson, long-time friend and archaeologist overseeing work on opening up a new mine in the region, was coming to spend a week or two with me before heading home to the UK at the end of his contract. We planned to spend much of that time at my beach house on a small island off the coast some distance to the north of Millhaven. I needed a break and was looking forward to it.

Tempted not to act on Mr Hensley's call, something made me give him an appointment. I reassured myself it wouldn't matter as this meeting's outcome would be a repeat of the previous one. Nothing would come of it.

The night's chill forced me indoors. I checked my emails before turning in for the night. As if guided by some psychic influence, Troy emailed me earlier this evening. Some last minute stuff would delay him for a few days. He would call me when he knew his likely arrival. Okay, I can rest easy about tomorrow's appointment. I'm still confident it won't come to anything, but it will fill in some time until Troy arrives … and this time, I will bill Mr Hensley for my time.

*****

As ten o'clock approached, I wondered if Hensley would bother showing up. I would have a quiet day if he didn't. While I sat compiling a mental list of all the things I might do with a spare day to catch up on outstanding tasks in the office, Hensley slammed open the door and marched in.

He hadn't changed much: still the same ruddy complexion, but carrying a bit more weight now and looking more dishevelled than I remembered. Gushing profuse thanks for seeing him, he flopped into the chair and dumped a carrier bag on the floor beside him. "I am grateful for this. I wasn't sure you would even talk to me after the way things went last time."

If he was hoping for soothing or conciliatory words from me, he was disappointed. "I must admit, I wasn't inclined to meet with you again. Before we begin, I must advise you that, after what happened last time, you will be billed for any time spent discussing or acting on your concerns." He looked sheepish but nodded in reply. "Good, now we understand each other, what is the reason for your contact this time?"

"Er… well, the problem is the same one I had last time. I am concerned about what is happening with some of my teams' night patrols."

"That does not fill me with any degree of confidence. Does you security firm do anything other than night patrols? I don't imagine there's much demand for such work during the day."

"There is a range of regular work, for example, escorting payrolls."

"People still are paid in cash?"

"Some smaller places continue to offer that option. Our courier service undertakes cash deliveries between businesses

5

and banks. So, the daytime work is not fulltime and not every day."

"That must make rostering people for the daytime jobs difficult. Are the night patrol officers used for that work as well?"

"No. My wife, our operations manager and I attend to the daytime jobs. The three of us work in the office, so it is easier for one of us to do it than trying to call in one of the night patrol blokes."

"Well, I still need to know all there is about your firm's night patrols. Did you bring relevant documents with you?" He scooped up the carrier bag from the floor and tipped its contents onto my desk. It took a few moments to sort it out. This time it was all here: maps, lists of night security patrols and their schedules, and route timelines showing times of arrival and departure from the various businesses on each route.

As she came in, Emily smirked at the sight of Mr Hensley at my desk. The smirk soon changed to curiosity when she saw what we pored over. After a few moments peering over my shoulder, she told Hensley, "This is quite detailed information; just what we need to understand your operations." It was at that point I realised my omission and introduced 'my colleague' to Hensley. Like a true gentleman, he bounced up off his chair to shake Emily's hand. Interrogation of his documents then continued for some time.

My ever-present watchdog, Emily, took on the self-appointed task of ensuring I didn't overload myself with cases and would be free to take a break when Troy arrived. She didn't seem too worried about the way discussions with Hensley were progressing, so we pressed on. After going over everything with him, I undertook to call him later in the day with my decision regarding accepting the contract.

It wasn't the answer he wanted, but accepted it and left. Emily made coffee and we settled at the desk to go over everything. After studying all Hensley's information in detail several times, we agreed Whittington Investigations should take on this case – and there was no better time to start than tonight. I called to advise Hensley. He sounded a bit taken aback by how soon we would begin.

Then Emily and I went about selecting our first night patrol to shadow. On a photocopy of Hensley's map of the chosen patrol's area, we marked the location of the premises and noted the time the patrol was due to check each of them. With that completed, we planned our first evening's surveillance of the selected patrol. Our plan was to monitor alternate locations on the patrol's route, with Emily and I leap-frogging each other from location to location until the patrol's shift ended back at the company's office at midnight.

I was pleased Emily took time off in lieu of the overtime payment for the long hours she worked over the previous few weeks. Big things were happening at her employers. It was being kept hush-hush for the moment but, whatever it was, it had Emily looking worn out and frazzled, and in need of time off.

Our plan was to eat early and be in position to begin surveillance by the time the patrol was due at its eight o'clock location. As my first site was across the other side of town, I needed to leave home not much later than half past seven to be in position a little before the patrol's arrival. We gathered up everything we might need for the night's activities and headed for my place.

It was while stopped at a set of lights, I remembered it was likely I would have a house guest for the next few nights. The unit Sam bought was being repainted and she would stay with me while it happened. They were supposed to start painting today, so Sam should arrive tonight. Soon after seven o'clock, she arrived to find us halfway through our share of the lasagne I cooked for dinner. Not wanting Sam to start quizzing us, I jumped in before she could ask questions. "There's lasagne for dinner if you want it. If not, leave it in the fridge. Apologies for eating without you, but we have to be gone in about another fifteen minutes."

"Where are you going? I thought you were going to be home tonight."

"I'm sorry but, when a job comes along, I have to take it if I want to stay in business. I'm working tonight and won't be home until after midnight. I'll try not to wake you when I come in. Look at the time. Gotta go!"

As Emily and I headed for the door, Sam called after me, "Ben's coming over tonight. He should be here any minute."

"That's okay. There's enough lasagne there for both of you. Just reheat it if you need to, and you could make a salad to go with it if you like." It was about ten minutes earlier than I intended leaving home. Emily, not needing to be in place quite so early, followed me down the driveway and then called at her unit to change before heading to her first location.

On my way to my first site, I stopped at a convenience store to buy a bottle of water. That put me back on my original schedule. I arrived at my surveillance place about five minutes before the security patrol was due. As I unclipped my seatbelt and settled down to wait, Emily called to confirm she also was in place.

Eight o'clock came and went but nothing happened. Ten minutes late, the patrol finally arrived but showed no apparent hurry. This location was a huge industrial site consisting of an enormous main building, with four or more outbuildings dotted around its perimeter. Tall security fencing surrounded the whole complex, and massive double gates guarded the entrance drive-way. No remote opener for those gates; one of the security guys manually unlocked and dragged the gates open for his mate to drive through.

They began their patrol of the complex with a drive, at not much more than a crawl, past all the buildings before parking out front of the main building. Then, together, the two officers walked around the building, rattling all doors to check they were locked. Their return to their vehicle ended the night's inspection of the property. One of them again unlocked the gates and locked them once the car drove out. The bloke on gate duty climbed back into the car and it turned right onto the street and drove off into the night. Somehow, their tour of inspection allowed them to make up two minutes of their lost time. They were only eight minutes behind schedule when they left for Emily's location.

A quick call to update her on the situation, and I sat using my voice recorder to make a note of the patrol's visit to this site. As I finished the brief recording, out of the corner of my eye, something caught my attention. I slid down in my seat until I could just see the complex across the road. Illuminated in lights coming from somewhere at the rear of the complex, a figure ran towards the gates. Then, the vehicle came into view. It drove through the now open gates and waited while they were locked. A man ran from the gates and scrambled in the waiting small pantechnicon. It turned left onto the street and sped off. The sign on the driver's door was so degraded, it was impossible to read.

My schedule indicated I should be at my next location within twenty minutes at the latest. That truck was more temptation than I could resist. A vehicle driving out of the complex so soon after the security patrol completed its check didn't gel. Something was not right. By the time I turned my car around, the truck was disappearing around the corner at the end of the street. It led me out to the ring road. After a short distance it turned off that road and onto suburban streets. It was heading for the harbour. Although I risked losing it if my assumption about its destination was wrong, I took a more direct route to arrive before it.

Plenty of people patronise the marina-side restaurants and cafés tonight. Parking was at a premium. I found a space and illegally parked. I won't be here long, I told my conscience. After scrambling out of my car, I wandered along the footpath beside the road. After about five minutes, I doubted the wisdom of my assumption about the truck. There was no sign of it. My more direct route to the marina wouldn't have put me more than five minutes ahead of the truck. "Bugger…! I've lost it," I hissed at the night.

I shouldn't be chasing after trucks anyway. I should be at my next location waiting for the security patrol to arrive. If I leave now, I might just about be in place in time. I manoeuvred out of my illegal park and headed away from the marina at a little above the legal speed limit. Even if I continued to drive over the limit all the way to my next location, it was doubtful I would make it in time. Still, it was worth a shot.

The road to the marina, after branching off a major road, passes through a small older light industrial area before ending at the new marina complex. Street lighting is in short supply along this road, and the industrial premises are deserted and in darkness at this hour. So, why is there light spilling out onto the road ahead? I lifted my foot to crawl through the illuminated area.

It looked like a nondescript three-bay shed with its two roller doors up. That's my truck! The truck I followed was parked in one of the bays. Whatever was in it was being transferred to a red van parked in the adjacent bay. I continued out to the major road, circled the roundabout, and started back, still at a crawl, towards the marina. About a hundred metres along the road, the truck passed me on its way back to town.

The road was so narrow, making a U-turn required something akin to a forty-four point turn. There was no option but to keep going until I came to somewhere that accommodated an easy U-turn. As I crept along the road in search of such a place, the red van rocketed out of the shed, bounced over the kerb and roared off ahead of me towards the marina. Without giving any thought to the matter, I sped up to maintain a safe distance as I followed it.

Diners were still enjoying their night out. The parking situation hadn't improved. I drove to the end and followed the van into the area reserved for boat trailer parking. There weren't many vehicles and trailers parked there tonight. The van seemed to have disappeared. I slid into a space between a couple of rigs. It was dark and nobody was likely to be patrolling the area at this hour. With the night vision binoculars from the glovebox hanging around my neck, and keeping to the darkest shadows, I found a position offering a good view of the area. ... And there was the red van.

Chapter 2

Beyond the trailer parking area and the boat ramp, a dock equipped with a huge travelling crane and cradle for lifting larger vessels ran out a short distance into the sheltered waters behind the rock wall of the marina. The dock was designed to carry heavy vehicles such as low loaders for transporting larger boats to dry-dock for maintenance. This is where larger vessels tied up to refuel and take on provisions and passengers.

After reversing none too confidently along the dock, the van driver parked alongside a large, expensive looking cruiser tied up at the end of the pier. The moment it pulled up, bodies swarmed down the gang plank to surround the van. A cargo net was lowered over the side of the vessel. In a well-practised operation, a number of large cartons transferred from van to net. The whole exercise so well-orchestrated that, as the net was hauled in over the side, the unloading crew jogged back on board and the van drove off.

I made my way back to the car and was idling at the give-way sign when the van flew past and out of the marina. A bus delayed my departure. Too big for the normal vehicle parking areas, it used the trailer area to drop off and collect passengers. Entering the area required making a tight turn. Not a problem for normal vehicles, but it required the long bus to back and fill several times to accomplish the turn.

Waiting at the give-way sign for the bus to unblock my exit, I wrestled with the question of whether to follow the van, or to resume the remainder of my night's surveillance schedule. The van, travelling at speed, would be long gone by the time I could follow it. A small gap opened. The bus mounted the kerb in a desperate attempt to enter the area. I planted my foot and shot through the gap without losing any paint in the process.

Displeased, the bus driver let me know with a long blast of the horn.

My phone rang while I was upsetting the bus driver. I hit the button to take the call but didn't answer until I was on my way out of the marina. It was Emily screaming, "Are you okay? Sonny, answer me. Is everything all right? Answer me."

As soon as I could divide my attention between driving and answering hands-free, I reassured her I was fine. "What's happening with the security patrol? Are they heading for my next location?" I mentally debated whether to admit I wasn't yet in place, or to leave Emily in blissful ignorance for now of my unscheduled activities.

"No. Something is not right. They are so late arriving. I think they must have checked another property before coming here. Maybe their route changed since our document."

"I'm confident it's current. Tell me what happened since their scheduled arrival time at your location. They were already eight minutes late when they left me."

"The street was deserted when I arrived. The patrol should have been here twenty minutes ago. I was about to call you when a vehicle turned into the street. I waited. It stopped further along. Two men got out and collected their private vehicles from a company's carpark. I waited to ring you until they all drove off. That's when a cavalcade of three vehicles entered the street. All private vehicles, one turned off onto a side street, one drove to the end of this street and disappeared around the corner. The third vehicle dropped off another bloke outside that same property before driving off. As with the previous two, that man collected his vehicle from the company's carpark and left. I waited until the street was empty again to call you."

"Are you saying the patrol still hasn't arrived?"

"Yes, there is no sign … Hang on. A vehicle just turned into this street. It's creeping along; can't be doing more than twenty kilometres an hour. Ah yes, it's the security patrol vehicle … and they are about to turn into the property they are supposed to inspect."

"By my calculations, they are more than half an hour late now."

"I make them about thirty-five minutes late. That's why I thought they inspected somewhere else before coming here. Anyway, let's see how long this inspection takes. In ten minutes, they should be on their way to you."

No need to explain I wasn't yet at my next location. After all, I was only a few minutes away from where I was supposed to be and should be there well in advance of the patrol ... unless they attempted to make up lost time somehow. About three minutes after Emily's call, I eased into an ideal parking spot across from the patrol's next premises.

Use this few minutes to relax and refocus, I counselled myself as I unclipped the seatbelt. I still had about five minutes before the patrol left Emily's location. While I waited, I recorded more of the night's events on my phone's voice recorder. Recalling what happened so far so preoccupied me, I didn't notice time slipping by. My phone vibrating in my hand brought me back to reality. Emily again.

"I don't know what's going on. The security patrol drove onto the site and stopped out front of the building to check the door. Then they walked along the side of the building checking doors as they went around to the back. I waited for them to reappear. That was twenty minutes ago. Their check on this place is supposed to take ten minutes. There are no lights or sounds coming from over there. I'm starting to get an uncomfortable feeling about what has happened."

This is not going according to script. "Stay there and keep watching. I'll be with you in about five minutes. If anything happens in the meantime give me a call." Ignoring the speed limit, I pulled in behind Emily's car just over three minutes later. As soon as I pulled up, she dashed over to occupy the passenger seat beside me.

"See, their car is still where they parked it when they first arrived. They haven't reappeared from around the back of the building, and there is no sign of activity over there. I don't suppose we should risk going to take a look…"

"No, I don't think we're going to do that for all sorts of legal reasons. My thinking is, we should sit here for another five minutes and, if nothing happens by then, you should go home." As expected, Emily began protesting. I ignored her and continued.

"I'm going to see if I can get law enforcement interested in what's happening here. In my line of business, and in line with my contract to undertake surveillance for the security firm, I have a right to be here and I would be doing the right thing by calling the police about my concerns. On the other hand, you might be subjected to a lot of difficult questions if you were found here with me. So, in these few extra minutes we're allowing those blokes to reappear, give me a blow by blow description of everything that happened from when their car arrived. That way, when the police want to know what's been happening, I'll sound like I've been here all night."

"Okay. Well, it happened just as I told you on the phone. Oh, there is one thing though. One of those 'blokes' is a woman." It took a couple of minutes for Emily to run through everything that happened again and answer the few questions I asked. With still no sign of movement across the road, it was time for Emily to disappear. She remained unhappy about it.

"Keep in touch. Call me every fifteen minutes so I know you're okay. If you don't call, I'll call you. If you don't answer, I'll be here in a flash. Is that clear?"

"I had a mother. I don't need another. I will keep you updated. Now, go home so I can do what I need to do." Emily scrambled out of the car and, within moments, I watched her taillights disappearing into the darkness.

Time to call someone, but who to call? After a moment's thought, I decided Sam might be a good place to start, although I wasn't sure what sort of reception I would receive. Sam's mobile phone rang for ages before switching to messages. Perhaps she left her phone in the car. That's unlikely, but stranger things have happened. In case that was the situation, I called my house's landline. No answer there either. My uneasy feeling about the security patrol is strengthening. When all else fails, and always against my better judgement, call Ben.

As I run down my contacts list, it occurs to me Sam might be called out on a job. If that were the case, it is likely Ben is there too. I chanced my luck. He took a while but answered as I was about to end the call and ring the police station. "What's up? Sorry I took so long to answer. I was climbing out of the shower when you called."

"Strange things are happening. You could put some clothes on and join me at my stakeout location or, better still, send a couple of uniforms to join me."

"If you need police assistance, why didn't you just call the station?"

"I didn't want to waste time trying to convince a communications officer that it is urgent." I barely gave him details of the location and event before he ended the call. Okay… I hope that's a good sign, and not an indication he is pissed off with me.

Thank you, Ben. A police car cruised along the street and stopped beside me. Through their open window, I explained my concerns about what was happening across the road. As expected, they said they would handle the situation, and that I should go home. Well, that isn't going to happen. As I climbed back into my car, the police drove across the road and parked beside the patrol's vehicle. After spending what seemed like ages checking that vehicle, the officers returned to their car and drove towards the back of the building.

A car's headlights came towards me. It slid in behind my car. Then I saw the unmistakable shape of Ben Richards striding towards me. Oh Lord, here we go. This probably won't be fun. He surprised me by wrenching open the passenger side door and climbing in. "Anything happening over there yet?" he asked as he opened the glove compartment and extracted my night binoculars.

"You don't need those. There's nothing to see from here. Your two uniforms drove around to the back of the building a while ago. Come to think of it, it's taking them a while to reappear."

"I'm going to take a look. Stay here and stay out of trouble."

Not bloody likely! I watched Ben open the door of his car and reach in under the driver's seat. I copied his example before following him. As I jogged after him, I shoved the Glock I retrieved from under my seat into the waistband of my jeans at the small of my back.

"I told you to stay in the car! I should have known better than to expect that to happen. Stay close behind me, don't do, or say, or touch anything, and for God's sake stay alert," he shouted over his shoulder.

"Yes sir, Master…" I murmured, and hoped he didn't hear.

It was not a pretty sight. The two uniformed officers had called for backup. In the meantime, they were fully occupied with what they found. The male security officer was dead. The wound surrounded by a dark red patch on the left breast of his shirt left little doubt about his status. His female colleague was barely alive, and the officers were doing their utmost to keep her that way until the paramedics arrived. Her several stab wounds were not yet fatal, but could prove so. Cuts on her hands and forearms attested to the fight she put up against her attackers. Attackers…? Was there more than one? Taking out two well-trained and armed security officers surely would require more than one assailant.

Sirens in the distance drew closer. "Let's go back out to the front," Ben said. We jogged out to where the security patrol car was parked as the first of the sirens wailed along the street. "Stay out of sight here beside this car. I'll stand out there and direct traffic around the back." With that, Ben jogged over to meet the first vehicle as it turned onto the site.

All manner of police cars and ambulances arrived. When the arrivals came to an end, Ben returned and told me to go home. This time, I knew there was no arguing with him, but a thought occurred to me. "Ben, before I go, there's something you should know. No vehicles or persons left this site since the security patrol arrived, unless they did so during that brief time we were at the rear of the building. The site is walled in on three sides by other tall buildings. There is no easy escape route from the rear of the property. Whoever did this has to be still here somewhere." For the length of a few heartbeats, Ben stared at me before springing into action. He moved away a few paces to make a phone call and then came back to me.

"Forget my earlier instructions. Go back and sit in your car. Keep watch on the front of this place, but keep out of sight while you're about it. Stay there until I tell you to go."

Ever obedient, I did as I was told … Ben would probably add 'for once'. I jogged back to my car, unlocking it as I crossed the street. With Glock in hand, I circled around to the passenger side and checked out the car's interior through the windows to make sure no one had made themselves comfortable in there during my absence. No intruders detected, I settled in behind the steering wheel. The wail of a single siren grew louder as it turned into the street.

The police car parked on the street out front of the site. Another siren. This time from behind the building. An ambulance with siren wailing raced out onto the street, and was followed soon after at a more sedate pace by the second ambulance. Figures seemed to be surrounding the building. Ben sprinted towards me, but went to his own vehicle. In my rearview mirror, I watched him open and close the rear door of his SUV. Then, with his protective vest in his hand, he was standing beside my open window. "Now you do have to go home. Go straight home and stay there. I'll talk to you tomorrow."

There weren't a lot of options. I drove home. On the way, I called Emily to apologise for having turned off my phone. She was climbing into her car. After having tried to call me several times, she was coming to investigate why I wasn't answering. "I know you sometimes turn off your phone when you're on a job and don't want distractions, but I hadn't been able to contact you for too long. I was worried."

By the time I gave her my brief report, I was home. I let myself in with all the usual rattling and banging that accompanies that procedure. There was no concern about waking up anyone. Amongst the last of the vehicles arriving at my crime scene was Sam's car. Earlier in the night I felt tired, maybe even exhausted. Perhaps it was adrenalin, but the weariness had disappeared. I sat in my office and transcribed my notes from tonight before taking a quick shower. I was asleep within moments of falling into bed.

*****

This morning found me sluggish and slow off the mark. What time Sam came in last night remains a mystery, but she was gone again by the time I surfaced this morning. That is inconvenient. I wanted to know – I *need* to know – how last night ended so I can work out what to do today. I'm confident the police advised Hensley Security Services of last night's tragedy. As I'm investigating on that company's behalf, I need to follow up with them today. It would not do to have Mr Hensley thinking everything that happened last night did so without my being aware of it. I also need to see if he has new thoughts on how the investigation should proceed – or if it should proceed at all. That will not be a great way to start my day.

After about half an hour in my office, I was about to call Hensley when Emily arrived. "How did the night end?" was her greeting. She received a shrug in reply. "How are we going to know what to do next?"

"Exactly… As I can't put it off any longer, I was about to call Hensley when you arrived. I'm not sure it will be a great conversation." At that point, the phone rang. "Ah, Mr Hensley, thank you for calling…" I shot Emily a look. She headed for the coffee machine. "I was waiting until a civilised hour to call you about last night. I assume the police contacted you, but I haven't been able to confirm that with them this morning."

"Yes, yes. Someone called sometime early this morning."

Hensley sounded vague and frazzled. Should I worry, I wondered. He rushed on before I could comment. "I know you are busy, but could you spare me some time this morning. I need to talk to you ... urgently."

"Of course; I hoped you might spare me some time for a catch-up. I'm free this morning. What time would suit you for a meeting."

"I can slip away now without anyone thinking it unusual."

"Okay, that suits..." He ended the call before I could say more. Why did he want to talk to me urgently? That word started a certain tightening in the pit of my stomach. I relayed the gist of the conversation to Emily as she placed a mug of coffee in front of me.

"Do you think he wants to cancel the contract? Does he somehow think our investigation is responsible for what happened last night? What have the police told ...?"

"Whoa, hang about. I don't know the answer to any of that. In fact, I don't know anything ... except that I won't shed tears if he does end this investigation." Emily's eyebrows shot up to her hairline and she shook her head in confusion.

"Why not...? Wouldn't losing the contract be a concern?"

"After last night's events, whatever is happening regarding Hensley Security Services is now a police matter. It will be almost impossible for us to continue the case without being blocked at every turn by their investigation. Let's not jump to any conclusions until we hear what Hensley has to say."

I had no sooner finished speaking than Hensley burst into my office. His face, redder than usual, evidence he had rushed over, or maybe it was a result of the distressing situation confronting him. He made straight for the chair opposite my desk. Emily waved her coffee mug at him. "Yes please; strong, black and no sugar." Emily shot me a look before retreating to the coffee machine.

"Mr Hensley, perhaps we should start with what the police told you about last night's incident." He nodded as he lifted his coffee mug with both hands firmly around it.

"That won't take long! They never told me much at all. The disregard they showed … I'm sorry, where were we? Oh yes, what did the police tell me? It was about one o'clock when they rang. My wife usually hears the phone before I do and answers it. She didn't last night … she's away for a couple of days. It took me a while to realise it was the phone ringing downstairs that woke me. I forgot to take the phone upstairs with me when I went to bed. Anyway, by the time I got to the phone, it stopped ringing. I stood there like a zombie for a couple of minutes waiting to see if they called again. Then someone was pounding on the front door. It was the police. They weren't too happy about my not answering the phone and wanted to know why."

Emily gave me a startled look. I dismissed it with a slight shake of my head. Why were the police ringing this man to tell him one of his employees was dead and another one was close to it? That didn't make sense, and I doubted it was standard procedure. Perhaps the rest of the story will clarify things. "So, what did the police tell you after waking you at that hour of the morning?"

"Tell me…? They hadn't come to tell me anything! They came to ask questions. It was like being in front of a firing squad except, instead of bullets, they were firing questions at me … Was I the owner of Hensley Security Services … were those two regular employees … what time did their patrol begin … what were they supposed to do at that location … where was their previous inspection … where were they supposed to go next … how many other patrols were out last night? I was barely able to get an answer out before they asked the next question – and none too gently I might add. Then they snapped their notebooks closed and stood up to leave. I thought, no you don't; you're not leaving until you give me some answers."

"Their performance was a bit odd. Did you get any answers before they left?"

"I raced over and blocked the door so they couldn't leave.

They tried to shove me out of the way, but I'm a big lump of a bloke and I trained with the Red Berets. It might have been a while back and I might not be as fit as I used to be, but I'm still no push over. I still can handle myself. I told them they were not leaving until I had some answers."

"That was ballsy, but it could have gone very wrong for you," Emily commented.

"Nah, two puny teenagers they were, still wet behind the ears like as not. They didn't sit down; just stood there glaring at me. So, I asked my questions; fat lot of good that did me. I asked what happened to my patrol car. It's impounded. I asked about Cass' injuries. They asked if she was family. I said no, just an employee. They told me, as I am not family, I am not entitled to any information about her. I was beginning to see red. I asked an important question: had they notified the dead officer's wife about his death? The arseholes just shrugged …. apologies for the language. That's when the red mist came down. I chucked them out. I told them not to bother coming back. I would only speak to a senior officer in future."

It took all my self-control to keep a straight face when he told me about chucking them out. The vision in my mind's eye of the event was wonderful. I do hope I can winkle out more in-formation on the aftermath of that episode, and the identities of the constables involved. I think I'm beginning to like this man.

"I take it the 'Cass' you mentioned is your female security officer who was taken to hospital in a serious condition?"

"I don't know what her condition was – or is now."

"What I can tell you is that she received multiple stab wounds and was in a serious condition. I don't know what her condition is now."

"You were there… when it happened, I mean?"

"No, not when it happened, but I was on the scene when the paramedics arrived. If I find out anything more, I will let you know. I guess the question at the moment is whether you want me to continue with this investigation. If you wish to continue with our contract, it can be only on the same arrangement as we originally agreed. I can't do anything about last night's incident. That is now a police matter and they will continue to investigate it. We have to let them do their job."

"Bollocks to that. Those blokes who came to see me last night couldn't find a feed in a fridge. Yes, I want you to continue with the investigation as we agreed. Not tonight though; things are a bit all over the place today. I'll give you a call tomorrow to let you know if things have settled back to normal."

Hensley's mobile phone was in danger of walking off my desk. It vibrated constantly with incoming calls the whole time we spoke. "Perhaps you should go and deal with some of those calls," I suggested.

He lumbered up out of his chair. "I'll call you tomorrow." And he was on his way to the door.

"That was interesting," Emily said as she walked back after closing the door behind him. "What do we do now?"

"Get a good night's sleep tonight, and see what tomorrow brings."

Chapter 3

Hensley departed and Emily went to check on her new laboratory. She still has a few more days off work. I hope we wrap up this Hensley case in that time, and before Troy arrives. Alone for the rest of the day, I needed to devote thought and time to what last night was all about. My list of questions about the incident – and Hensley's security patrols in general –grows by the minute.

I checked out the properties fronting onto it as I drove along the street where it happened last night. The business where the patrol was attacked had two sources of income according to the signage on the main building. It seems McGregor's is a basic transport firm specialising in import/export operations. It also operates as a removalist firm for household relocations. Might prove worthwhile checking them out.

It would be surprising if McGregor's diversified operations proved important in any way. Still, it would be worth knowing about the other businesses on this patrol's route. Last night, it was too dark to see any signage on the first property I monitored. Security lighting was installed throughout the complex, but it was low wattage and only illuminated the building to the height of the doors. I parked across the street from the site.

This is a warehousing operation that also runs a light transport service throughout the region. Surprised by two transport operations based in such close proximity and on the same security patrol route, I pulled out my phone. A check on Google brought up the firm's online advertisement. It didn't tell me much more than I already knew, except that it claimed they made daily trips to service the surrounding mining towns.

Instinct urges me now to check out the nature of the other businesses on this patrol's route. A semi-trailer trying to reverse onto the site blocked the street, so I spent another five minutes waiting to drive away. It gave me time to mentally collate what

I knew so far: not much of any import. And what about that shed the red van came out of? What's its story? Seems like I have plenty of research to do back in the office.

On my way back to the office, a sudden change of direction took me along the marina access road. The shed is closed and looks deserted today. Mounted on posts out front, a faded, splitting plywood sign tells me this is a metal fabrication workshop. Another faded small sign fixed to one end of the front of the building suggests at least part of the establishment is a paint and panel workshop. The business looks down on its luck. The site is untidy, littered and has tall dead grass protruding from amongst dead metal objects, and the shed is in need of maintenance. Today, the place did nothing to change my mind about its relevance to my case. My gut is telling me they were up to no good in there last night.

Back at my desk, I scanned today's newspaper for a report on the security patrol's attack. No mention of it. No mention of last night's incident has me curious. Is it being kept under wraps? Only the police could do that. Why would they? The only reason I can think of is that it is part of some bigger story … some bigger operation! Now that's an interesting thought. I shall need to be particularly nice to two astute coppers I know.

While I intended checking on the nature of the businesses on the patrol's route, I found myself unable to settle to the task. My subconscious kept nagging at me, but I couldn't work out what it was trying to tell me. To avoid sitting staring at the wall, I entertained myself rifling through the information Hensley provided. Every document got no more than a cursory inspection as I went through the pile twice. Something pulled me back to the list of patrol officers. I read through the names associated with each patrol a couple of times before what my subconscious was nagging me about became obvious.

I ran a highlighter across the names of the patrol we were monitoring last night: two blokes. So when did one of them morph into a female? I couldn't swear they were two males who checked on that first property I monitored, but I felt certain they were men. I wish I knew what that tells me. All it indicates is that something fishy occurred between when the patrol left my site and its arrival at Emily's location. And whatever that was, might explain their delayed arrival at that second site. But something else about the security patrol needs investigation. Another cup of coffee might help.

A thought occurred to me while I stood by the coffee machine: who were the two patrol officers who were attacked? Another look at the list showed only two teams were male and female combinations. Hensley had referred to the injured woman as *Cass*. 'Cass' could be the shortened version of Cassandra, but I couldn't think of any other names that might be shortened in that way. I looked at the two male/female combo teams again. No Cassandra mentioned. Then it jumped off the page at me. One of those two teams included a Marie Cassidy. This had to be the team that was attacked. And that suggests her partner – perhaps that should be ex-partner – was Jason Knight.

Gaining traction on this investigation is slow going, but I now have two names. That had me wondering about Marie – or Cass, if you prefer. She was in a bad way last night. I wondered if she made it through the night and about her current status. My guess is they took her to the base hospital. Not being family, they were unlikely to tell me her current condition. After devoting a few moments thought to the situation, I called the hospital. "I wanted to enquire about Marie Cassidy… No, I'm not family. I'm a work colleague. I wondered if it would be all right for me to send her some flowers."

The brusque initial reception I received softened. "No, it's a bit early to be sending flowers just yet. She wouldn't be allowed them in her room. Wait a couple of days before checking again. She might be in a position to receive flowers or other gifts by then."

From that brief conversation, I assume Marie is still alive but remains in a critical condition. My attention swung to her dead partner. Hensley's comments indicated Jason Knight had a wife. I can relate to the terrible experience it was for her to have a police officer wake her in the middle of the night to give her the news her husband was dead. It brought back with amazing clarity my own such experience when my husband was killed at work. From my brief glimpse of Jason Knight last night, he looked young; maybe only in his early-twenties. Had they been married long? Were there any children? I'll put those questions to Hensley when he calls me tomorrow.

Time to return to the businesses on the patrol's list for last night. None of them required any more than a ten or fifteen minute inspection. That posed a new question to ponder. Even allowing for coffee and meal breaks during the shift, the remaining time allowed the patrol to undertake a significant number of short duration inspections. The number to inspect on last night's route didn't seem enough. Even allowing generous travelling time between locations left a lot of unaccounted for time during the eight-hour shift. Perhaps that's another question for Hensley tomorrow. At this rate, I could end up with a long list of questions for Hensley ... that is, if he calls me tomorrow.

Emily arrived while I continued poring over Hensley's documents. "I'm surprised you are still here. I thought you might have decided on an early day and be gone by now." I checked the time; not yet four o'clock.

"I hadn't planned an early day, but I can't see much point in spending more time here. How has your day been?"

"Not exciting, but good; I spent time at the new lab."

"How is it coming along? I remember you saying it was close to being finished."

"Yeah. It should be ready to occupy by the end of the week. If that is the case, I will spend all next week moving in and setting up."

"That gives me precious few days when you might be available to assist with this case. By the way, you never said why this new lab is being built. With the mining industry stagnating the way it is, I wouldn't have thought you needed a bigger and better laboratory."

"Uhmm ... yes, there is that, but other stuff is happening as well." I gestured for her to tell me more. "I can't say anything; can't tell you what's going on. It's all hush-hush until we move in. There are so few of us who know about it, I can't risk saying anything even to you. It would be too easy to trace any leaks back to me ... not that I'm suggesting you would blab it about town..."

"So it's a 'watch this space' situation for a week or two yet?"

"I'm afraid so. I will tell you as soon as I can. All I can say is that it might provide opportunities for Whittington Investigations in the future."

That was not helpful, but I nodded my acceptance, and shrugged to indicate not knowing didn't bother me. But it damn well did bother me. What can possibly be happening in the area of minerals testing that my colleague, friend, and chemical engineer, Emily Inneston, can't tell me about? And then she has the gall to tease me by suggesting I will benefit from it. I think I'll try parking this one in the back of my mind somewhere. Today already has produced more questions without answers than I need.

Emily left soon after. I shut the office and went home. There was a nice leg of lamb in the fridge that would go down well for dinner tonight ... and might woo the two coppers who most likely will be there to help me eat it. Like so many of the best laid plans, it didn't happen that way. As I was driving home, Sam called to say she would be late but didn't know how late it would be when she could get away. I asked if that also applied to Ben. He would be late as well, but she wasn't sure how late. Okay, forget the lamb. We will have steak and salad when everyone finally arrives. Anyway, if both coppers are working late, they are not likely to be in the mood to be forthcoming with information.

Not long after I arrived home, Emily came. As we prepared the salads for dinner, I thought it wise to plan our strategy for later. "Ben and Sam don't know you were involved with the surveillance last night. It should remain that way. I plan to ask a few simple questions about the police's investigation. It would

28

be good if you could feign complete ignorance of the event. It might not work, but take your lead from me and we will see if we learn anything." Emily and I have worked this stunt successfully before. It only works because Emily is a quick thinker and knows what I am trying to achieve.

It was about eight o'clock when Ben called to say he and Sam were about to leave the police station, and asked if they should bring take-away. Dinner was relaxed, but conversation was scant. I put it down to everyone being tired after the previous late night. Food seemed to revive all of us a little. I eased the conversation around to where I wanted it to go until I could ask my first question.

"What's the latest on the condition of that woman who was stabbed last night?"

"Where... here in Millhaven?" All three of us nodded in reply to Emily's question. "I didn't hear or see anything about a stabbing on the news."

"So, the police are keeping the incident under wraps, are they?" I looked hard at Ben as I asked the question. Both he and Sam gave half-hearted shrugs. "Okay, I get the picture. Did either of you end up having to tell the dead bloke's wife?" Ben's face remained impassive. Sam sat upright in surprise. She shot Ben a look. He didn't receive it.

"Someone was killed as well?" Emily did her bit again. "Was this part of the same incident?" It was time to see if I could shake something out of the two cops.

"Yeah. One dead; one in a bad way," I said in the most matter of fact way I could manage. "The bloke looked very young. Did he have any kids?" Sam, not as seasoned as Ben, cracked first.

"You think he was married and he might have kids...? What gave you that idea?" Sam, now perched on the front edge of her chair, looked a bit agitated.

"About what ... the kids? I don't know if he did have kids. Like I said, he looked young. Still, there could be kids wondering why their daddy hasn't come home."

29

"Sonny, you believe the bloke killed last night was married?" Sam was becoming more agitated by the moment. "Why do you think that?"

"His boss told me Jason Knight was married. He asked the constables who came banging on his door last night if they had advised his wife. The question wasn't answered."

"Who is Jason Knight?" Emily asked cautiously, as she too sensed how uptight Sam had become.

Then Ben joined the conversation. "Where did that name come from?" His demand wasn't too pleasant. "How confident are you about the source of the information?"

"Confident; Hensley's has a woman member in only two of their teams. The critically injured one is known as 'Cass'. I believe she is Marie Cassidy, who is teamed up with Jason Knight. Unless there were changes to that team last night, or my logic is wrong, the dead security patrol officer is Jason Knight."

An almost palpable silence settled over the deck. The two cops spent more than a few heartbeats eyeballing each other. Emily fidgeted in her chair. I knew she was uncertain whether she should do or say something. I gave her a slight shake of my head. She relaxed. It was up to me to liven things up again.

"Okay guys, what vital nerve did I manage to hit with that delivery. If this is supposed to be 'cops-only' information, you should tell me about it to avoid having me say the wrong thing to the wrong people. And Emily should be included, as she will be involved in my case associated with the incident."

Ben cleared his throat. "Perhaps we could have coffee and adjourn inside before we tackle the issue." Halleluiah, a break-through... maybe! I assessed Ben's call for coffee as a play for time to put some words together that would shut me up. While I dealt with the coffee machine, I dashed off a quick text to Hensley: We need to meet as soon as possible - it's urgent.

Everyone had settled with their coffee when my phone vibrated. 'Hensley', the caller's ID, sent me out onto the deck again to take the call. "I hope you don't mind me calling you straight back. I wondered if I could help you with something now rather waiting until tomorrow."

Seated at the table, I pulled out my pocket notebook, took the top off my pen with my teeth, and anchored the notebook firmly to the table with the elbow of the arm attached to the phone. There followed a barrage of rapid-fire questions, some of which I hadn't thought of until part way through the call. I had only two questions when the call started but, like Topsy, the list grew. "Describe those two constables who visited you in the middle of the night; anything and everything you remember about them."

"Let me think ... young, skinny, a bit scruffy looking ... their supervisor must be lax about the way his troops are turned out. Both could have done with a good scrub and a haircut, and their uniforms didn't look like they had seen an iron in a while. One was short and square – built like a brick outhouse – but still skinny-looking somehow. He was gingery blonde with fair complexion and blue eyes. The other bloke was a bit taller, skinny, with dark hair and eyes and sort of greasy-looking. I'd say the short one was about five foot seven or eight inches – sorry, I still speak the old language – and his mate was about five feet ten inches. Neither of them had polished their boots in a long while. I was in the armed forces back home. Those blokes would never have passed muster in my day."

"That's good info. Did you notice their vehicle? Was it a standard police vehicle?"

"After I chucked them out, I stood watching until they drove away. It was an unmarked, but red and blue flashing lights mounted on the dashboard came on when they started the car. Is there a problem with them?"

"No. I'm just gathering information at this stage. Now, I want to ask you about your vehicle. When you asked the constables about it, you said they told you it was impounded. This was the vehicle the attacked patrol used?" He confirmed those details. "What signage do you have on your patrol vehicles, and is it the same on all your cars?"

"We didn't go overboard with that stuff. Kept it simple and all the vehicles are the same: company logo, company name – Hensley Security Services – and a landline and mobile phone number. That's it. Oh, and a couple of older cars have an advertising skin on the rear window. Some time ago, my wife got the bright idea we could make extra cash hiring out the cars' rear windows for advertising. It was a crap idea. Only brought in a couple of contracts and, as soon as their twelve-month contract ended, we scrapped the idea."

"Okay, so now you are missing a patrol vehicle. How will that impact operations? I assume it is still impounded." His response was silence. I let it last a few seconds before firing off the question I really wanted to ask. "You are missing a vehicle, aren't you? Could you check which one it is, please?" I heard tapping on a keyboard and then a long silence before he came back to me.

"I don't understand… I checked. All … the cars … are here. I checked the CCTV. They are all parked in the compound where they are supposed to be. We have no patrols working tonight as a mark of respect."

Maybe Hensley just discovered something that will keep him awake tonight. While my original questions were dealt with, a bundle of others occurred to me during the call. By the time I explored them all, it was a long phone call. Before returning to the others, I sat for a while to consider all I had learned from.

"Well, look who has joined us," Ben announced as I returned to my chair and now cold coffee. "You were so long, we all need another coffee." Emily said she would make it, and Sam went to help her. Once we were alone, we sat in silence for a few moments before Ben asked quietly, "Are you all right. Was the call upsetting; bad news perhaps?"

"Eh…? Oh, no. But it has given me food for thought … and some of those thoughts are heading in an unpleasant direction." The return of the other two with steaming mugs of coffee created a brief pause until everyone settled again.

Then Ben, watching me over the top of his mug, asked the question I knew was coming. "…Anything of interest you want to share with us? We are well-trained good listeners." Yep, there it was. Ben knows me too well, probably even better than I know me.

"Yeah, perhaps there is, but only if you answer a couple of questions first." There was a collective shuffling as the others sat up and moved forward in the chairs in anticipation. Ben appeared to consider my proposal before answering.

"Okay, but the usual provisos apply. Fire away."

Chapter 4

His provisos wouldn't stop me accepting Ben's invitation. "Is there a Hensley's car in the police vehicle pound at the moment?" Ben and Sam exchanged a look and shrugged. Ben answered.

"The short answer is: don't know. But last night's security patrol vehicle should be held for forensic investigation. I doubt it would go to the pound before that."

"The car probably wouldn't provide any useful evidence anyway, as the crime scene was contained to an area some distance from it," Sam added.

"Right then, next question: were two constables in an unmarked sent to question Hensley Security Services' owner at about midnight last night?"

"Two constables would not be sent, and two constables would not be in an unmarked. Anyway, nobody went to Hensley's because we didn't know Hensley's firm was involved." Ben's tone indicated his growing frustration.

"Why not? There was signage on the car and on the patrol officers' shirts. What about the officers' IDs? Didn't they have personal IDs like a wallet or driver's licence on them, as well as their work IDs?" I watched shock register on Sam's face. Ben studied his hands clasped tightly in his lap. "Hello. Is anyone going to answer?"

"Hang about! I'm thinking. Give me a moment to do that," Ben snarled.

You may take as long as you need, Ben, because I think I know the answer to all that. It felt like an eternity before he answered. His measured reply was carefully chosen words directed at Sam, not me.

"I … suspect … we … have a … problem. Yes…?" Sam nodded but didn't look at him. Ben returned his attention to me.

"What other bombshell do you wish to drop?"

"None really, but is it possible to find out if the vehicle from the crime scene was impounded? I mean, to find out now without having to wait until the morning." Ben had his phone out and was on his way out of earshot by the time I finished speaking. The three of us sat in silence and without making eye contact while Ben made his call. Out of the corner of my eye, I saw him put his phone away. We had to wait a bit longer before he rejoined us.

"No car came in last night or today, and definitely none with a company logo on it. It wasn't taken to forensics either."

Deep furrows creased Emily's brow as she looked hard at me. "I'm confused. Hensley isn't missing a vehicle, and the police don't have the one from last night, so where is it? Was there a serious crime last night? Was a car involved in some way? Are you lot sure you know what you're talking about? If you do, what happened to the bloody car?" She cast her eyes around the group as she finished speaking. The two cops seemed to be fascinated by their footwear. The exaggerated wink Emily dropped me went unseen by the others.

No one appeared keen to respond, so I jumped in to bring the focus back to where I wanted it. "Here are some facts you might find useful. The phones went crazy at Hensley's this morning as staff rang in to find out what was happening. By some mysterious means, they all knew an incident happened to a patrol last night." I raised an eyebrow at Ben to see if the significance of that statement sunk in. He remained stony faced, and I continued. "Mrs Hensley, who is a director or something but not a partner in the business, is away visiting family and friends. Hensley doesn't know when his wife will return."

"She picked a good time to be away," Emily observed.

"Yeah. Jock, a long-time employee and friend who is helping out in the office for a couple of hours every morning while Mrs Hensley is away, was helping field this morning's phone calls. In between other calls, Hensley heard Jock tell a caller: 'No, Cass is not here. No one is here today… Uhmm, let's see … No, she wasn't on morning shift … Sorry, mate; can't help you with that'. Later, Jock told Hensley the caller was someone looking for Cass. The same man called back again around six o'clock this evening. He is Cass' boyfriend and told Hensley he hadn't seen Cass since she left for work last night, and she was not answering her phone. Hensley didn't think it his place to explain her absence."

"Phone…? Did she have a phone with her?" Ben demanded of Sam.

"No. No phone or anything else. It probably was in her handbag in the car. She wouldn't lug her handbag around while they carried out inspections, so she probably left it in the car with her phone in it."

"Would that be in the car that isn't missing and isn't impounded?" Emily quipped. Ben scowled at her but, undeterred, she added, "Wouldn't security officers carry at least a work mobile with them on their rounds?"

"Good point, Emily," I managed to say before Ben cut in.

"The other officer … What was his name? …Knight… Anyone query his absence?"

"Jason Knight," I began, "married for just over a year and the youngest of Hensley's employees. His wife is expecting their first child around the end of next month. She was having a few problems but refused to go into hospital for bed rest for the remainder of her term, and went home for her mother to look after her instead. She probably isn't aware yet of what has happened."

"Jesus, that's a good job for some poor copper from wherever she is staying at the moment. Maybe suggest they have the paramedics on standby when they tell the wife," Ben told Sam. "Are there any other interesting facts you'd care to share with us?"

"Oh, yes. I'm not finished yet. All Hensley's patrols have two shifts off in rotation every week. It means they don't have the same nights off every week. The company runs two shifts each day. A night shift from four o'clock to midnight, and a morning shift from midnight to eight o'clock. Some teams remain on the same shift all the time, while others will work as required, but work the same shift for the whole week. Cassidy and Knight had worked together for only about three months. Wait for it! The really interesting thing about Cassidy and Knight is that they were rostered off last night and tonight for their weekly break."

"Why were they there? Were they filling in for another team who didn't come in?" Emily asked.

"Not that anyone is aware of. The team rostered on that route last night most likely were the two men I observed at the first place I staked out. And, before you ask, I don't know what they have to say about last night. They are rostered off tonight and tomorrow night. They're good mates and planned a couple of days of camping and fishing. They were to head off as soon as they came off shift at midnight."

"Maybe they had Cassidy and Knight cover the rest of their shift for them so they could get away early. One of those un-official mutual swap arrangements that happen between shift workers," Sam suggested.

"That's something for your lot to look into," I replied. "There is something else for you to think about." I looked at Ben. "The patrols are allowed a coffee and a meal break each shift. They take those at whatever time suits, and usually when their route takes them close to an appropriate place. Somehow, when the swap occurred between the two teams, more than half an hour was lost. The first team was running eight minutes behind schedule when they left the first property I observed, but the replacement team was about thirty-five minutes late arriving at the second venue I monitored. Knowing what caused the lost time might prove useful."

"I assume you will share that information when you find out," Ben said.

"No. That's not how this works. I have amassed enough unanswered questions related to my case. Any excess unanswered questions to accumulate I am shoving across to you. Their answers probably are more relevant to your investigation than mine."

"Who is going to look into that disappearing car?" Emily asked.

"Oh, that's one for the cops to investigate. It's on the list of questions I've shunted across to them. And there is another one they can add to their list: who were the supposed two 'police constables' who banged on Hensley's door in the middle of last night … when the police didn't know the victims had anything to do with Hensley's?"

"Of course, they weren't police constables. That car does bother me though," Sam admitted. "Anyone got any ideas?" She looked at Ben. He didn't respond.

I suppose I might as well help them out. "Think back to what it was like at the crime scene once everyone started searching the property. Two blokes in police uniforms could emerge and be free to walk around. They might even supervise the loading of the patrol's car onto a tow truck or low loader. Was it likely anyone would question them or what they were doing?"

Sam's jaw dropped as she stared at me, but she managed to keep her mouth closed. Ben ruined the moment with his rumbling chuckle. He too watched Sam's reaction to my helpful input.

There wasn't much else to be said. The evening broke up soon after. I walked Emily to her car for a few quiet words. Some of those questions I relegated to the cops we would be exploring ourselves first thing in the morning. My hope was Hensley would keep his nine o'clock appointment with me to assist with the process.

After loading the dishwasher, I made noises about going to bed. Ben took the hint and stood to take his leave. When I went for a shower, Sam was seeing him out. The impromptu meeting they held outside lasted some time. Sam was still out there when I fell asleep.

*****

Sam and I danced around one another making breakfast this morning. Conversation was scarce, not due to tension between us, but because each of us was preoccupied with planning our days. Memories flooded back of having a houseguest from when Sam stayed here not so long ago. I sensed a little of the same emotion again today. Both of us are used to being on our own and aren't comfortable sharing space with someone else. There are exceptions of course. One of those exceptions will be when Troy Donaldson comes to spend a few days with me before returning to the UK. Come to think of it, there's been a distinct silence about that for a couple of days. I should follow-up before I become too engrossed in the Hensley case.

With my first appointment not until Hensley arrived at nine o'clock, I was in no hurry to leave for my office. Sam was long gone before I finished the day's first coffee. As I walked out to my car to leave, Ben called. "Do you know where Hensley's missus is spending her time away from here?"

"No. I never asked. It probably didn't occur to me that it might be relevant to my case. I could ask Hensley when he comes at nine o'clock … and no, you are not invited to attend." Knowing Ben, I wouldn't put it past him to arrive at my office five minutes after Hensley was due. His chuckle told me my guess was right on the money.

"Yes please, if you can ask about the wife without being too obvious. Don't know if it is important, but it could be useful."

"Okay. My gut tells me he might not be in contact with his wife, or she would be back home by now." Ben's interest in Mrs Hensley's whereabouts created doubts to occupy my mind all the way to the office. Have I missed something? Have I over-looked a possible angle on the patrol's attack?

Forget about what happened to the patrol, I told myself as I unlocked my office. That's not part of my brief. That is, it's not, unless it relates to the anomalies I am supposed to investigate. By the time I was sitting behind my desk, I had convinced myself Mrs Hensley's whereabouts might be important. If Ben is interested in where she is, maybe I should be too. A quick skim of my notes of my discussions with Hensley confirmed there had been no mention of where Mrs Hensley's family and friends were located, yet I felt I had a vague recollection of the comment 'up north'. No time left to wonder about it. Hensley arrived.

He rushed in out of breath (that might be due to not trusting the lift and having climbed the stairs instead), his face the colour of a ripe plum, and perspiring heavily. Close on his heels, Emily followed him in. "Goodness, Mr Hensley, here, sit down," she said as she pushed a chair towards him. "Are you okay? Can I get you a glass of water?"

"Please...," he croaked. Emily dashed to my miniscule kitchen to fill a tumbler for him.

"Take a moment to relax and get your breath back," I suggested. I watched as he drank the water. "Why were you rushing about and getting yourself into such a state?"

"Oh, it's nothing..." I stared hard at him. He squirmed in his chair. "You'll think I'm losing the plot, but I thought I was being followed. I undertook a fair bit of *housecleaning,* if you know what I mean, and then looked like making myself late for this meeting."

"Who do you think was following you ... or what made you think you were being followed?" Emily dragged a chair over to the desk and slid onto it. Her eyes had grown large. "Is there a reason someone would be following you?"

The three questions I asked Hensley received only one long shake of his head in response to all of them. I tried again. "Do you think they followed you here?" I was half tempted to lock the door in case someone sinister came barrelling in. Hensley shrugged off my question. Okay, one more try, "If you are not sure someone was following you, don't know why anyone would be following you, and don't know if they followed you here, can you think of any reason why anyone would be interested in you?" Again, a shake of the head, but more enthusiastic this time.

Congratulations, Mr Hensley. You have stirred up my intrigue. Something tells me there is a more sinister story running beneath this case than I know about. Time to play hard and fast with this client if I'm to make any progress. One last ridiculous question occurred to me. I decided to try it to see if it shook anything loose. "Does your wife think you are playing away from home and is having you followed?"

"What...? No, of course not. Why would she think that?"

"She is away at the moment. Maybe she is not just visiting family as you claim. Maybe she left you." There were those eyes of Emily's again; as large as saucers this time and focused on me ... but she remained silent.

"It's like I said. She is visiting family and friends. Yeah, we've had a couple of rows lately. What married couple doesn't? We're both tired that's all. There's nothing wrong, and nothing like what you are suggesting." I had aroused his temper. Let's see if he is as forthright with everything else I want to know.

"Okay. Has she returned?"

"No. I'm not sure when she will be back. Her mother's not too good at the moment."

"I see. I thought the incident the other night might prompt an early return. I assume someone told her about it."

Hensley looked sheepish and dropped his voice to not much above a whisper when he answered. "I don't know if she knows. I haven't been able to contact her. Aarrgh, there's nothing strange about that, so don't be giving me a funny look. She was to spend a few days with some friends out on a property where they don't have much mobile reception. I don't know if that's where she is at the moment, or if she is with her cousin out on his yacht somewhere. Her trip didn't have a firm itinerary. It was more a case of seeing when people were available for her to spend time with them. They all knew she was coming, but there were no firm dates. In the end, her mother's becoming ill at the same time as things were quiet for us here influenced the timing of her trip. I never know where she is likely to be at any given time. She will be moving around a bit within a big geographical area."

"…Up north somewhere, I think you said." He nodded but didn't offer to enlighten me further.

That's enough on that topic. Now it's time to find out exactly what this case is about. "Why were Cassidy and Knight on patrol the other night? It was supposed to be one of their nights off, yet there they were getting themselves attacked at the property to be inspected shortly before 8.30p.m. No, Mr Hensley. Don't shake your head at me. It's time for straight answers, so stop mucking me about!"

"I … I don't know why they were there."

"Okay… If that's how you want to play it, this investigation is over. I wish you well sorting out whatever anomalies you think you have with some of your patrols' operations. I'll show you to the door and let you out." I stood up and walked around my desk. Hensley didn't move. "I said I would show you out … and I meant it. I have nothing more to say to you, and I would appreciate you not wasting anymore of my time. Move it, Mr Hensley!"

"You don't understand…"

"That is quite possible since you haven't told me anything. But I will tell you something for nothing: I think you're mixed up in something dodgy – up to your ears in whatever it is – and Whittington Investigations does not want any connection to it. Is there anything in what I said that you don't understand?" More head shaking from Hensley. "Good, then lift your arse out of that chair and get out of my office."

"No. No, please wait. It's difficult…" I was on my way to the door and kept walking without hesitating. "All right; I'll tell you what I know. Please sit down and let's start again." I turned to face him and gave him a hard look before continuing to the door. "No. Stop, please stop. I promise I'll tell you all I know, if you will just hear me out. Please…" I stood my ground.

Hensley gave Emily a look that beseeched her to intervene on his behalf. I gave Emily the slightest nod. She rose to the occasion. "Sonny, perhaps we should allow Mr Hensley another five minutes to tell us what he knows. If it looks like he's not playing it straight, I'll ring security and have him turfed out. Maybe his behaviour so far might interest the police in their investigation. Perhaps I should ring the police instead of security if he keeps playing his silly game."

Well done, Emily. Her threat hit the mark. Hensley slumped in his chair like a deflating airbed. I resumed my seat behind the desk and said, "Well, Mr Hensley, the ball is in your court. Do you intend to run with it, or shall we blow fulltime and make a phone call?"

"It's a long story and much of it is speculation."

"You have wasted too much of our time, so get on with it," Emily snapped. Hensley rested his elbows on the desk and cradled his head in his hands. Without lifting his eyes to either of us, he started speaking and it continued for the next half hour.

Although much of his story was repetitive, there was enough information in it to understand why he was concerned. And, although he didn't allude to it in any way, some of what I heard not being said, suggested Mrs Hensley might not be above suspicion. By the end of his story, I was convinced I needed to know where Hensley's wife was and what she was doing ... oh, and with whom might be important too.

At the end of his spiel, I found myself unsure of what questions to ask. There were gaps in the information he provided, but it was clear those gaps existed because he didn't have the details to pass on. While Emily gave him that mouthful about wasting our time, I deftly started the recorder in the top drawer of my desk. I don't always use it to record client interviews and, if I do, I always erase the recordings after I transcribe them. In this case, I hadn't started the recorder at the outset of the interview as it didn't look worthwhile.

Now, the monumental task of transcribing Hensley's story was ahead of me. No doubt, once I revisited everything he said, there would be a whole host of questions I want to ask. That would be for another day. Hensley looked wrung out in spite of yet another cup of coffee, and I needed time to digest his information.

As I opened the door to let him out, I again assured him I would call him tomorrow or the day after if I needed more from him. Then Emily and I were alone, with the coffee machine working on our behalf this time. Emily stayed about another half hour, then left me alone to ponder the morning's outcome in peace and solitude. With everything about the case spread out before me, I attempted to make sense of it.

That's what I was doing when my phone startled me back to reality. It was Ben telling me he was bringing food for dinner, and asking how much longer I would be before heading home. The answer was simple. It was seven o'clock and I was starving. It took me no more than about two minutes to gather up all I wanted to take home with me, lock the door, and be haring down the stairs to my car. Ben drove up about five minutes after I arrived home.

Chapter 5

Sam didn't come for dinner. The painters finished yesterday and cleaned up today while Sam inspected the place. Then, between work intrusions, she replaced furniture and aired the unit. Her preparations for moving back into her unit continued this evening. Tonight would be her last at my place before returning to her unit tomorrow.

Ben took advantage of Sam's absence. It was only after I objected, he postponed the inquisition until after dinner. As soon as we left the table, it began. For the next half hour or more, Ben quizzed me about what I managed to elicit from Hensley this morning. My carefully worded answers didn't amount to much. Truth is, I hadn't learned much from Hensley. There wasn't a lot share with Ben ... including my speculations.

Several times during our conversation, Ben commented I looked tired. I didn't feel tired but, at the rate my mind was working to avoid saying anything I didn't want Ben to know, I was in danger of suffering mental exhaustion if we continued. It was a relief when he left around nine o'clock. On leaving the office, I intended working after Ben left tonight, but I weakened and went to bed.

*****

Ben seems more attuned to me than I thought – or like! I slept until well after eight o'clock this morning. Sam had left my spare room empty by the time I surfaced. It was wonderful to have the kitchen to myself as I strived to become human again. Despite my best efforts, it was almost ten o'clock by the time I dragged myself up the stairs to my office.

Any lingering zombie-like tendencies vanished as I unlocked the door. The sound of heavy footsteps thundering up the stairs at pace made me fling open the door and rush inside. There are other offices on this floor, but somehow, I knew whoever was pounding up those stairs was coming for me. I attempted to close the door, but was too slow. A huge lump of a bloke barged the door open again and lumbered into my office.

Although almost plastered against the wall when he flung the door open, I tried for some measure of control over the situation by demanding, "What the hell are you playing at? Who are you, and what gives you the right to barge into my office?"

"Thank God you are here…"

"Never mind about thanking God. I'm asking the questions, and I want answers … and now, if you don't mind."

I saw all the fire go out of him. He shuffled from foot to foot in his embarrassment, and I watched the pink tinge rise from his throat to his temples. "I'm sorry. I do apologise for barging in like that. It's just that I rushed over here as soon as I found it … and I half expected it to be a dead end. Please, may I talk to you for a few minutes?"

"As it happens, I don't have any appointments for a while. Take a seat. I don't know about you, but I need a coffee."

"Yes, please. I am desperate for coffee."

The time it took the machine to produce two mugs of coffee gave me time to gather myself again and prepare for whatever story the bloke might deliver. As I settled myself behind my desk, something about the man struck me. There was a familiarity of some sort. He noticed me looking – hopefully not staring – across at him.

"What's wrong? Why are you….?"

"No. I'm sorry; I was wondering if we had met before?" He shook his head. "I didn't think so, but somehow you looked familiar. Perhaps you should introduce yourself and tell me why you are here."

He sat up straight and gave me a hard look. Something of the anger present when he barged into my office returned. It seems he didn't feel the need for introductions.

"What has happened to my father? Where is he?" His demands were low and guttural. This was not a happy bloke.

I'm beginning to wonder if I shouldn't have gone back to bed and stayed there this morning.

"I don't know. Perhaps, if I knew who you are, I might be able to work out who your father is. Whether I might know anything about him or his whereabouts is another matter." There it was again, his embarrassment returning as he climbed down off his high horse.

"I'm sorry, I'm not doing this well. I'm Xander Hensley. That's Alexander Hensley, Frank Hensley's son. Coming here was a long shot. I knew that, but it was the only hope I had. Do you know my father?"

"I have met him a couple of times. What made you come here, and why are you asking me where he is?" I felt my stomach tighten.

"I flew in this morning. My father was supposed to meet the plane. He didn't show. I tried ringing him on every number I could think of, but he didn't answer on any of them. It's not like him. I started walking and eventually found a taxi to take me to the house. No one was there. It was too early for the changeover of shifts, so nobody was around downstairs. Although it was early, Dad would be in the office by then. So, I went upstairs to look for him."

"How did you get in? Was the place unlocked?"

"No, I have keys. I've always had keys to everything in the place."

"So, you let yourself in through the front door … and then what?"

"No. When the taxi let me off, I went around to the backdoor to let myself in."

"Why the backdoor? Don't you have a front door key?"

"Yes, but I've always gone in through the backdoor. The stairs are just along from the door. After I let myself in, I took a few steps straight ahead so I could see the whole office area. I called out … no one answered … I went upstairs. There was nothing unusual about that. It's my standard practice. The only unusual thing was that my father wasn't downstairs in the office by then."

"Okay, so you went upstairs. What did you find there? I take it your father wasn't in the middle of having breakfast." Xander shook his head as if to clear an unpleasant thought or memory. "Walk me through it step by step please, Xander." He took a deep breath and paused for a moment before launching into his walkthrough of events.

"I called out as I walked up the stairs. The old boy is getting on a bit, but he still can handle himself. I didn't want to surprise him. There was no response, so I went through to my room. It's the same room I've always had, and it's kept as I left it. After dumping my bag, I roamed around the place calling out for Dad."

"You didn't check his bedroom? He might be ill."

"You don't just go barging into your parents' bedroom…"

"Only private investigators' offices…?"

"I said I'm sorry about that. But your parents' bedroom is different. You know… what you see might be embarrassing. Oh, I don't mean I'd be embarrassed, but the oldies probably would be a bit upset about it. After banging on the bedroom door a few times and calling out, I opened the door and looked in. The bedroom was empty. Someone had slept in there last night. The bed was dishevelled. Dad would never leave his bed like that. When he wasn't there, I thought he might have gone to meet me, and we had crossed somewhere along the way. I tried ringing his mobile and his work mobile. No answer on either of them."

"So, how did you end up at my office?"

"Short on ideas of what else to do, I went all over the quarters. Maybe he left a note, or there might be some other clue about what was going on. On the notepad by the landline phone, I found your name and phone number…"

"You found my details, and came barrelling in here hoping to find what?" My voice was a touch sharper than I intended, but it reflected my level of indignation.

"No ... nothing like that ... Oh, I don't know. Your information was the only clue I found in the whole place. It had to mean something. That's what I told myself. Then, the night shift ended. The patrols were returning to base. Jock was in the office trying to deal with the officers, the phones, and everything else. I slipped onto a chair and helped him until things settled down."

"Did he offer any clues about where your father might be?"

"After he gave me my usual welcome ribbing, Jock wanted to know why Dad wasn't on the job. He couldn't tell me anything. I told him I had to go to follow up on something. He said he would be okay on his own for a while and told me to go and do whatever I had to do. I came straight here."

I took a few moments to study my desktop while I thought about what else I could ask. Nothing came to me. Hensley's disappearance was worrying. The pit of my stomach was not a happy place. Xander brought me out of my reverie.

"Why did he have your details next to the phone? Are you working for him ... investigating something for him?" I shrugged and flapped my hand in the universal 'maybe-yes, maybe-no' gesture. "Your lot investigate divorce type stuff; spouses playing away and such situations. Is that what you were doing? Did he hire you for a bit of grubby spying ... or did she want *him* watched?"

Now, there was an interesting response from out of left field. "I would tread carefully, Mr Hensley. You are about to find yourself apologising again, this time for offensive accusations and pig-ignorant behaviour. I don't know about other private investigators, but my case load is considerably more diverse than you suggest. Is there anything else you can tell me about this morning; anything Jock said that might be pertinent?"

"No. It seems everything is normal. At least, it would be if my father was there."

"There is one thing. How do you come to be in Millhaven this morning? You said your father was to meet your plane. It sounded as though that was to be quite early this morning. There are no flights into Millhaven at that time of day."

He chuckled. "I have a pilot's licence and own a Cessna. I left at first light and Dad was supposed to pick me up at the aerodrome shortly before seven o'clock."

"I think I would like to go over the quarters at Hensley Security Services and maybe talk to Jock if he is available. There are a couple of things I need to do first. Perhaps you should go back to help Jock, and I will join you when I finish here."

Xander looked a little crestfallen but didn't argue. There wasn't anything I needed to do, but I thought Xander having some time alone with Jock in the quieter part of the morning might shake something interesting loose. After making a few rough notes in my pocket notebook, about half an hour later, I walked the short distance to Hensley's establishment.

The front door was closed, so I went around and entered through the open backdoor. Both men were busy in the office. Phones never stopped ringing, and Jock seemed in a foul mood. I heard him bellowing at Xander as I came in. Rather than risk making things worse, I hung back and waited – and hoped – things would settle down in the office. They didn't. The snarling and bellyaching continued. I quietly made my way upstairs.

On my way up, it occurred to me Xander hadn't mentioned Mrs Hensley so far, except for the one veiled reference to her checking up on her husband. There was a whole truckload of questions I wanted to ask about her. I hoped Jock didn't injure or maim Xander before I had a chance to ask them. The discourse in the front office became louder by the moment. My patience was running out.

In the end, I bellowed down over the ruckus in the office. "If you two could tear yourselves apart, I would appreciate your presence up here, thanks Xander." An immediate heavy silence descended over the downstairs area. For a few heartbeats, nothing happened. Then followed the sounds of scraping chairs and shuffling papers… and Xander bounding up the stairs.

"What the hell are you two arguing about down there? I would think you had more serious matters to occupy your minds than the trivial things you were squabbling about."

"We weren't arguing. We weren't even squabbling." Xander looked seriously confused by my outburst.

"Well, what were you doing … apart from yelling loud enough to waken the dead?" Oh God, that might not be the best choice of phrase, given my suspicions about Frank Hensley's possible fate.

"We were discussing… Okay, we did get a bit loud, but we weren't arguing. We were discussing Dad's apparent disappearance and everything else that's happened in the last few days … and trying to work out where that leaves everything here. Do we just carry on as though nothing happened, or what? Jock can't manage the business on his own, and I can't be away from my own business for too long. My business partner can't manage that business on his own either."

"Right, well now that's cleared up, can you notice anything missing from up here, or anything disturbed?"

He shook his head, but I persuaded him to accompany me on a tour of the quarters anyway. Xander was a bit tentative about going into his father's bedroom. I dragged him through the door with me. "This is my father's private place. I never come in here. I feel like I'm trespassing in somewhere sacrosanct."

The fact he wasn't a regular visitor to the room meant he couldn't be sure if everything was as it should be. We didn't waste time. A quick look around and we were out of there. Xander seemed to think our inspection had covered every room but, by my counting, we missed one. "What about that room behind your father's? The one across the hall from yours, we haven't looked in there."

"No, we haven't, but that's a spare room. It's a sort of store-room; junk room, more like. I haven't been in there in years."

"Good time to take a look then. Let's go."

I watched his jaw drop as we stepped into the room. This was no junk room. This was a woman's room, albeit an untidy one. While there were no pink frilly bits decorating the room, there were clothes strewn everywhere … and they were either b a woman's or belonged to a raging transvestite.

"I wanted to talk to you about Mrs Hensley, perhaps this might be a good time to do that." Still looking stunned, he followed me out to the small sitting room and flopped into an overstuff armchair. I selected one a little easier to climb out of across the low coffee table from where Xander sat slumped and shaking his head in disbelief.

"Tell me about your mother. What's her name?"

"My mother…? What do you want to know about her for? She's been dead a long time, and highly unlikely to have anything to do the current situation here."

"I'm sorry. I thought the woman, Mrs Hensley, is your mother."

"No! She's not." A little too emphatic to ignore, I thought, and proceeded with caution.

"Perhaps, if you explain the relationship, I might avoid upsetting you further."

"Sorry. Yes, of course. The woman you call Mrs Hensley is Gina Burtell. She stuck with her previous name. I think it had something to do with some property ownership issue, or something like that."

"How long ago were your father and Gina married?"

"Uhmm … quite a few years ago. I'm not sure when."

"You don't remember their wedding? I would think it a memorable event. Where were they married, do you remember that?" He shrugged and was shaking his head again. "You did attend the wedding …?"

"No … It must have been while I was overseas."

This is all a bit odd. Xander and his father were close, but he didn't attend the wedding…? It might have nothing to do with my current case, but my gut is suggesting otherwise, and instinct tells me to dig deeper. Winding him back a bit and then walking him forward through events leading up to now might prove useful.

"Were you overseas long?"

"…On and off for about ten years."

"Did you go to different places, and maybe come home here between trips?"

"Yes … well no, not exactly …"

I kissed the last of my patience goodbye and gave him my best shrew rendition. "For Christ's sake, this has gone on long enough. Either you answer my questions – or tell me why you won't – or I am out of here and you can do what you like about your missing father and what's been going on with his business. What's it to be? Don't waste any more of my time."

Jock down in the office probably heard every word I said. When angry, my voice usually descends to a deep growl. Today it didn't. Today, even the neighbours probably heard it. Xander's mouth hung open and that startled rabbit look was back.

"I was in the Army. Went in straight from High School…"

"Then, smarten up soldier! Come to attention and provide the information I'm asking for. How was I supposed to know about your stint in the Army?" He claimed 'everyone' knew he went into the Army. "Well, I didn't until now. So, shall we start again? This time, I want straight answers to every question."

He nodded and apologised again – several times. While that happened, I tried to get my head around where I was at with my questioning. The short answer to that was: nowhere. So, I began a recap of what little I did know.

"Okay, tell me about when you left the Army and what happened then."

"I left the Army about four and a half years ago and came back here. Dad wanted me to come into the business with him. I didn't know what I wanted to do with the rest of my life, so I hung around here for about eighteen months, learning the ropes and helping run the business."

"Was your father married … I mean, was Gina here when you came back from the Army?"

"Uhmm … yes …. Ah, no. She didn't arrive on the scene until just before I left here. In fact, her arrival probably triggered my departure."

"You didn't get on?"

"We got on okay, but she was a bit pushy; seemed like she wanted to take over. I couldn't see the three of us being in the business working out. A mate from the Army and I talked about setting up our own business. I was working out how to tell Dad I was leaving when Gina arrived, and provided the excuse I needed. A couple of weeks later, I headed south and started the new business with my mate."

"It sounds like Gina just 'arrived'… no announcement; no fanfare, no wedding. Is that how it was?"

A shrug and a nod. "Yeah, pretty much like that. But Dad was okay about me leaving. He understood my reasons and was chuffed about the new business we set up."

"What is the new business? Is it in security services like this one?"

"Hell no. We both are IT professionals and the business started out offering those types of services. It's doing well. About twelve months ago, we added a cyber security arm to the business. My mate and I run that side of things, and another mate now manages the rest of our business. Both my mate and I are licensed pilots, and each has our own plane so we can be anywhere quickly to deal with whatever job comes up."

"Let me recap what I think we have established: Gina Burtell is not your mother, probably is not married to Frank Hensley, and hasn't changed her name, possible because of something to do with property ownership, but more likely because no legal process offered the opportunity anyway. What prompted you to fly into Millhaven at this time?"

"Dad called me late last night. He said something had come up. He wanted me to come home, and it was urgent. I drove to the hangar straight after his call, got the plane ready and flew out as soon as it was light enough for a legal take-off. You know the rest."

"Did he give you any clues about what happened?"

"No, but he sounded a bit … I think 'tense' describes it. He didn't sound right, and didn't want to chat. I knew it was serious."

"Has Gina contacted anybody here; you or Jock?" He

shook his head. "I noticed keys and a mobile phone on the floor in the bedroom. Perhaps we should check that phone." Xander appeared surprised. He hadn't noticed the items that were on the floor. My gut told me someone had tried to hide them by kicking them under the bed. The carpeted floor probably prevented them disappearing from sight.

There were two sets of keys, a mobile phone and, further in under the bed, an open wallet. After photographing the situation with my phone, I dragged the items out into the open. Xander identified one set of keys as the master set for the building. The second set contained the key for Hensley's private vehicle, the remote for his garage door, and another key Xander couldn't identify. Hensley's wallet contained almost four hundred dollars and a collection of cards. A photo of Xander in uniform occupied the owner's ID pocket of the wallet.

A check of the phone showed the only recent message received was Xander's providing his expected time of arrival at Millhaven. The only missed calls in the relevant time period were from Xander after his father failed to collect him on his arrival. None of this reduced the uneasiness I felt about Hensley's possible current situation. Jock interrupted my thoughts. He yelled for Xander to come downstairs.

"Go and help Jock with his problem. There is nothing more you can do up here. I'll be down as soon as I have another quick look around."

While Xander thudded down the stairs, I began a new slow and methodical search of the living quarters, this time without someone looking over my shoulder. Twenty minutes later, I stood considering my findings. That didn't take long. There wasn't much to consider. Only one thing stood out in my mind. Apart from the keys, phone and wallet under the bed, there was nothing to suggest anything happened up here. As I started down the stairs, I saw Xander go out the backdoor. A few moments later, a car drove out of the vehicle compound behind the building.

Chapter 6

Jock ended a phone call and slumped back in his chair as I slid into the chair recently vacated by Xander. "Bad day…?" An inane opening, but all I could manage on the spur of the moment. "I saw Xander leave as I came down."

"Aye. There's a payroll run booked. One of us had to do it and one of us had to mind the shop. He chose to do the run. Anything I can help you with while I have these few moments of peace. I'd swear every man and his dog has phoned or dropped in this morning."

"Everyone except Gina perhaps…?"

"Yeah, not a peep from that one; not answering her phone and no other way of contacting her that I know of."

"You might not want to talk to me, Jock, but anything you can tell me about how things were around here of late might prove useful." He signalled he didn't know what I meant. "Was there any tension, did anything unusual happen? Were there any rows between anyone – whether associated with the business or otherwise?"

"Nah, much the same as usual. There's always a bit of tension in the air of late. Don't think Frank and Gina were hitting it off too well before she went holidays. Frank was edgy yesterday, but I put that down to what happened to the team the night before. There might have been something else going on that I didn't know about. Frank wouldn't call Xander back here unless he needed him for something serious."

"I understand you have worked for Hensley's operation for some time. So, I imagine you know Frank and Xander, and even Gina, well. And you are familiar with the routine around here. Have there been any changes or anything radically different happening over your time here?"

"Of course there have been changes. I've been here more than 25 years. Things are bound to change over that time." I encouraged him to give me examples of the more significant changes. "Well, let's see now. The business has grown; expanded its operation quite a bit. And then there was the death of Mrs Hensley … and Xander left to go into the Army. Frank was so proud the lad was following in his footsteps. They are close, more like good mates than father and son. I think Frank always hoped Xander would come back into the business and take over one day. Of course, we mustn't forget Gina's arrival on the scene. She would consider that a major event and, in a way, I suppose it was."

"How was that? Tell me about Gina's arrival. From my discussions with Xander, I don't think Gina and Frank are married."

"O-o-h, I think she had intentions of getting a ring on her finger – and her claws into the business. Circumstances gave Frank just enough time before she had a chance to herd him down the aisle to work out that it might not be a smart move. But, yeah, her arrival caused a few changes around the place."

"Xander said you started out here as one of the patrol officers. Why did that change?"

"Aye. In the early days there was only Frank and me. In those days, we managed the patrols between us. Not too many businesses were worried about security, so it was easy for the pair of us to manage. Then we added payroll and banking runs during daytime trading hours. That's when Mrs Hensley started helping out a bit whenever we needed her in the office during the day. If either Frank or I didn't have a run to do, we would man the office so Mrs Hensley could do her housework."

"As you said, the business grew quite a bit over the years, and it now employs quite a few patrol teams. I take it you don't do any of the night patrols these days."

"Mrs Hensley's illness was short. She wasn't available, so I came to help. I continued on after she died. Then, Frank came off the road full-time, so a patrol replacement for him was employed. As the number of clients expanded, more patrol officers were employed. That meant the workload here at base increased as well. Back in those days, most workers were paid by cash, so there was a fair bit of daytime work as well as the night security patrols to cover. I had a bit of a health scare around that time and needed to take things easy for a while. When I was well enough to do a few hours a day, Frank asked me to help out in the office. Over the next couple of years, the business grew, we got busier, my helping out in the office became a full-time job. Then, along came Gina. She was dead set against anybody who wasn't 'family' being involved. I didn't want to go back to doing night patrols, so I ended up doing only a few hours in the office whenever they were too busy to cope during the day."

"I'm not developing a great opinion of Gina, but perhaps I'm misjudging her. She had a bloody cheek pushing you out because you weren't family, when it appears she wasn't either." Jock shrugged but offered no argument.

How long would Xander be away? There was still quite a bit of work I wanted to do before he returned. Jock appeared to be in an expansive mood and happy to answer questions. I decided, as time was running out, I needed to ask the couple of hard questions I had in mind to see how he responded, and if they shook anything loose.

"You may or may not know that Frank came to see me a few months ago." Jock shook his head. Okay, don't give up just yet I told myself.

"There was only the one visit. Nothing more happened until a couple of days ago. He told me the reason for his visit was still the same as before. We began working the case for him that night, without much idea what we were looking for. Even Frank wasn't sure there was anything to investigate. That first night on the job was the night of the tragic attack on the patrol. Did Frank discuss his concerns with you, or of his intention to talk to Whittington Investigations?"

"No, not a murmur. I don't suppose you can tell me why he engaged you…?" I shook my head. "Okay, let's see. Private investigators are hired to look into straying spouses; to find evidence to support a divorce application. So, my guess is, it was about Gina." Jock raised his eyebrows at me in question. "About bloody time he woke up to that woman. She'll take him to the cleaners, she will."

58

"I sense you are not a fan of the woman. Why is that? It has to be based on more than the fact she pushed you out and possibly marginalised your friendship with Frank."

"There is something about her that shrieks devious and deceitful. I don't think she's at all fond of Frank. Doesn't show it if she is. Argh, I'm telling tales out of school but, almost from the day she arrived, I felt she had an agenda. I'm sure she's been up to something. I don't know what, and I've no evidence to suggest it's true, but something is not right there. Not right about the way she is in this business."

"Perhaps it would be useful if I knew what her role was here. Since talking to you and Xander I saw Gina as just another body working in the office, answering the phone and dealing with enquiries. Doing the usual routine office duties. Is that the case?"

"Yes, that's part of what she does. But, over time, she assumed greater responsibilities. She took it on herself to do all the daytime runs. Before that, Frank and I shared the responsibility. Whoever was free did the run. That's how it started out when Gina arrived. She soon changed that. Then she took to meddling in the rosters."

"What does 'meddling in the rosters' mean?"

"Frank is responsible for the rosters – or so he thinks. He draws up the rosters and keeps an eye on how the teams are going, just as he always has. But she comes along and changes things: swaps partners around, shuffles teams around so they no longer operate according to the roster. I've never worked out why she needs to change them. More importantly, she never bothers to tell Frank anything's changed. A few times he's been caught out when things went wrong, and he challenged the team that should have been on patrol about it. He ends up looking a fool, but he is so smitten with the woman, she sweet-talks him and feeds him a line about why the changes were necessary."

Plenty of food for thought in all Jock comments, but I'm not sure how relevant they are. Perhaps it's time to change tack and focus more on the night Frank disappeared. "I've had a good look around upstairs, both with Xander and then on my own. There is no evidence to suggest anything happened up there; no damage or evidence of a scuffle. If his keys and his wallet weren't still there, I'd be inclined to assume he'd gone off somewhere of his own volition. Instinct tells me that's not the case. Have you noticed anything here around the office area that's out of the ordinary in some way?"

"Not if you ignore the mess just inside the front door. Something unpleasant happened there. I thought Xander would call the police, but then you showed up. Anyway, I haven't touched anything. Come to think of it, I'm not sure Xander is even aware of the mess. He came in through the back door when he arrived, and only ventured as far as this office before going upstairs. You can't see the front door from here. You have to go around to the front of the counter to see the area in question. None of our employees use the front door. Everyone uses the backdoor, so I don't think anyone came in through that front door this morning. It remains undisturbed from last night, if you want to take a look."

I wandered around to the front of the office counter, but still couldn't see the front door area until I took a couple of paces away from the counter. Quite a scuffle occurred there.

Furniture was knocked over. There were some breakages of what looked like nice pieces of glassware. Strange stuff to have just inside the front door of a security firm's office. A carpet square occupying the area immediately inside the door bore a couple of worrying stains. Almost lost in the pattern and colours of the carpet, I'm sure forensics would prove the streaks were blood, human blood. And, more precisely, Frank Hensley's blood. My stomach did a couple of major flip-flops before tightening into a lead ball. Never doubt your instincts. It looks like mine were spot on from the outset this morning.

Jock came to join me as I inspected the damage. "Jock, the shards of glassware and what I can see of these bits of furniture seem a little unusual for this operation. Is there a story to it?"

"That's Gina's doing. Before she arrived on the scene, we had a couple of chairs over there facing the counter. If a client came in while we were busy with someone else or on the phones, they sat and waited until one of us was free to deal with them. That wasn't good enough for Gina. She wanted to spruce the place up; had grand ideas for the whole of this space. She started in the area near the door without consulting Frank first. He wasn't too happy with this part of the 'refurbishment' and demanded to know what else she planned. Let's just say, her grand plan came to an abrupt halt at that point. Frank wouldn't even have new tiles laid." Jock's obscene chuckle suggested he enjoyed Gina's being taken down a peg or two.

"Has anyone notified the police about this?" I asked as I gestured across the wreckage.

"No; not my place to do so. I suggested Xander do it, but he didn't. Not that he didn't want to call them, he was too pre-occupied with his father's disappearance to do it."

"How much longer before Xander is likely to return?"

Jock checked his watch. "He should be back about now – unless something goes wrong to hold him up."

I would prefer Jock hadn't added that comment about some-thing going wrong. From the way this investigation is going, Murphy's Law seems at work here. I recited it in my mind: any-thing that can go wrong, will go wrong ... And probably in the worst possible manner, I added for good measure.

Twenty minutes later, when Xander still hadn't returned, I felt compelled to act. With my phone in my hand, I told Jock I intended calling the police. He did not look pleased, and argued to allow Xander a few more minutes before making the call. While reluctant, I agreed to allow Xander to be thirty minutes late before I called them. A car drove into the car compound in the twenty-ninth minute of our waiting period. Xander had returned.

He looked flustered and pre-occupied as he strode into the office and hung the car keys in the key safe. "Everything go all right?" Jock asked in a flat voice and without raising his eyes to look at Xander. A short pause followed before Xander flung himself onto the other office chair.

"I don't know. I'm not sure." Jock jerked upright and swung around to face Xander. "Oh, no need to panic – I don't think... Well ... no ... Uhmm ... the run went okay. There were no problems collecting the client and taking him to the bank. As I left the bank, I thought I might have picked up a tail, so I chose a more convoluted route to return the client and his payroll back to his workplace. …Told him the radio said there was a traffic snarl along the route we normally took. He was okay with it."

"That wouldn't have delayed you for almost half an hour, would it?" Jock demanded.

"Of course not; my alternate route added only a few minutes thanks to more traffic lights to contend with. I still wasn't convinced I wasn't being tailed, so I drove into the city heart, parked and did a bit of housecleaning. That …"

I'm sure I know what 'housecleaning' means but I asked for clarification anyway. Jock explained. "If you're on foot, you go in and out of places … in the front door and out the backdoor or some other exit. You go at a quick pace, without running or appearing to be hurrying, and you never stop. You keep on the move – doubling back and darting off on tangents all over the place – to lose anyone following you."

"Yeah, I did a bit of that," Xander continued, "and ended up upstairs in a department store where I had a clear view of my car in the carpark below. When no one appeared interested in the vehicle, I headed back, taking a tour of Millhaven to get here. Maybe I'm being paranoid. I'm not sure there ever was a tail."

It was a good time to drag their attention back to the incident that occurred at the front door last night. Xander claimed he didn't know what I was talking about. I led the two men around to the scene of the scuffle. "Whatever happened to Frank Hensley is a matter for the police, and I am calling them now." I directed my next comments to Xander. "Once the police become involved, there will be little I can do for a while without trampling all over their investigation … and they will not allow that to happen. Xander, you have a decision to make. When the appropriate time presents, do you want me to continue the investigation your father hired me to undertake, or do we rule a line under it now?" He didn't hesitate.

"No. You keep going. Whatever concerned my father

enough to hire you needs to be followed through. Anyway, it might have nothing to do with the police investigation. I want you to continue your work. Don't worry about being paid. I am still authorised to operate on the business bank accounts. You will be paid."

"Good, but I wasn't thinking about my bill. Things are going to be confused around here for a few days, making it almost impossible for me to resume my original investigation. What I propose is to undertake background research and look into a few other matters. This will be 'office-based' work, so you won't see me around the place, but I will be available if you need to contact me by phone or email. We need the police investigation to be well advance before I pick up from where I left off."

Neither Jock nor Xander questioned with my proposal, so I called Sam. She arrived about five minutes later accompanied by another detective and a uniformed officer. While the other two officers spoke to Jock and Xander, I gave Sam everything I knew about Frank's disappearance. With that done and the police investigation beginning to hum about the place, I headed for the solitude and comfort of my office. A text message arrived as I let myself in: Troy Donaldson.

Troy, having finalised whatever work delayed the completion of his contract, was now free to come to Millhaven. Everything in life is conditional. Troy's impending visit was no different. He would catch tomorrow's flight from Brisbane to return to the mine site where he expected to spend a day or two before flying to Millhaven. By tomorrow, he would be more definite about his arrival.

It felt like I had been waiting for that information for an eternity. Sometimes life smiles on you. My proposed way forward with the Hensley investigation allows me to get away for a few days guilt-free. Troy's impending arrival means I need to work my tail off until then to have the Hensley case background research completed before taking time off.

I hadn't progressed much beyond booting up my computer when Ben rang to ask what was happening about dinner tonight.

My answer was short and simple. "Nothing. I'll be working late." I didn't dare mention I would spend some of that time working in my city office in case Ben decided to bring takeaway to have dinner with me anyway. Apart from that, I still hadn't really told Ben about Troy's visit or our plans for the time he would be here. I fear life is about to become complicated.

Chapter 7

It was five o'clock and all I had managed since returning to my office was a list of background information I wanted. Such research is time-consuming. It takes you off on tangents and eats up time. I groaned inwardly when Emily bounced into my office. So far today, nothing went according to plan.

"I knew you would be working on tonight … and if I rang to see if I could help, you would fob me off. So, here I am with laptop computer. What can I do? Oh, as I haven't seen you today, maybe you better bring me up to speed before I begin."

First, I sent Emily a mental apology for my earlier groan at her arrival. My overview of the Hensley case took up the next fifteen minutes. "So, for a while, the case will be restricted to office-bound research. Here's a list of the information I think we need to better understand the world of Hensley Security Services. My gut tells me finding out all there is about Gina Burtell should be our primary focus."

Emily threw one of my lounge chair cushions on the floor, set up her computer on the coffee table in that corner of my office and began work. While she organised herself, I locked the door to tell any latecomers the office was closed for the day. For the next hour, the heavy silence was punctuated only by the occasional sound of a car horn or the screech of brakes from out on the street.

A little before seven o'clock, we stopped to review progress. There was preciously little to review. Emily glanced at the clock as someone's stomach growled. She abandoned her cushion on the floor to stroll about the office to revive the circulation in her legs and backside. As we finished our review, Emily stopped pacing and spun around to face me. "How certain are you that this Gina Burtell person actually exists?"

Ever astute, Emily had arrived at the same place as I had a

few moments earlier. I held serious doubts about Gina Burtell. "After the last hour's work, Emily, the only thing I'm certain of is that a woman – a real person – calling herself Gina Burtell does exist. Who she is might be significant to this investigation. I need to think about how we sort that one out before we go much further."

"Good luck. I haven't a clue how we might track her down. But I know we need food to keep us going. You devote your thinking to finding Gina while I go in search of something for dinner." Before I could argue, Emily was on her way out the door.

After staring at the wall a while, a lightbulb moment happened; a weak lightbulb but worth a try. I called the number. Confident Hensley's office would be deserted, I was shocked when Jock's brogue purred in my ear. "You've reached the office of Hensley Security Services...." Damn! Answering machine ... I tried my luck when the message ended."

"Jock, it's me, Sonny Whittington. Can you spare a couple of minutes to speak to me?"

"Aye Lass, what can I do for you? I can spare as much time as you need. The patrols are out now. Things are quiet around here. If you wanted to speak to Xander, he's gone up to bed. He didn't sleep much last night, and today exhausted him. We shared a couple of bevvies and he went to crash for the night. If there is anything I can do to help..."

"Thanks, Jock. I prefer to talk to you, so it's good you are alone. Here's my question: I imagine there are all sorts of rules and regulations governing who may work in the security industry and who may drive for the likes of payroll runs. Am I correct?"

"Aye, you just about have to be able to walk on water, and a reference from God himself would be handy. What do you really want to know?"

"So, the company needs to keep comprehensive personnel files for all its employees and others who operate for the company."

"We do ... and I'm thinking you're really enquiring about the 'others'. If I'm right, that includes the likes of Frank, Gina,

Xander and me. And, if I take a wild guess at where this is heading, I'd say you were interested in what's in Gina's file."

"Well spotted, Jock. I know such files are supposed to be confidential, but is taking a peek a possibility?"

"Come to the backdoor after eight o'clock. Xander will be asleep by then, so we won't be disturbed. I assume you prefer Xander didn't know about this."

"Yes, for the moment. Thanks, Jock. I'll see you soon after eight o'clock."

Moments later, Emily arrived with food. The aroma of roast dinners wafted through the door with her and had me almost drooling by the time we were settled with food in front of us and tools in hand. Conversation was sacrificed in favour of eating until we dispatched a significant portion of our meals. I was about to tell Emily I would be leaving soon, but she jumped in ahead of me.

"Our new lab is ready for occupation. I'll be working in there from the start of next week. So, you should get as much work out of me as possible before then."

"That's fortuitous. Troy should be here in the next couple of days. We will head up to my beach place for a while. That's why I worked late tonight. We can't go tramping all over the cops' crime scene, so I'm doing as much as possible in the office before I leave with Troy. Can you tell me about this new laboratory of yours yet?"

"They're keeping it under wraps until next week, but I'm more comfortable talking about it now. It's added as a new wing to our existing labs. You're aware what passes for a forensic lab here in Millhaven has struggled for a while and hasn't earned many accolades lately. The Government decided to contract out its forensic laboratory operations in regional centres. My mob successfully tendered for the contract. After all, we have a qualified forensic scientist on board now."

"That would be you, I presume."

"Yes. I will manage all the labs, but will work primarily in the forensic lab. One or maybe two of the staff from the existing forensic set-up will come across to work with me. I'm hoping it's only one of them. It will not be helpful if the other bloke comes too. I suspect he and the bloke who retires tomorrow are the cause of the long-running problems in that lab."

"Am I correct in thinking everything from future police investigations will come through your new lab from next week?"

"Yeah, and we are to inherit the backlog of work from the existing lab. We are going to have to hit the floor running next week. I'll spend bits of time in the new lab between now and then to get as much as I can done beforehand."

"Well, congratulations are in order … and I can see how – with careful management – this new arrangement might benefit Whittington Investigations. Nevertheless, I will do nothing to jeopardise your position there."

"Never thought you would. Now, what else are we doing tonight?"

"Nothing more; I plan a big day tomorrow, so a good night's sleep is required. Anyway, I must meet someone in a few minutes, so let's get out of here."

With the residue of dinner cleared away, Emily left. A couple of minutes later, I followed her. It was almost 8.30p.m. when I parked about a block away from Hensley's and set off on foot. The backdoor was open, so I knocked gently and went in. Jock met me. "I just checked on Xander. He's sound asleep. Poor bugger had a rough day." Jock noticed my frown. "What? Why the frown?"

"I'm sure Xander is worried about his father. Who wouldn't be? But, he's not a boy anymore and he's served overseas with the Army. I wouldn't have thought today would knock him around as much as you suggest."

"There's more to the story. Frank and Xander always were close. That became even stronger after Xander's mother died. They were more like best mates. Even after Xander and his partner set up their new business, Xander would fly up once or twice a month to spend the weekend with Frank. If there was something on, like the football grand final, he would organise tickets, come up, collect his father and fly off to wherever it was being played. Sometimes they went out fishing on a charter boat for the weekend, or spent the weekend camping in the national park."

"Okay, I get it. They were close."

"Aye, but in more recent times, that changed. They still talked on the phone every day, but Xander didn't come home so often. I think this is his first trip back in a couple of months. Now, I'm not privy to exactly why, but I do know it had something to do with Gina. So, apart from being worried about his father, and being given a rough time by that young detective, Xander is overwhelmed by guilt. He feels he has let his father down; let something – whatever it was – come between them. Then, when his father needed him, he wasn't here. It became worse when he heard what happened to that patrol the other night. He started putting two and two together in relation to what happened to his father, and didn't much care for the answer. Xander rarely drinks. I gave him a good stiff scotch tonight and it knocked him out for a while. I wager he won't be too bright when he wakes up." Jock chuckled at the thought of it.

Jock unlocked a cabinet and ran his finger across the top of the file pockets. "I assume you'll be wanting to look at Gina's file first." I confirmed his assumption. He checked the name on the file tag before lifting out a relatively thin folder.

"Don't think we'll find out too much about the lady in this folder." Jock placed it on the desk in front of me. "I don't know what's in there. I've never looked in the folder; never looked in any of them for that matter. Maybe I should check my own while I'm here."

My misgiving about how thin the file was proved well placed. It held little of interest: a sketchy CV that didn't shed much light on what she had done or where she had been in the past, a couple of other documents of no consequence to me … but no copy of Gina's driver's licence. That is the one document I hoped to find in her file. I queried its absence.

"Dunno…," Jock said. He flicked through the contents of

the file again. "No, it's not here. But it has to be... For compliance with industry regulations, we are required to hold a copy on file. So why isn't there a copy in here?"

"That's my question, Jock, and it seems it's one neither of us can answer. Let's have a quick flick through Frank's file. Maybe it went in there by mistake." Jock left Gina's file on the desk and retrieved Frank's file.

Not interested in details of Frank's life, I flipped through the file with no more than a glance at each document. A copy of his driver's licence was there as it should be, but there was nothing to do with Gina. I handed Frank's folder to Jock to replace in the cabinet. He ran his finger across the file pockets, stopping at the one with Frank's name on it. As he replaced the file, he murmured, "That's odd."

I took a couple of steps to peer over his shoulder. "What's odd? Just point it out before you touch anything."

"See at the back there. There's an unnamed folder. Not in a pocket, it has slid down under the other pockets hanging in the drawer. I wouldn't know it was there except, when I pushed all the pockets to the back of the drawer, they didn't quite go to the end of the hangers. There's a corner of that folder sticking up that's stopping them." He turned his hand palm up towards me in a 'what-now' gesture.

"Oh, I think we must look at that file. Don't you agree?" He grinned and began easing the folder out from under the others. I had to admire his restraint. He handed me the folder without glancing at its contents.

"Come now, don't dally about, Lass. Open it so we can see what secrets it holds." Maybe not as restrained as I thought, but he had the right idea. Within a second, the file was lying open on the desk. "Who the hell is this person?"

"I was hoping you could tell me. I don't recall seeing her before. But then, I hadn't ever seen you or Xander before today." I took my time looking through the file, scanning each page for clues to the identity of the person. When almost at the end of the file, I asked Jock, "Have you seen anything so far that sheds light on who this is?"

"Nothing. All we know so far is that it's a woman, and she has a funny name."

"Foreign sounding name …," I murmured as I flipped over a document to reveal the last sheet of paper in the file. "Well, whoever she is, here's a copy of her driver's licence."

"Eh…? What have you found?" Disappointed, Jock had abandoned the file and flopped onto his chair. At my mention of the driver's licence, he sprang up and almost pushed me out of the way to see it. "Jesus, that's Gina!"

I was about to ask him if he was sure, but it seemed pointless, so I settled for a different response. "…Not according to this licence. It's a woman with a strange name, not Gina."

"I don't care what it says. That's a photo of Gina. Taken a while back I'll grant you, but it is Gina."

"Perhaps you might give me a photocopy of this document…?" I suggested.

"Copy the whole bloody file for you, I will. I'll be interested to see what you find out."

"Best we don't mention anything about tonight to Xander. I'll come back first thing in the morning. I think I need another look at Gina's room upstairs."

With the copy of the rogue file tucked in my bag, Jock walked to the backdoor. He surprised me by following me out and locking the door behind him. "Where is your car? I'll walk you to it." I argued there was no need as it was only in the next block. "The way things are around here at the moment, it's safer if I walk you to your car. Then you can drive me back here to the backdoor." It seemed a bit over the top, but I know when I'm beaten. I didn't argue.

It was nudging eleven o'clock when I arrived home. So much for the good night's sleep I advocated to Emily. The thrill of the chase was coursing through my veins. I wouldn't sleep if I went to bed now, so I might as well do some more digging into Gina's identity. Around midnight, it occurred to me that Gina might be Gina. Maybe the name in the file is an alias Gina used at some time. Bugger! Such thoughts are not helpful at this hour of the night.

*****

Not the brightest this morning although I managed to drag myself out of bed at my usual time. After abandoning my research and going to bed around one o'clock, sleep was a long time coming. The tantalising clues uncovered last night failed to solve the mystery of the woman's identity. Disappointment does not make a good bed mate.

As I lingered over a second dose of caffeine with my breakfast, Sam's name came to mind. I had no doubt Sam Keller, as Millhaven's lead detective, had more than enough work to occupy her without my adding to it. Nevertheless, I could justify asking her to look into the rogue driver's licence as it might be linked somehow to Frank Hensley's disappearance and the earlier attack on the security patrol officers. I was clutching at straws but, by the time I finished breakfast, I convinced myself to call her. I walked through to my office while her number was dialling.

"Hi Sonny, sorry I took so long to answer. I was in the shower. What has you ringing me so early in the morning?" I gave her a brief overview of the situation without providing specific details. "That's intriguing. I have a meeting with Ben at eight o'clock. How about I come to your office as soon as that finishes? Geez, look at the time. Gotta go or I will be late for Ben." Before she ended the call, I confirmed I would be in my office all morning. Then it was my turn to be on my way into my city office.

Nine o'clock came and went. I was debating whether I needed another coffee when Sam arrived with Ben in tow. That resolved the issue. Coffee all round required before we get down to business. Once seated at my desk with our coffees, and before I opened the photocopied file, I ensured they both understood the source of what I was about to share with them would not be disclosed. Ben launched into a strong protest. I stood up, dropped the folder into my filing cabinet and locked it. "I'm sorry, guys. It seems your visit is a waste of time." I dropped back onto my chair and raised my eyebrows at Ben in expectation.

"Okay, okay," he growled, "It seems said file and the information it contains dropped to earth from the sky some-time in the recent past. Now, may we get on with it?"

After retrieving the file and beckoning them to follow me to the coffee table in the corner of the room, I locked my office door before joining them around the table and opening the file. Half an hour later, we all sat back to ponder its contents in silence. So far, so good, but I needed to push things along.

"I have it on good authority, that's Gina Burtell's photo on that licence, albeit a younger Gina. What I don't know, and therefore can't share with you, is which one is the real woman. Whether the identity of the woman has any bearing on your current investigation of all-things-Hensley or not is something for you to find out. But, I would like to know the outcome of your deliberations." After giving them a copy of my photocopy of the photocopy of the licence Jock gave me, there was nothing else to discuss. Emily was about to knock on the door as I opened it for Ben and Sam to leave.

She announced she wasn't available this morning and would check in with me again after lunch. That suited me. While she played in her new lab, I would check on Gina's bedroom at Hensley's. After loading the few things I needed into my bag, I walked the few blocks to the security services' building.

The atmosphere in the office was subdued. Jock dropped me a wink as I walked in. I didn't know what it meant, but decided to be cautious until I found out. Xander had no objections to my searching Gina's room again, but the police had gone over it since I was last there. "Will you be okay to find your own way around up there?" he asked. His face almost beseeched me to say 'yes'. I left the two men in peace and climbed the stairs to the quarters.

Evidence of the police's presence was everywhere. The place hadn't been trashed but there wasn't much that hadn't been disturbed since my previous visit. I found it odd that Gina's room seemed to suffer hardly any disturbance. Everything looked as it was the last time I checked the room. I didn't waste time. The last thing I needed was for Xander to become curious about what was taking me so long upstairs and come to find out. While I wasn't doing anything illegal, I didn't want an audience while I was about it.

Chapter 8

My search started with the dressing table just to the right of the door. Then I intended working my way around the room.

Nothing of any interest lurked in or on the dressing table. The next piece of furniture was positioned under the window. It was a small table with two drawers. My search confirmed Gina used it as a desk. I thought it strange she required a desk in her bedroom when there was a huge office space at her disposal downstairs. I moved onto the bed and its two bedside cabinets. A bed is a bed. Nothing else to say about that.

My attention turned to the identical bedside cabinets. Made of fine-grained timber, each cabinet featured a shallow drawer at the top with a small cupboard space underneath. The drawer of the cabinet on one side of the bed contained much what I expected: small packet of tissues, a pen, a nail file, and a pocket-sized book of crosswords. The cupboard underneath held a pair of fancy bedroom slippers adorned with a few sequins and a fluffy piece of ostrich feather.

On the other side of the bed, the cabinet told a different story. The cupboard area was empty but contained dust and detritus that suggested it once held material, some of which was paper. The drawer above, although now empty, contained similar debris … and one other interesting item. An oil stain not quite the size of my palm adorned the bottom of the drawer. I checked underneath. The oil hadn't seeped through to the underside.

Did that mean whatever caused the stain wasn't in the drawer for long. Or, perhaps the thing wasn't very oily. What would leave an oil stain in a bedside drawer? A well-oiled hand-gun might. But why would Gina keep a weapon in this drawer? I sniffed the drawer, and then rubbed my hand over the stain to pick up any oily residue. A sniff of my hand confirmed what I already knew: a well-oiled weapon left this calling card. I need to ask if Sam and Ben know about it. After clicking off photos with my phone, I moved on.

A built-in wardrobe was the last piece of furniture to search. So far, my hunch had struck out. I didn't hold out much hope of striking it lucky with this cupboard, but I was in for a surprise. What appeared to be a built-in cupboard with double doors proved to be something else entirely. I flung open the doors expecting to be confronted by a wall of hanging garments. Instead, I was looking at a short passageway into a space behind the bedroom.

Inspection of the space revealed it once was a storeroom, but now converted to a walk-in wardrobe. While there was no evidence of it outside, on the inside of the space, the now blocked off doorway from the main hallway was visible. Original shelving remained along the far wall of the space. The right-hand wall of the entrance passage formed the end of a long hanging space that extended to what was the outside wall of the building.

Apart from the configuration of the space, there was little else to suggest this was a wardrobe. Only five forlorn-looking garments hung there. Fabrics and styles of the garments suggested they were long past their prime. On the other side of the space, a handful of items remained on the shelves. These included a couple of pairs of lacy knickers in need of new elastic, and three old tee shirts with frayed and stretched ribbing at the neck. Two well-worn pairs of shoes resided on the shoe rack running along the floor under the bottom shelf.

"What a forlorn looking space this is," I told the universe before returning my attention to the hanging space. A significant collection of empty hangers was pushed towards the far end. They came to rest against a white melamine-finished storage unit. Incongruous with the rest of the space, the shiny white unit is of the type available from most hardware stores. Measuring 400 millimetres wide and 450 millimetres deep, the unit contained three shelves, three standard depth drawers, and one deep drawer at the bottom. Nothing remained on the shelves or in the first three drawers. The bottom drawer refused to open in spite of my best efforts.

No dust on any of meant all shelving was in use until recently. This appeared to be Gina's only wardrobe, so where were her clothes? She either had few clothes, or a mountain of suitcases accompanied her on holiday. If the latter were true, why would she take so much with her when it was supposed to be a short trip? The state of this wardrobe – and the rest of the bedroom – said she wasn't planning on coming back.

Deep in thought, I wandered out and sat on the bed. No other conclusion came to me: Gina was in the wind. Nobody could contact her or had heard from her. She planned to disappear. She did not intend returning. What precipitated her hasty flit from where she worked so hard to ingrain herself? Perhaps the other entity, the one on that driver's licence, is her real identity. Maybe answers to my questions lie in that identity's story and not in the life of the mysterious Gina Burtell. As I sat there trying to piece together what I knew, or thought I knew, about the woman whose room this was, I remembered the stubborn drawer in the wardrobe.

A more determined attack on the drawer produced the same result. The only thing all my pulling and shoving did was to pull the unit out a bit from the wall and skew it slightly away from me. I went down on my knees to attack the drawer and stopped. Something was not right. I could see a sliver of the rear of that drawer. It appeared to be a void. There was no back end to the drawer.

I scrambled to my feet, pulled the unit out of the hanging space and turned it around to see its rear. The drawer front remained in place, but the board across the back end of the drawer was missing. Nothing, except dust and cobwebs remained in the resultant void. Nothing, that is, except for the clear outline of something secreted here for some time. Only a narrow strip at the edge of the void was visible, but that was sufficient for me to make out the outline of the box-like object. Judging by the build-up of dust around the outline, it was there for some time. With the remainder of the void a black hole, I reached for my torch.

Illuminated by my small LED torch, I could see the missing object's outline covered most of the base of the 'drawer'. A few pieces of paper at the far end of the void appeared overlooked when the object was removed. With my torch held between my teeth, I scrambled around on the floor to photograph the whole of the void. I overcame the temptation to reach in and drag out the pieces of paper. Gina Burtell might not be part of the police's investigation, but she might become a key player. Sitting back on my heels, I called Sam. It dialled out. As I put my phone away, I wondered what to do next. The answer to that came when my phone rang.

Expecting it to be Sam calling me back, I didn't check the caller ID before answering. It wasn't Sam, it was Ben. That's odd. "Are you with Sam at the moment?"

"No. Why?"

"I tried calling her, but she didn't answer. Then you called straight after."

"You won't get Sam for a while. She's gone onto silent mode. Are you in your office or are you working right now?"

"Working...sort of."

"Why did you want Sam? Or, should I ask what's happened now?"

"That's uncalled for. Anyway, you called me. What did you want?"

"It can wait. Have you found something relevant to Sam's investigation?"

"Uhmm ... maybe ... she needs to see something to decide if it is."

"Stop mucking about. What have you found ... and where are you?"

"I'm in the living quarters at Hensley Security Services ... and, yes, I think I've found something relevant to the Hensley investigation."

"I'll be right there."

Damn! I don't need Ben. I'd prefer Sam to have a look. I don't know who this new Ben is, but I want the real one back, the one I've known for almost as long as I can remember. If I knew what caused the change in him, it might be easier to understand.

About five minutes later Ben thundered up the stairs to the living quarters. I took him to Gina's bedroom and showed him the walk-in wardrobe. After his quick inspection of the space, I pointed out what to me appeared anomalies. The last thing I showed him was the bottom drawer of that storage unit. I shone my torch in so he could see everything, including the paper jammed at the far end of the void. "I haven't touched anything; just photographed it."

"Good; focus the torch of those bits of paper." He reached in and began removing them. There was more than I expected. Once all the pieces were removed, he spread them out on the floor to examine them. Two pieces looked like they came loose from a larger multipage document. I had no idea what they were about as they were in a foreign language. The other smaller pieces reminded me of receipts and the stubs torn from deposit slips. I wasn't sure as Ben crouched over them, preventing me from getting a good look.

As I tried reading over Ben's shoulder, he gathered up all the paper and dumped it into an evidence bag which disappeared into his pocket. He stood up and began a methodical inspection of the space. My frustration continued to develop. Finally, I demanded, "Do you agree this wardrobe suggests she has no intention of returning?"

"It does look that way. What about the son, does he know what's going on here?"

"He is a stepson, and he, like everyone else, believes his stepmother has taken a short break to visit family and friends. To further complicate matters, no one knows who her family is, or where they are other than 'up north somewhere'."

"Sounds a bit far-fetched; do you buy it?"

"Yeah, I do. Even Hensley told me he didn't know where she would be at any given time or how to contact her. By the way, you still haven't told me why you called me."

"Oh yes, I rang to tell you the name on that driver's license appears on several databases. There are a number of people who would like to speak to the owner of that name if she ever materialises. I now have various people searching for an image to compare with the image on the license. It's unlikely there'll be a quick response to that, or perhaps any response. And, in the end, it might be that the name on the license does in fact belong to the image, and that the image is of the real Gina Burtell. I don't know if that has any major impact on your case, but I think our interest in her possible involvement in our investigation increased substantially today."

"Do you know what language was in those documents?" I nodded towards the evidence bag in his pocket.

"Languages never were my strong point. Someone much cleverer than me will sort that out."

With nothing further we could do upstairs, we went down to the office. The phones were quiet, leaving a heavy silence hanging over the area. "I wanted to let you know I was leaving. Thanks for allowing me to have another look around upstairs. I'll let you know if anything develops. I assume you know Superintendent Ben Richards." Both Jock and Xander looked a bit startled when Ben came down the stairs with me. It was obvious he hadn't introduced himself when he arrived. Neither man responded. "He wanted to talk to me and came here when I told him this is where I was." Both Jock and Xander nodded and I think they relaxed a little.

Not long after I arrived back at my office, Emily arrived loaded with lunch. She wanted to know if I'd uncovered any-thing interesting, but I wasn't sure what to say. Had I uncovered anything interesting? I let Emily go on believing it wasn't a fruitful morning.

Halfway through lunch, the call came in. Troy would be arriving tomorrow. That resulted in a concerted effort on our research for the rest of the day. Troy's arrival tomorrow would curtail work on the Hensley case for a while. Then cancellation of Troy's flight further delayed his arrival. He didn't arrive till the evening flight, so that provided a bonus extra day to work the case. Just before leaving the office to collect Troy from the airport, I phoned Hensley's to confirm I would not actively work the case for a few days, but I would be available if they needed to contact me.

Troy's plane had landed when I pulled into the designated area for collecting passengers. He looked tired and frazzled as he loaded his bag into the car and climbed into the passenger seat. "You have no idea how much I'm looking forward to a hot shower, a hot meal and a good night's sleep," he chirped as I drove out of the airport.

The hot shower worked. He was brighter afterwards, and chirpy as we tucked into steak and salad on the deck. It wasn't a late-night, but conversation never strayed far from planning the next few days and tomorrow's preparations for our stay at my beach place.

*****

We both were up early this morning. Troy undertook the usual pre-trip check of the boat and motor before accompanying me to the supermarket. After lunch in a bistro at the marina, we spent the afternoon loading the boat and car in readiness for an early departure tomorrow.

Emily dropped by on her way home to say hello to Troy, and for any last-minute instructions I might have for her. Apart from keeping an eye on everything for me and collecting the mail, there was nothing else for her to do. Emily wouldn't have spare time anyway. With her new forensic lab commencing operations, she and whatever staff she has will be busy clearing away the backlog of work inherited from the previous lab.

At about seven o'clock, Sam arrived to update me on their Hensley investigation before I left town. That didn't take long. How long does it take to say 'nothing new and no further progress today'? Oh, and of course, she wanted to say hello to Troy. It seems everyone is keen to drop by tonight, and say hello to Troy – everyone except Ben. I hadn't heard from him today. He didn't answer either of my calls. Something very not good happening there, and I am going to have to sort it out when I return from the beach.

After Sam left, I loaded my computer, files and everything else I wanted to take with me into my car. Troy stopped me as I was about to head for bed. "Where are we going tomorrow and what does it involve?" I realised I had never explained our trip.

"We're up with the larks in the morning to drive four hours north along the highway towards Wickham, before turning off for the boat ramp, and then travelling about eight miles across Regents Bay from the boat ramp to my cottage in a tiny bay on Riposte Island."

"What else is there beside sun, surf and sand?"

"No surf; just sea, a big shed, cottage and a bunch of rainwater tanks. That's it."

"Can't wait…" His comment seemed genuine enough.

My early night meant I spent a long time in the dark waiting for sleep to arrive. Early nights being such a rarity for me, I had difficulty falling asleep. It began to concern me as I knew we hoped to be on the road by 3.30a.m. and I would be driving to the boat ramp.

I shouldn't have worried. After fitful and not restful sleep, my alarm rattled me awake just before three o'clock. Troy's bedroom light came on almost simultaneously. Within no time, we were in the kitchen for a quick coffee before we hit the road. As we would be at my beach place by ten o'clock, we agreed, after settling in, a late breakfast on the deck overlooking the ocean was the way to go.

Nothing unexpected occurred with our travel. Traffic was light. We arrived at the boat ramp at about seven o'clock. By splitting the tasks between us, we had the boat in the water, the car parked, and were idling out into the channel by 7.30a.m. Light breeze and a glassy sea had us at my beach house about twenty-five minutes later. Due to all the usual faffing about getting the tractor out of the shed, hauling the boat out, and unloading everything into the cottage, it was over an hour later before we were on the deck with breakfast.

Our first day at the bay was spent familiarising Troy with my place, the bay and the rest of the island. After a glass of wine with lunch, we both disappeared into our rooms to catch up on last night's missed sleep. A large chunk of the afternoon was gone by the time I resurfaced ... and I needed coffee. While the coffee machine did its thing, I unpacked my computer and set it up in the corner of the open-plan living area that is my office when I'm here. Troy joined me in the kitchen as I took the first sip of coffee. "Any more of that going? After being lured out of my den by the aroma, I need a cup." We took them out onto the deck.

The afternoon sea breeze was up and loaded with the briny smell of the sea. I thought the breeze stronger than the forecast suggested it would be. Clouds gathered on the horizon. "With this breeze behind them, those clouds will be here soon enough," I told Troy. "If we are lucky, they might bring a shower to wash the dust off everything and freshen up the place."

"It would be nice to fall asleep listening to the rain on the roof. How about we pick a few oysters off those rocks when the sun loses some of its sting later this afternoon?" Armed with appropriate tools and a bottle of cold white wine and two glasses, that's how we filled in a pleasant half hour.

The first sprinkle of rain arrived at dusk, changing our plans for a barbeque in favour of pasta indoors. We sat on the deck after dinner and talked as we watched the lightning bouncing off the clouds. Troy wasn't sure when he would leave for the UK. He suspected there would be some extra little thing to do before he left. It might mean spending a few more days at the mine site after we return from the island.

Troy asked about my Hensley case. I didn't realise how little there was to tell until I tried outlining events. It seemed that only added interest to the story for Troy. He began speculating on what might be the cause of the various aspects of the case. Before long, I joined in and found myself suggesting all sorts of wild hypothetical scenarios. The weather intervened to prevent us being subsumed by fantasy.

A light continuous misty rain replaced the earlier sporadic sprinkles. With the lightning moved on, there was nothing more to see, and the breeze, having moved a little more to the north-east, now brought the misty rain in onto the deck. We moved back inside and, after cleaning up the kitchen, Troy went to his room to read. My sleep this afternoon left me disinclined to an early night. Instead, I spent several hours typing up my notes on the Hensley case and going over everything in the file in the hope something might start to make sense.

I went off to bed none the wiser about the case. In the short while before I fell asleep, I felt my concern for Frank Hensley deepen. As if that wasn't enough, my gut kept telling me digging into Gina Burtell's whereabouts and real identity would uncover nothing good.

Chapter 9

Morning dawned without making much impression on an almost uniformly leaden sky and sea. Overnight, the Northerlies arrived, bringing huge breakers rolling in from the Pacific Ocean. The rhythmic crash and thump on the beach of each wave turning over cubic metres of sand marked its arrival. I wandered out onto the front deck to assess the morning. It offered not even a glimpse of watery sunshine.

I stayed up well after midnight last night, not only to work on the Hensley case but also to email a report and final invoice to my previous client. This left me a bit slow off the mark this morning. There was no sign of Troy. He went to bed earlier than I, and probably woke at his usual time this morning. Perhaps he went to the shed to tinker with something rather than wake me by wandering around in the cottage.

No sign of Troy in the shed or that he had been there. He wouldn't go for a walk along the beach. Only the foolhardy would take on that wind and flying spray. Flecks of spray adorning all the glass panels in the front of the cottage bore testimony to how unpleasant the beach was this morning. My search for Troy unsuccessful, I wandered through the shed and around the cottage, checking the wind hadn't caused damage or shifted anything during the night.

With all my internal systems not yet fully functioning, I was half way up the stairs to the side deck of the cottage before I realised one of the boats was missing. What the...? How could we lose a boat during the night? It had its trailer's safety chain securely attached. Hauling the trailers out of the water and up the beach without attaching the safety chain invited disaster. While it was a windy night, it would require a cyclone to blow the bigger of the two boats off its trailer. Even if that happened, it is likely the boat would be on the beach – probably damaged – but not disappeared from sight.

Intelligent thought slowly returned. The tractor we use to haul the boats up the beach was attached to the big boat's trailer. With the threat of rain last night, the tractor was parked in the shed. Therefore, Troy used the tractor to launch the big boat this morning. Why would anyone try to launch anything today? Launching the smaller boat in this rough sea would swamp it. Waves rolling in over the transom would fill it in no time. The bigger boat invited much the same problem. But, somehow, Troy launched the bigger boat without sinking it before getting it off the beach.

His need to launch any boat today mystified me. Neither of us needed to be anywhere. When Northerlies were forecast for the next few days, we both looked forward to staying indoors and reading the books we brought with us. Leaving no note or message for me was unlike Troy. While his taking the boat out this morning continued to gnaw at me, I decided to adopt a wait-and-see approach for a couple of hours ... or, that was my initial intention.

I found I couldn't muster any interest in anything for breakfast other than coffee. After sitting at the breakfast bar nursing my mug of coffee for about fifteen minutes, my concern for Troy's safety turned into anger at what I saw as his cavalier attitude to safety, and to me. Where had he gone ... and why hadn't he told me or left me a note? The satellite phone wasn't much use thanks to the heavy cloud cover. I went in search of my mobile phone.

It was on my bedside table. On my way to my room to get it, I realised I hadn't checked Troy's room. Maybe he hadn't gone anywhere and was still curled up in bed. I eased open his bedroom door. No Troy. Maybe he left me a note in there somewhere. A quick check of the room proved I was clutching at straws. I grabbed my phone and went to sit at the breakfast bar again.

When Troy failed to answer my third call, a lead ball formed in the pit of my stomach. I tried rationalising the situation to myself. In this wind, it would be hard to hear your phone ringing.

If you are travelling in the boat, it is hard to hear a phone above the sound of the motor. Perhaps he was ashore somewhere and left his phone in the boat. They were all credible explanations, but I didn't buy any of them. Then it struck me. Of course! Why didn't I think of it before? I hadn't checked to see if Troy's mobile phone was still here. No, it wasn't. He took it with him. "Call me, damn you!" I shouted to the empty cottage.

It took a little while, but rational thought returned. The big boat was missing. Therefore, Troy had gone out in it. He had his phone with him but wasn't answering; not a good sign given the circumstances. Never mind why, where would he go? Nothing came to me. Okay, which *way* would he go from here? That assumes he did leave and didn't go down and drown in the swell close in to the beach. Perhaps checking the beach might be a sound move.

Hard to tell whether it was misty rain or spray and foam carried in on the wind soaking me through to the skin. Sand stung my legs, arms and face as I inspected the beach. Bugger this wind, it's making it almost impossible to do anything. The trailer's tracks remained clear on the sand above the tide mark. That was some feat Troy accomplished. He had to launch the boat once he had the trailer in the water, and then had to leave it anchored on the beach while he moved the tractor and trailer back up above the high water mark. All that without having the boat break free, capsize or be swamped.

Deep in thought, I wandered back up from the beach and found myself in the shed again. Since I am here, it won't hurt to look around, I told myself. There was nothing relevant to Troy's disappearance. I had to try to find Troy.

A few minutes later, I was kitted out in dry clothes and a spray jacket, and had everything I might need loaded into a backpack. I stood at the edge of the deck, slapped a cap on, pulled my untidy pony tail out through the opening at the back, and hefted my backpack over my shoulder. One last check on the laces of my hiking boots, and I was down the stairs and heading for the beach... and bracing myself mentally for the physical work ahead, and what I might find along the way.

There was only one way Troy could go: south. To go north would necessitate punching through the breakers rolling in around the tip of the island. Going south meant travelling with the wind and the waves, and not against them. I put my faith in the logic of those thoughts and marched to the southern end of the bay. Then the first of the physical stuff began. A wall of rocks tumbled down from the top of the island and out into the bay. It effectively hemmed in my bay from the next one. The only way on foot to the next bay was up and over those rocks. I headed up the slope to where the rocks were not so wet and slippery.

It was hard work and, in spite of the wind and drizzle, I sweated under the spray jacket. At the other side of the rockfall, a decision was required. Should I climb down onto the narrow rocky beach of this next bay, or stick to the high country and loop around the top of the bay. Staying up the slope lengthened the hike to the other end of the bay, but the foam building up on the narrow strip of beach below suggested the high ground was the best option.

By sticking to the higher ground, I saved myself a good deal of climbing and time. Nevertheless, it took me an hour to cross the four bays to reach Windy Point which is the south-western most point of the island. I sheltered in the lee of a couple of big rocks, which also provided a little overhead protection from the rain, and tried Troy's mobile again. Still no answer. Every fibre of my being told me no good news was coming.

After a handful of trail mix and a swig of water, I headed around the point and crossed the next bay. This south-westerly side of the island afforded some protection from the northerly wind, but the cold, light rain continued. Half an hour later, I crossed a large flat bay and its sand spit jutting a long way out into the bay. To cross the rocky divide beyond the sand spit and enter the next bay meant climbing a few metres higher up the hillside. When I reached a long flat rock platform, I stopped to survey the long arc of the island's coastline stretching out before me.

Beyond this point is the start of mangrove country where there are no beaches. The tidal areas are thick with mangroves. Occasional narrow inlets run back through the trees, some reaching back to the rocky base of the hill that is the island. While those inlets are inviting for crabbers and fishermen, many have come to grief in them. Rocky ledges lurk not far below the surface, unseen in the dark water shaded on three sides by over-hanging mangroves. Once in an inlet, it is almost impossible to turn a boat around to exit again… and trying to reverse out of these inlets doesn't often succeed.

With nothing of interest visible from my vantage point, I wiped the rain off my binoculars and pressed on. Strangely enough, sticking to the higher ground made crossing the next area easy going. No boulders were in my way, and the build-up of leaf litter and other soft material underfoot made for easy walking. I strode out, making good time crossing this first swampy part of the coastline. It was almost half an hour into my trek high above the mangroves that I saw it: something white in the entrance to one of the inlets some distance ahead.

If it was possible, the knot in my stomach tightened. I dug the binoculars out of my backpack. With trembling hands, I lifted them to my eyes. And there it was; my worst fears confirmed. It was my boat lying at a crazy angle up against the mangroves. Water sloshed in and out over its starboard gunwale now low down to the water in the inlet. The boat's port side was propped up on mangroves some distance above the water. Was the boat damaged? Hard to tell from up here, but it seems likely.

I checked what I knew of that inlet. A large rock, less than a metre under water, occupied about half the entrance to the inlet. My recollection is that it is on the same side as the boat but should be further ahead in the inlet than where the boat is. Still, from up here, it's tricky to judge. Maybe Troy tried to enter the inlet and hit that rock. Maybe that rock is closer to the entrance than I remembered. Why would Troy try to enter that particular inlet – or any inlet along here?

My pulse raced. My breathing became shallow. Where was Troy? He wasn't on the boat, and there was no beach here. Those of us who know this island and its waters know there are crocs around. Every so often one is seen in the area, usually along here in the mangrove area. There are no reports of any hanging around in my bay, but I exercise caution. On any other occasion, nothing would coax me down into those mangroves … but today, I have to know what happened.

There was no easy direct route from my vantage point to the boat. I decided the best approach was from a little further along the hillside. 'Easier' was not the word to describe it. The descent to the mangroves required clambering over a whole landslide of various sized rocks and, closer to the bottom, there was the added joy of scrambling through gnarly tangled bushes, some with needle like prickles. After losing some skin on the rocks and bleeding from numerous scratches, I broke through the first of the mangroves to find myself in a small clearing.

About the size of a small bedroom and walled in almost completely by mangroves, the area sloped gently towards the inlet. A track about as wide as a person and almost devoid of vegetation ran through the mangroves and down to the water of the inlet. I spotted the clearing from high up on the last rock I climbed over, and headed for it. While the clearing came as a surprise, nothing prepared me for what I found there. I caught my breath, and for a moment, my feet refused to move.

After breaking through the last of the brambly vegetation, I took a couple of steps across the soft ground of the clearing before stopping to survey my surroundings. That's when I saw him. With arms and legs positioned as if he were climbing, Troy was face down on the ground at the high edge of the clearing, tucked in under overhanging vegetation, he remained hidden from view until that moment. His face was turned away from me. I couldn't tell if he was breathing.

The next thing I was aware of was my heart hammering violently as I crouched beside him. His hair was matted in the dried blood across part of his forehead and down the left side of his face. I choked back tears. He was alive. Troy was breathing. It was weak, but he was breathing. A quick frisk found no broken bones, so I eased him onto his side. That caused a low, but reassuring groan. With my backpack on the ground beside him, I extracted everything I thought I might need.

With a tissue moistened with some of my bottled water, I cleaned his head wound. In spite of my being as gentle as possible, Troy moaned throughout the exercise and often tried to pull his head away. Perseverance paid off. At last his wound was revealed … and I did not like what I saw. Luck had been on his side today. It was a glancing injury. Had it been a direct hit, it would be a different story. Troy would not be breathing, and he probably would still be in the boat – or feeding the fishes.

My efforts to deal with his wound were primitive. I threw a small first-aid kit into my backpack almost as an afterthought. About as big as a small tin of chocolates, it didn't contain anything too sophisticated for dealing with what to my untrained eye looked like a bullet graze. Nevertheless, I swabbed it with antiseptic solution – that caused plenty of reaction – and covered it with a wide dressing strip. By the time I finished ministering to my 'patient', I thought he seemed a little more aware, although not yet awake.

After making him as comfortable as possible, I repacked my backpack, keeping out only the bottled water. Unsure what to do next, I sat down and leaned back against the stump of a long-gone tree. Might as well get comfortable, I told myself, this could be a long wait. I turned my attention to Troy. "Please regain consciousness soon," I whispered. I couldn't see any evidence of crocodiles having frequented the clearing but, the longer we stayed here, the more likely we could become 'lunch for the taking'. With nothing to do but wait, I filled in time by letting my mind ponder the options available to us.

It was sometime during this process that my eyes drifted back to Troy. Did that happen? Was it real, or wishful thinking? No. There it was again: the merest flutter of Troy's eyelids. "Come on, Troy. You can do it. Come back to me." After repeating my encouragement a few times, my heart skipped a beat when his eyes half opened for a fraction of a second. More encouragement required! It took another five minutes before his eyes opened to give me a blank stare. He wriggled around a bit and moaned a couple of times, but that was good. He was coming back to me.

The slow process of rejoining me in the real world felt as though it took longer than it did. After about ten minutes, Troy replaced me against the old tree stump. In slow, short swigs, he downed about half a bottle of water. Thank goodness I decided to pack a second bottle. The only way we had of getting back to my cottage was to retrace the way I came. I wasn't sure Troy was up to the challenge. He assured me he was. It seemed wise to allow him to rest as long as possible before tackling the long trek home. With my eyes and ears peeled for any hint of crocs showing an interest in us, I questioned him about what led to his current situation.

He appeared distracted, didn't offer any clues about this morning, and complained of a headache. Not surprising given his wound. A scrabble through my first-aid kit produced a card of analgesic tablets. After gulping down two, Troy closed his eyes and leaned his head back against the stump. I didn't want him falling asleep. At some point in my first aid training, I remember being taught concussed patients should be kept awake. Troy assured me he was not falling asleep. In spite of his reassurances, I kept my eyes glued to him. Suddenly, his eyes flew wide open, almost startling the life out of me.

"We have to get out of here."

"Eh...? O-k-a-y, but is there something I should know about?"

"There are crocs here." He pushed himself upright and winced. His hand flew to his wound. "I'm serious, Sonny. I'm sure there are crocs around here. That's why I tried to get as far from the water as I could. I just didn't get too far before I blacked out." Troy gave me a lopsided grin as he finished speaking.

"Uhmm … Yes, I agree getting away from here would be a good idea. The only problem is, the first stage of our way out is rough going. No, don't argue. I came down that way to find you, so I know what's ahead."

"Well, stop wasting time and let's get to hell out of here." Troy insisted, and I wasn't inclined to argue.

I helped him to his feet. His legs were wobbly. He leaned heavily on my shoulder for a few moments before straightening up and putting on a brave show of being ready to go. After hoisting my backpack over my shoulder, I led the way to the path through the brambles I created on my way in. Everything was fine until we reached the base of the rocks. As I was about to indicate our path up and over that rocky outcrop, I noticed what looked like an easier track off to my right. A quick reconnaissance from ground level indicated it did offer an easier climb until at the very top of the rockfall. One huge boulder blocked the end of the track. Nevertheless, I decided this was the better way to go. We would deal with the boulder when we reached it. My assessment of the situation proved correct. While navigating our way around that boulder was tricky, overall, this proved much easier than the track I used before.

Once over the rocks, we made good time all the way back to Windy Point. Troy held up well, and I kept the pace moderate to ensure he would make it back to my cottage. The climb over the rocks at the Point was relatively easy and, once we are over the top, we stopped in the lee of a rock for some trail mix and water. After a rest stop of about fifteen minutes, we hit the track again. The trek home was easier than earlier this morning. The gale force winds had abated to a cool gentle breeze, and the rain now confined itself to the occasional patch of drizzle.

The last part of our journey would be the toughest for Troy. That last climb over the rockfall leading down into my bay was tough. Troy would be nearing exhaustion by the time we faced that. How best to handle the situation occupied my mind for most of the way. By the time we reached the rockfall, I had decided the best course of action was to leave Troy on this side, and climb over the rocks by myself. Then, I could launch the small boat and motor around to collect him and take him back to the cottage. Now that the weather was behaving itself, there would be no problems launching the small boat.

I might have had a grand plan, but Troy would not agree to it. He insisted he was capable of climbing over the rockfall with me. We took another rest break before attacking that last climb. A few minutes rest, more trail mix washed down with water, and we were on our way. As I led the way across the rocks, I felt weariness starting to take over. If I felt this way, how is Troy coping? I kept a close eye on him but, he showed no sign of exhaustion, we kept going.

Back at the cottage, the first order of business was a hot shower and dry clothes for Troy, followed by proper attention to the wound on his head. When I joined him in the kitchen after I showered and changed, he announced he was starving. "A sandwich of some sort and a cup of tea I think is what's called for."

Tea…? My coffee-making skills are good; my tea-making skills not so much. Maybe Troy discovered that fact in the past. He volunteered to make the tea while I made sandwiches. We settled back and ate our late lunch in silence. Then, as we sat sipping our teas, I asked the BIG question. "Whatever possessed you to go out in the boat this morning? Where were you going, and why? It was a filthy morning. I don't know how you launched the boat safely, but I'm dying of curiosity. Put me out of my misery and tell me the story."

Chapter 10

For a few moments there was nothing but the rhythm of waves on the beach as we sat on the deck looking out at clouds scurrying across the still leaden sky. Troy cleared his throat and confessed, "It all seems a bit naff now."

"Even naff will do. I'm listening, so please go on." Another short pause while Troy scuffled his feet on the deck and squirmed in his chair. I let him take his time, as I watched the ever changing greyness of the sea.

"Right. Well, it started last night. After my nap yesterday, I didn't sleep much and woke a bit after midnight. I knew I wasn't going back to sleep, so I sat on the deck to watch the storm."

"I didn't hear you get up." That surprised me. I'm a light sleeper, and any unusual sound wakes me.

"At the time, the thunder and lightning were continuous overhead. I didn't need to turn on a light, the lightning lit up the whole place. It was a spectacular storm. I'm unsure of the time, but it was after one o'clock; maybe closer to two o'clock. Anyway, through a momentary break in the sound of the storm, I heard a boat close by. I grabbed your binoculars and came back out to search for it. It was directly out front when I saw it … a largish ugly looking boat heading north without any lights. Not even the port and starboard lights showed. To be out in that storm was stupid. There had to be something critical brought them out in that weather at that time of the night."

"Agreed. Your description doesn't remind me of the vessels I'm familiar with from around here. I assume you tracked it."

"Yeah, I thought it was heading for one of the bays near the north point of the island, but it didn't come in. It continued out through the entrance to the bay to meet up with a large yacht just out front. The wind and drift of the tide took them around behind the rocky northern tip of the island, so I couldn't see what went on out there. The yacht must have been just inside the main shipping lanes running past this island, but it had no lights on either – not even a running or masthead light."

"Whatever went on, it sounds like they were up to no good. Why else would you want to stay dark while you were doing whatever it was? Let's not jump to conclusions, but it's likely they were transferring something from one vessel to the other. I don't know what, or who, or in which direction the transfer was made, but it's what instinct tells me last night's event was about. Did any of the boats come back through the bay?"

"Yeah. About four o'clock, the same boat headed south past here. I tried following it, but the rain was too heavy to see clearly, and I lost sight of it. I tried going back to bed, but my mind kept conjuring up questions about what I saw. I couldn't go back to sleep. Curiosity won out. As soon as it was light enough, I took the boat and cruised south along the island to see what I could find. The storm had abated, so launching the boat wasn't difficult … well, maybe a bit tricky. It was only a short lull in the storm before it returned more ferocious than before. Until I encountered that boat and was shot at, my only concern was how I was going to pull the boat out when I came back here. With the storm so vicious, I knew I wouldn't be able to bring the boat ashore without swamping it."

"Isn't it amazing how a gunshot brings everything else into perspective? I suppose you've already told me how the rest of the story panned out, unless there's something you forgot to mention."

"No, that's what happened. My concern now is what to do about your boat. On a good day, we could still go back to the boat ramp in the small boat. But, what do we do about the big boat? We can't leave it there stranded in the mangroves."

"Preferably not, but I haven't worked that out yet. I want to know what we're dealing with before I worry about the boat."

I looked over at Troy. He stifled a yawn, and had slid down in his chair. "I need to ponder things a bit longer, and you need some rest. Take yourself off for a nap, and maybe take another couple of analgesics before you go."

Once he was in his room, I documented all he told me about last night. By the time I completed my notes, it was well after four o'clock and I was desperate for coffee. Coffee late in the afternoon keeps me awake at night. Today I was prepared to risk it. My mug was half empty when Troy emerged from his room. He stopped at the coffee machine before joining me on the deck.

Nothing much emerged from my deliberations while he napped, but one thing was clear to me. "We should be prepared to accept last night's event as a once-only show that won't be repeated again any time soon. On the other hand, as we don't know what it was about, we can't be sure it won't happen again – even as soon as tonight." Troy nodded. "I propose keeping watch tonight in case something does happen. We could split the night into two shifts and take one each."

"I seem to remember sitting on a beach keeping watch in shifts through the night some time ago, only it was on Crete. As I recall, life became a bit hairy not too long after."

His reference to our involvement in disrupting the illegal trafficking in cultural artefacts brought a flood of memories rushing back, not many of them pleasant. "I remember it too, but I think things here already are 'hairy' … unless you don't consider your head wound as such." He gave me a wry grin and threw up his hands in resignation.

We agreed Troy, having had a nap this afternoon, would take the first shift while I slept until one o'clock when I would relieve him. Our experience on Crete was that it doesn't end up working that way. While we both remembered it, neither of us chose to mention it. Troy suggested I should have an early night to maximise my sleep time. An early night was pointless. I'm used to late nights and wouldn't fall asleep until my usual time. An early night would result only in much tossing and turning. I had no doubt we would spend the night keeping watch together.

With dinner dealt with and nothing worth watching on TV, by nine o'clock all lights were off and we were settled on the deck for our long night's vigil. The first couple of hours passed easily. Time slipped by as we revisited our time on Crete, the time and place where we first met. We chatted about various shared events and the other people involved, and dug deep into our memory banks for the names of some of the students and staff there with us on the archaeology school's dig.

Midnight slipped by, but conversation dried up after that. There were other things we could talk about, like the support Troy gave me when I returned from Crete to find James, my mentor and business partner, battling terminal cancer, and through the long journey afterwards as I set up on my own. But these remained still sensitive subjects; raw memories best left undisturbed. We lapsed into a comfortable silence.

At two o'clock, I went and made coffee by the pitiful light of a pocket torch with almost depleted batteries. Coffee and munching a couple of biscuits didn't occupy much time. Silence descended once more. By three o'clock, my eyelids felt heavy and I longed for something – anything! – to wake me up. It seems Troy was at the same stage. He stood up and stretched before prowling around the deck. Not satisfied, he went down the stairs and prowled around in the shed for a minute of two. I heard a couple of soft yelps as he collided with things in the dark. When he returned to his chair, he seemed alert again. I decided to give it a try, and wandered around the deck a few times before settling again.

Not long after my stroll, my ears pricked up. A boat was coming. Which way was it coming, and where was it going at this hour of the morning? It was still out of my field of vision, so I turned my night glasses to the entrance to the bay. From Troy's details of what happened last night, I half expected to see a vessel hove-to near the entrance. Willing it to be there did not make it so. I turned my attention to the boat approaching from the south. It slid into view as I adjusted the binoculars. "That's strange," I murmured, more to myself than to anyone else.

"What's strange?" Troy demanded, and reached for the other pair of binoculars. It took him a moment of fiddling to adjust the focus.

"It's a long way out across the bay, over closer to the mainland side of the bay than to this island. That's an unusual course to take." I shot Troy a quick glance. He still fiddled with his glasses and was becoming agitated. "What's the problem?"

"I can't really see anything. I thought I could make out a speck close to the horizon, but I'm not sure."

"Those binoculars aren't quite as powerful as mine and they are not night glasses. Here, look through these and tell me what you see. The boat is directly in front of us now. It's running without lights; dangerous practice on any water at night. Is it the same vessel you saw last night?"

"Y-e-a-h, I think so. Yes. Yes, it is, but it is behaving differently. It's on a different course tonight. I wonder where it's going this time." He handed the night glasses back to me.

"It looks to be heading for somewhere on the mainland, and that's what is strange. Only the occasional crabber or fisherman goes near that stretch of the coastline. It's bordered by a strip of marshy mangroves stretching back some distance to become wetlands. There are a number of small tidal creeks draining the area, but they are too small to take a boat."

"Maybe they are going to run a net out or throw in a few crab pots. Are there any other boats in the area?"

"No, there are no other boats I can see. And, there are better and more accessible places for crabbing and fishing around this island than over there. The water out from that coastline is littered with snags and rocks."

Troy grabbed his glasses again and fiddled with the focus. "Geez, even a hint of moonlight would be handy tonight."

"I don't think our friends on that boat would welcome moonlight. I suspect they are up to no good and a moonless night suits them fine." The boat continued along the coast at not much above idling speed. Then it happened. "Christ...! They're changing course. They've turned in towards the mainland. Hang on a minute, I remember there is one navigable creek along that stretch of coast. It's the only one a boat can enter, and then only on high tide."

"High tide is at four o'clock ... about now."

"And this one's a big tide. They had enough water to get into the creek about an hour ago. On tonight's big tide, they'll probably be able to stay in there for a couple of hours before the tide drops too low for them to come out again. Whoever they are, there is no way they could travel along that coastline and into that creek without a sounder. Even experienced locals who know this area wouldn't attempt it in the dark without one. So, why can't I see the light from the sounder's screen? It's so dark out there, and they have no lights, so the glare of the screen should be visible. It's not."

"Short of using some form of auto pilot arrangement, I don't know how they do it without a sounder … and a sounder has a backlit screen."

Troy drummed his fingers on the armrest of his chair for a moment. "If that creek leads into such 'nothing' country, why would anyone take a boat in there? From what you've said, the boat I saw waiting at the entrance to the bay last night was too large to enter that creek. So, my question remains: why would that boat enter that creek in total darkness tonight?"

"If you think of an answer, let me know. I've been thinking about the country that creek opens onto. Past the mangroves, it opens up to basic wetlands. I've been up that creek twice … long ago. If I remember correctly, the creek runs inland far enough to go beyond the mangroves and a little way into the wetland area. Hundreds of hectares of land in that area are owned by an old bloke; a virtual recluse. It used to be a prime grazing property in its day. The bloke's owned it for years. When he got too old to work it, he let it run down and revert to nature. So, these days, I imagine it's mostly covered in scrub."

"Would that old bloke be interested in whatever that boat is up to?"

"No. He's a recluse, and has been known to fire his shotgun at people who come calling. Apart from a couple of long-standing friends in the community, no one goes near the place. I remember someone from up this way telling me recently the old bloke was ill and in hospital. On his release, he was to stay in town with friends for some time for after-care. That was a few weeks ago, so I'm not sure whether he's back home again or not."

"…Or if he will ever go back home again."

It made sense. Maybe old Sammy was not well enough to return to the property and remained in town somewhere. It also is possible the old bloke might've died. I wouldn't hear about it unless I spoke to someone from up this way. The more we talked about it, the more convinced I became old Sammy wasn't at home these days.

Troy broke into my thoughts. "Two questions for you: what do we think they are up to in there, and what do we do now?"

"What we do now is easy to answer. We wait to see if they come out again. How long they stay up the creek might influence our thinking on what they are doing. Do you have any thoughts on the subject?"

"The only thing that comes to mind for me is drugs, but I don't have any ideas about details of the operation."

For the next half hour, we speculated on likely scenarios. When we exhausted all rational possibilities, we lapsed into silence again. Since the boat's arrival on the scene, I was alert and didn't feel tired. Now, sitting in silence again, I felt my eyelids fighting my efforts to keep them open. "If they plan to come out of the creek, I hope they do so soon," I murmured. "Anyway, it will become light soon, and the tide is on its way out. If they don't reappear soon, they risk being seen exiting the creek in daylight, or being stuck in there until the next high tide."

"Who would see them once it became light? They knew I came from somewhere on the island – maybe even knew it was from this bay – but they think they eliminated me from the equation, and that I'm croc lunch by now. Maybe they don't know you're here. Nobody checked on me or tried to salvage the boat. From our trip past all the bays on this side of the island when we first arrived, we know there is no one else here at the moment. If we were able to determine that, I'm sure they did too, particularly if it is of some importance to their operation."

I thought about all that but, to avoid causing concern,

I refrained from mentioning something else. Troy hadn't mentioned it, and I'm not sure it occurred to him. Being the only people on the island puts us in a vulnerable position if having people around doesn't suit the other mob's plans. The other thing I hadn't mentioned to Troy, mainly because it's a naff thing people tend to scoff at, is that my gut instinct is telling me whatever is happening here on the island somehow is linked to Frank Hensley's disappearance and whatever else is happening with his security service in Millhaven.

While pondering why my instinct should tell me that, I took my eyes off the target. Troy nudged me in the ribs and gestured towards the creek on the other side of the bay. "Our friends are returning. It's quite light now. Should we worry about being seen sitting out here on the deck?"

He was right. Any keen eyed body on that boat, or maybe one with binoculars, could see us here. "Quick, before they turn to head back through the bay, move further around on the deck." I pointed to the corner of the deck about two metres from where we were sitting. "Over there; those small trees in the garden bed out front will hide us from view but, if we keep our eyes peeled on the bay through the gap in the trees, we will see the boat if it heads back this way."

We didn't have long to wait. Soon, the boat cruised past on its way south, but this time it was on a different course from the one it used earlier. This time, its course brought it across the bay to travel south in close to the lee side of the island. While they might've wanted to create the impression of a boat coming back from a night fishing trip, I believe it more likely they were checking for inhabitants who might be aware of their night-time activity.

They were barely out of sight when I heard Troy give a low whistle. "Whew, I'm pleased we moved when we did. I don't think they would be too happy finding us sitting here on the deck watching them." And then, there was that question again. "So, Sonny, what do we do now? Do we tell someone about this? Who could we tell?"

"Good questions, but there is a bigger one. What could we tell someone? We don't know who they are or what they were doing. That makes it hard to work out who to contact. And, without those details, it will be difficult to get anyone interested in what we have to say."

Dawn had arrived. I needed coffee again and it seemed like a good time to do something about breakfast. This morning, we breakfasted inside and in silence. When I was about halfway through my coffee, Troy asked if I was all right.

"Yes, I'm fine. Why do you ask?"

"You haven't said a word since we came in for breakfast, and the furrows that keep appearing on your brow tend to suggest something is bothering you."

"I'm trying to think through a few things. It's a bit like trying to guess what picture the jigsaw puzzle would produce if you hadn't lost half the pieces. Given other circumstances, grappling with our curiosity would be a challenge. But the circumstances, as we know them, suggest curiosity is not the worst of our situation. I need to think a bit more before I try making phone calls."

"Okay, I'll go off to my room to read. Let me know if you resolve anything."

"Troy, I don't think either of us is going to do any reading this morning. Unless you are in much better shape than I am, you will be asleep before you open your book."

It wasn't an idle comment. A few minutes later, the cottage was locked up tight and silent as we caught up on lost sleep.

Chapter 11

At around ten o'clock I woke with a thick head. No sign of Troy. Rather than risk a repeat of yesterday, I checked his room; still sound asleep. Good; it gives me time to mull over events of the last twenty-four hours. I need to know what's happening in the bay, as do the authorities. How to gather more information is the question.

I don't want to go anywhere near the south-west coast of the island. It would put my remaining boat at risk ... and worse. If they use their rifle again, they will ensure they do a 'proper' job. I could fly my drone over the area, but it's likely to meet the same fate as my boat. This calls for something more removed from the island, and the Fisheries Department's spotter plane might be the answer.

Their plane flies random sorties over the no-go fishing areas of the marine park. I tipped Fisheries off on occasions about potential illegal activities in the marine park areas. A call to them now would appear nothing out of the ordinary. The problem is, they might capture an image of what's happening on the coastline, but it probably won't show any associated activities. "I wonder if my contact is still with the Department," I murmured as I found him on my contacts list. No answer.

While there is nothing unusual about my call going unanswered, doubts crept in. Fisheries were included in recent Government cutbacks. I was unaware how they were impacted but, for other departments, reduced funding resulted in staff reductions. If Fisheries were the same, my contact might now find himself spending more time on the water rather than managing operations. Contrary to my usual practice, I accepted the invitation to leave a message.

The Fisheries issue dealt with for the moment, my concern turned to Troy's gunshot wound. It must be reported to the police. My long-time local contact is no longer attached to

Wickham precinct. He transferred on promotion to somewhere out west about six months ago. I haven't dealt with the local police since, so haven't cultivated a replacement contact.

Cold calling the local precinct will result in my speaking to any number of people without achieving anything. I'll receive the usual run-around. The logical thing to do is to call Ben and ask for a contact name at the Wickham precinct. But, that would invite a full scale interrogation by Ben before he was forthcoming with a name – if he was forthcoming at all!

No other option; I dialled Ben. He was a long time answering, and then came the predicted inquisition.

"Why would you want to contact the Wickham police? I assume you are still at your beach place."

"Yes, we are still at the beach, but there has been an incident. I need to report it to the police and don't want the usual run around. So, do you know someone up this way I might speak to about it?"

"I know a couple of blokes up there. I'm not sure either of them need you bothering them. Maybe you should tell me about this 'incident'." I tried saying I didn't want to go through the story twice. "Okay. It can't be too serious then, not serious enough to be bothering high ranking police officers." I relented and gave him an abridged version, emphasising the damage to my boat and Troy's injury.

"It does not sound like your situation is safe. How is the patient?"

"Troy's sleeping now. We sat up all night to monitor activities. He is catching up on sleep, but I think he is concussed. I tried calling Fisheries to ask them to do a fly-over to determine the situation further along the coast, but no one answered."

"Stay put. Don't go outside … don't turn on any lights … keep the place locked and looking deserted. I'll call you back shortly."

Frustrating though it is, I suppose it's the best I could hope for. I know Ben will ring his contacts, but I would prefer to call them myself. The next twenty minutes seemed to last an eternity. In such a hurry to pick up my phone when it rang, I fumbled and dropped it, before finally catching it against my midriff. When I answered it, Ben was yelling 'Sonny … are you there, Sonny? Sonny, pick up the phone'. I yelled back, "Yes, I'm here. Sorry I was so long … dropped the phone. What's happening?"

"You should see a plane go over soon…"

"Hell, I hope that doesn't alert them someone has reported them."

"No. It will appear perfectly normal."

"What about the police?"

"Yes, I spoke to them. They organised the fly-over, and will wait for the results it. I'll call you when I know more. In the meantime, my previous instructions remain in place. So, should anyone become interested, it should look like no one is occupying your cottage."

Ben ended the call before I could argue or ask questions … probably why he ended it so abruptly. This is not how I intended it. Hanging around waiting for something to happen was not part of my plan… And I am rubbish at doing nothing. After yet another coffee and wiping down all the kitchen benches once more –there's not a lot of bench to clean in a kitchenette! – I took to prowling around in the open plan living area. The sound of an approaching light plane halted my perambulating.

In defiance of Ben's instructions, I risked opening the blind a fraction on a front window. Planes, with the exception of the Fisheries spotter plane, usually fly over well to the east of the cottage. This one's path was to the west of here. Coming in from the north, it flew the length of the bay closer to the mainland side. It appeared to be heading in to land at the private airstrip on a mainland cattle property about twenty kilometres south of the boat ramp. Regardless of how I feel about being sidelined from the action, I admired the flight's deceptiveness. Nobody would suspect it was anything other than a private plane coming in to land at the private airstrip.

I don't know what I expected but, as soon as the plane disappeared from sight, I hovered around my phone. It was unlikely the police, Fisheries or anyone else would know any-thing yet. It would take time to receive a report from the spotter on the plane, and to study any photographs before they understand what is happening further around the island's coastline. Regardless, the waiting escalated my frustration.

Will they share their information with me anyway? As Ben alerted them to the potential situation here, they would be justified in not seeing any need to talk to me. I hope they keep Ben in the loop, and he sees fit to keep me informed. That last thought depressed me. If Ben's dark mood of the last few days persists, he might be perverse enough not to tell me anything. Such thoughts were not helpful. I headed off to my room to read a book.

An hour and many pages later, I abandoned the book. While I kept turning pages, I have no idea what I read. My mind focused on only one thing: what did the plane discover? It was another hour and a half before my phone startled me when it sounded so loud in the silent cottage. At last! It was Ben.

After the long wait, and when he was so obtuse – cryptic almost – I was tempted to crawl through the phone to shake the information I wanted out of him. I found myself yelling at my phone. "Stop messing about. Tell me what they discovered. If you can't, give me the name of someone who can."

"Jesus... keep your hair on! I was about to fill you in on what's happening when you started your ranting-wild-woman performance. Now, shut-up and listen. Yes, the flight proved worthwhile. It collected several pieces of interesting information ... And no, I am not going to give you details over the phone."

I went to protest but, before I opened my mouth, again I once more was told to shut up and listen. This time, the tone suggested it might be a wise move. There was a moment's silence to let the air settle between us before Ben continued.

"Sometime in the next hour, a prawn trawler will arrive in the bay and anchor in close to the northern point of the island. I think the trawler owner has a cottage in a bay somewhere near there. I don't have anything else for you now, but I will call you later when I know more."

Again his abrupt end to the call gave me no opportunity for questions. If his call was designed to ease frustration, it didn't.

It only exacerbated the situation. I was back prowling the living area and in danger of starting to climb the walls. I hate not knowing what's going on; hate not being able to conduct my own investigation and assess the information *I* gather; hate having to rely on other people.

With another coffee on the breakfast bar in front of me, I sat down to think. My first thought was: how come my yelling over the phone at Ben didn't wake Troy. For a moment, I was tempted to check on him but decided, unless he didn't surface for dinner, there was no cause for concern. Then it was time to return to Ben's call. He told me only two things: the flight was worthwhile, and a trawler was heading for the bay.

Since he was determined not to discuss the flight over the phone, I focused on the impending arrival of a trawler. It wasn't hard to work out whose trawler it was. Ben's scant information made it easy. The owner, whom I had known for many years, was the only trawler operator to frequent the island. Decades ago, his parents established a family beach place in the small bay tucked into the southern side of North Point. "Okay, easy to work out," I murmured aloud, "but why would Ben bother mentioning Robbie's trawler's impending arrival?" It took several sips of coffee to awaken my grey cells.

It's amazing how things clarify with serious thought aided by caffeine. Ben's mentioning the trawler suggests there is more to the story than the simple arrival of the boat. I suspect those on board are not interested in trawling for prawns. If they go ashore at North Bay where Robbie's family's set-up is, there will be nothing suspicious about the trawler's presence.

What happens then? I assume police are on board. A whole lot of bodies suddenly swarming over the island is bound to attract attention. Any attempt at a random trip by the trawler past the area of interest would lack credibility. Trawlers and large fishing boats never venture into that part of the bay. The only other way to approach the area without broadcasting their presence is on foot and, now the weather has cleared, such an attempt is risky.

My deliberations were going nowhere, my coffee was cold,

and I was over sitting at the breakfast bar. I wandered over to a window and parted the slats on a blind for a glimpse of the outside world. A trawler entered the bay. My assumption was correct. It was Robbie's trawler and it was heading for North Bay. "Pity I still don't know what happens next," I reminded the universe … and was startled when I received a reply.

"For starters, you could try making me a coffee." Troy, still with numb face and tousled hair, came in search of caffeine to kick start his system. "After so much sleep, I should feel ready to take on the world. Instead I feel like death."

With fresh mugs of coffee, we settled at the breakfast bar and I updated him on what he missed while asleep. There wasn't much to tell. I didn't even have any worthwhile speculations to share. Troy grasped the situation at once. "If the police have arrived, what happens next? All their subterfuge up to now will be to no avail once they start whatever it is they plan to do. My still half-asleep brain is telling me things will get hairy … like, maybe there will be more shots fired and people will be hurt – or worse. And while we are on the subject, what will be our involvement?" While he spoke, he focused on pushing his mug around in circles on the benchtop. When he finished speaking he looked up at me. His face told me those were not idle questions. He wanted answers, answers I didn't have.

There's nothing like the application of a degree of pressure to speed up the thought processes. "I have no idea what our role might be, or if we will have any involvement. I have worked with the police from the Wickham precinct on a couple of occasions, but the bloke I worked with is gone. The situation here is not the same as it is for me with Ben at home. Nevertheless, there are some preparatory precautions we might undertake right now."

Troy stood up. "Okay, I'm ready. What do we do?"

"First, you can drag out some gear for us to work on. In the big laundry cupboard, there is a panel behind the ironing board, brooms and other paraphernalia. Slide it to one side. In the gun safe behind the panel there are a rifle and a shotgun. Bring them out so we can work on them." I gave Troy what he needed to open the safe.

Instead of dashing off to find the safe, Troy remained anchored to the spot. His eyebrows had climbed up to meet the soft sun bleached curls falling over his forehead, and his mouth gaped slightly. "What's up? Is there a problem? A gun safe...? A shot gun and a rifle...?"

"Yeah. They were put away clean, but it won't hurt to give them another once-over so they're ready in case we need to use them. It's the sort of activity I do in the shed but, as we're supposed to remain hidden, we'll have to clean them here on this plastic sheet spread over the table." He still didn't move in the direction of the laundry. "I assume you are familiar with, and can use, at least one of those weapons."

"You forget, I'm off a large rural estate where shooting things – both for the pot and sport – is a major part of life. Yes, I know how to use both those weapons."

"Okay, unless something else is bothering you, go fetch those weapons, please." Troy shook his head in disbelief as he started on his way to the laundry.

By the time I had the table set up and the cleaning gear laid out, Troy brought the two guns. After half an hour, the job was done and both weapons were reassembled on the table. "I think I'll fold up this piece plastic and put it on top of that bookshelf in the corner, and then the guns and ammunition can go on the plastic so everything is handy if we need to use them."

"Where is the ammunition you want to put with the weapons?"

"In that closed compartment at the bottom of the gun safe..." Any further information I was about to give him was cut short when my phone rang. As I picked it up to answer it, I called out, "Have you found it?" Troy answered in the affirmative.

"Incoming...," was all the caller said.

"Incoming what?"

"No. Incoming who ... Me ... I'm climbing over the rocks into your bay now. Thought I better alert you to my presence on the off chance you are feeling a bit nervous."

"Good thinking; I'm amazed you found us. Follow the gully around behind the cottage and come up the back stairs. I assume we still are pretending none of us is here."

"Yes, no one is here. When I come up those stairs are you going to let me in?"

I had forgotten the back door, like all the others, was locked, and I rushed to open it. Ben rushed straight up the stairs, in through the backdoor and almost collided with Troy coming out of the laundry with a box of ammunition in each hand. With some difficulty, I stifled a giggle. The look on Ben's face was priceless as he eyed off Troy's 'cargo'.

"Even for you, this is something of an overkill – no pun intended. Which one will you be using for whatever you're planning to do?"

"Me…? I won't be using either of them. I have my Glock. If you want to use one, you and Troy can sort it out between you."

"No, I do not want to use one. What were you planning to do with them?"

"You know me, always prepared. If the cavalry requires assistance – or we are required to defend ourselves in the event the cavalry's offensive fails – we are prepared. Now, as soon as you recover your breath, you might like to tell me what the game plan is … and why you are here." We made ourselves comfortable around the dining table. Ben, in his usual manner, took the chair at the head of the table.

"The reconnaissance flight showed quite a set up in a small sandy bay on the south-west coast of the island. It also showed where your boat is stranded. The area is under surveillance since the flight data was analysed, and we know the boat associated with that set up left for the mainland about half an hour ago. The 'game plan' as you call it is for the officers who came over on the trawler to take a smaller boat to the bay just this side of where the camp is located. They will proceed on foot over the rocks and down into the next bay to explore the camp."

"If they are up to no good, they might not be inclined to leave their camp undefended."

"Give us some credit. An advance party of a couple of officers will check out the camp from a suitable vantage point above the bay before the rest of the troops sweep over the rocks and into the camp. And yes, we share your opinion. It is unlikely the place is left unattended … And no, we don't know how much time we will have to carry out the operation, as there is no way of knowing how long the boat might be away."

"What's your role in all of this, and why are you here?"

"I am joint leader of the operation. And I'm here because you have yourself in another one of your situations … And it's possible whatever you've gotten yourself into might be relevant to what's happening in Millhaven."

"Troy and I could be the advance scouts. We could take my small boat to one of the bays close by and then hoof it across the hill to check out the camp. It would allow the whole of your troop to be available for whatever comes next. How do you feel about it, Troy?"

"I don't have a problem. It sounds like a plan to me."

"No. That's not how it's going to work," Ben said. His slight hesitation before he spoke told me there wasn't total opposition to my suggestion, so I promoted it further.

"You know my suggestion is sound. I know the area well and we would do a much better job as a reconnaissance party than your officers. If we are sprung, you and the cavalry swarm into the bay to rescue us. Of course, if we do encounter some-body minding the camp, we could claim to be a couple of nature lovers on a hike around the island who dropped in to ask for a drink of water. Your lot wouldn't have to disclose their presence if we didn't need to be rescued. It would allow you to plan some other covert activity based on what we discover."

Discussions seemed to be going nowhere for a while. Then, after agreeing to consider my suggestion, Ben said he needed to return to the others. He left almost as abruptly as he arrived. He wasn't gone more than five minutes when my phone rang. Ben again.

"How soon can you have your boat in the water to go around to one of the bays near the camp?"

"About five minutes… The tractor is already hitched to the trailer. We only have to run it down the beach, float the boat off the trailer, and scramble aboard. How soon do you want us to leave, and how do you want us to communicate with you once we're moving?"

"Use the boat's radio to communicate, if you're on the water." He gave me the discrete channel number. "How is phone reception in that area?" I assured him it was good, especially from elevated areas on the hillside. "Okay, if you are on land, use your phone to call me."

As he finished speaking, I heard footsteps on the back deck and reached for the Glock in my backpack. Before I had it out, Ben marched in through the backdoor. "I thought this might be more useful than the arsenal spread out on the table." He held out a Smith & Wesson handgun. I nodded towards Troy before a worrying thought occurred to me.

"Troy, I know we've discussed your proficiency with the guns on the table, but how are you with a handgun?"

"Oh, I think I can manage. I don't like them but, somewhere back in my long lost youth, I was the champion of my university's pistol club."

Ben had placed the weapon in Troy's hand but kept hold of it during our exchange. Reassured by Troy's comments, he let go of the weapon and said, "It seems you might know how to use one of these, but don't do anything stupid, like shooting yourself. The paperwork would be horrendous and I don't need it."

While these exchanges took place, I stuffed the few items I considered necessary into my backpack and was ready to go. Ben came with me to launch the boat while Troy organised his own pack for the trip. Ten minutes after our conversation ended, Troy and I were on the water and heading for a bay on the south-west coast. As I turned the boat to follow the coastline along, I caught a glimpse of Ben galloping north along the beach of my neighbouring bay.

Chapter 12

"We are on foot and about halfway up the hillside. My boat is tucked into a small creek running back into the mangroves two bays prior to the one with the camp. No problems so far, but we should be overlooking the camp in a few minutes ... will keep you informed. Where are you and the cavalry, or are we operating alone on this one?" Apart from keeping him informed, my short call to Ben was to find out whether backup might be close at hand if we should run into trouble when closer to the camp.

"Call if you need help. We are tucked in close to your damaged boat waiting to hear from you. The intention now is to move up to the bay prior to the camp – the one where you are now and to wait there until we hear from you. Update me as soon as you have eyes on the camp."

After sharing Ben's information with Troy, we set off to find a vantage point overlooking the camp. Finding a suitable path across the craggy divide between our position and the bay where the camp is located necessitated climbing a few metres higher up the hillside. In spite of the hard going, we found a vantage point with a good view of the camp below, while shielding us from the campsite.

The waiting played on our nerves but waiting was all we could do. I filled in some time taking photos of the camp with my small digital camera. Troy began fidgeting beside me on the hard rocky perch. About to chastise him for his restlessness, he was spared when I caught sight of movement below. A man wandered out of one of the tents and perched on a crate. His need for a smoke brought him outside.

It seemed he had nothing more pressing to attend to, and was content to remain perched on his crate long after finishing his cigarette. With nothing else to do except wait and watch,

I studied the make-up of the camp. There were two main tents, much larger than the others. By the gear outside it and a glimpse of tables through the tied-back door flaps, I assumed one of those to be the kitchen/mess tent.

I turned my attention to the other large tent. It is only a small bay, but somehow they managed to set this tent a little distance from the others. While the gap wasn't great, it made it appear separate somehow. It had a more 'industrial' look about it. Arranged in neat stacks outside were pallets and drums. I counted at least ten pallets in a stack and three or four others strewn about beside it.

Drums were stacked two high and in rows of four across and four deep; 32 drums at least. A couple of crates similar to the one the man occupied were dumped beside the tent. Twin tracks leading from inside this tent and down to the water captured my attention. Perhaps the location of this tent was governed by the gentle slope of the beach in that part of the bay. From the tracks, and by the sheets of metal laid in bottom of the tracks, it was reasonable to assume a wheeled vehicle of some type ran between beach and tent. An idea began to develop.

"Troy, that ugly looking boat we watched going about its business last night, how confident are you it was the same one you saw earlier?"

"I'm sure it's the same one. Why do you ask?"

"Think about its appearance…"

"It was ugly."

"Y-e-s, but, is it possible it might be a barge of some sort?"

"Now you mention it, its front section could drop down as a ramp, and would explain its ugly squared-off looking nose. It's big and a bit up-market looking, but it could be a barge. What are you thinking? Does it have something to do with what they might be up to?"

"I don't know. It's just a germ of an idea so far." I didn't mention those tracks on that beach were influencing my thinking. With nothing more to be learned from the tracks, I turned my attention to the rest of the camp.

Apart from the two large tents, there were three medium sized tents and one small one. The medium sized ones are those described in camping goods catalogues as 'sleeping six persons'. The small tent looked as though it might sleep two if they were friendly. The man had emerged from the small tent. There is plenty of accommodation, but it doesn't look like a recreation camp or corporate retreat venue. So, whatever its operation, the camp involved a number of people.

As I sat churning over all the visual evidence I collected, the man vacated his perch and headed towards the small tent. He didn't go in. Instead, stopped at the entrance and looked in, as though checking on something inside. Satisfied all was well in the tent, he went into one of the medium sized tents and came out moments later with an armload of fishing gear. After stowing the gear in a small dinghy on the beach further along from the main camp, he set about pushing and shoving the dinghy into the water.

This is not good. Things could go pear-shaped if he encounters Ben and his merry men in the neighbouring bay. I whispered into my phone. "Ben, a problem has developed. A bloke is about to go fishing in a dinghy. I don't know where you are, but there isn't time for you to try to make a run for a hiding place."

"It's all good. Call me again when he is on his way."

I didn't know what 'it's all good' meant but hoped it was okay. A couple of minutes later, the fisherman was on his way and heading towards the southern end of the island. No fish there, I thought as I called Ben. After explaining the dinghy's direction, I added an afterthought. "Where are you and the others? I don't know how far around this bloke is going but, if you go motoring away from this area, he might see you."

"Like I said, it's all good. We are back where the trawler first dropped us at what is now our base in Robbie's family's set-up."

"I don't think there is anyone else in the camp. I'm going to…" The phone went dead before I could finish. "Bastard…," I hissed, "how bloody rude!" A moment later my phone vibrated.

I checked the caller ID and was ready to give Ben an earful for ending my call like that. It didn't work out that way.

"Sonny, get out of there now. Get away from that bay. We have received word the camp's boat is making ready to leave the mainland. Get yourselves away from there, and get you and your boat out of sight somewhere if possible."

"Before you so rudely cut short our last conversation, I was about to tell you I think the camp is deserted and I was going to take a quick look around. I could still..."

"NO! Do not jeopardise this whole operation by pulling one of your wild cowboy stunts. Get back to your boat now and make yourselves scarce ... NOW!"

For a second, I was about to ignore Ben's instructions. Then common sense kicked in. Our discovery would ruin everything. So far, we had no hard evidence of any criminal activity. I nudged Troy in the ribs. "Come on, we have to get out of here and back to the boat in double-quick time. Let's go."

There's nothing like a bit of emergency to get things moving. By jogging over the relatively flat parts of our track and hopping from rock to rock where possible, the only slow parts of the trip back to our boat were where we had to clamber carefully over jagged rocks. Without breaking stride, we leapt into the boat and I turned the key. Staying as close to the shore as was safe, I headed for my cottage. We tore along with my mind in hyperdrive trying to figure out where to go to be out of sight. Ben was silent and no help.

As I approached Windy Point, I eased back on the throttle for a quick look at the bay from around the Point. No crafts on the bay, and a quick check of the mainland through the binoculars also found no boats. In a snap decision, I opened the throttle and raced for my cottage.

My phone rang as I dragged the boat up to its customary place on the beach: Ben. "Where are you?"

"At my cottage; I'm just pulling the boat out."

"That boat is leaving the mainland."

"You said that before, but there is no sign of it."

"Their departure was delayed. One of them went off alone and they had to wait for his return. As soon as he reappeared, they all piled aboard and made ready to leave. They are leaving the beach now. Get inside and go into hiding again. Go now!"

I jumped down from the tractor and yelled at Troy. "Come on; we have to get inside. The boat's on its way back." We galloped from the beach, up the stairs and through the front door. Troy's momentum carried him through as far as the breakfast bar. As soon as I was inside, I propped, turned, locked the door and closed the drapes. Then we both leant on the breakfast bar for a few moments to collect ourselves. About fifteen minutes later, with my pulse and breathing almost normal again, I heard the boat.

"It looks like another storm is building," Troy said to break the silence. Heavy black clouds were gathering in the distance.

"Maybe, but we tend to miss the worst of the storms when they come in from that direction. It might be only a squall, and we'll get a bit of rain and wind."

Troy filled in the rest of our day reading his book, while I typed up my notes and drew a pencil sketch of the layout of the campsite. Using my phone, I photographed the sketch to send to Ben. My phone startled me when it rang while I was doing it. Ben again. "Is the backdoor unlocked?"

"Yes. Come right in." I didn't need to issue the invitation. He bounded in through the backdoor while I was speaking.

"Ah, good," he said when he saw my sketch. "That's what I came to talk to you about. What can you tell me about all this?" He gestured over the sketch. I explained what I thought to be the kitchen/mess tent and the accommodation tents. Then he interrupted. "What's this other big tent over here? And here where it says 'tracks', what's that about?"

"Didn't those tracks show up on the photos from the fly-over?" Ben shook his head. "Maybe that's not surprising. They are fairly well camouflaged."

"What sort of tracks are they, and what goes on in that tent to need tracks down to the water?"

"I don't know what they're for yet, but I have some thoughts on the matter. The tracks look as though they are used by a wheeled vehicle; not a big one. They are too close together to be for a large vehicle."

"Small tractor perhaps?"

"No, I don't think so. These tracks have strips cut from coloured sheets of roofing material in the bottom of them. A four-wheel drive tractor like the one I use to pull the boats out wouldn't need anything like that. With a heavy load on board, it still could travel over sand with ease. It took me a while to pick up the sheet metal in the bottom of the tracks, even with the binoculars. It blends in well with the sand, and there is a light sprinkling of sand over it. I don't know whether the sand is deliberate or a consequence of use."

"Whatever it is, might it be used to run a boat on a trailer down to the water?" I shrugged and then shook my head. "Why else would some form of wheeled vehicle need tracks running down to the water?"

"Have you seen their boat?"

"No, but everyone who has, says it is a big ugly thing."

"They're right. It is big and ugly ... and I think it might be a barge of sorts. Its large snub nose suggests it opens up to form a cargo loading ramp. So, my question is: what, requiring the use of a wheeled vehicle, are they transferring between boat and tent?" Ben ignored my question. He appeared engrossed in my sketch.

"This area you have marked as 'drums' was a bit hard to make out in the plane's photos. Tell me about it."

I explained how they were stacked and the number involved. "I'd say, by the colour of the paint on them, they are oil drums."

"We suspected they were drums in the photos, but couldn't see them clearly enough to be sure. You know this area and boating better than I. So, why would anyone stockpile such a supply of oil?"

"No reason I can think of. There is something odd about those drums. I think they are important to the purpose of that campsite. Is there anything from your end to shed light on what's happening here? We are fed-up with being cooped up out of sight. What did they do on the mainland today? I doubt they went shopping at the beach's small general store, and the café under the lifesavers' clubhouse only opens on some weekends."

"Nothing new to report. Today's trip to the mainland appears nothing more than visiting friends occupying a couple houses there. It involved quite a bit of drinking and swearing. It's likely the bloke who went off on his own had a pre-arranged assignation at another house somewhere in the same area. For now, we wait until their next move." I encouraged him to keep in touch as he strode towards the backdoor.

"Well, that wasn't particularly helpful," Troy muttered as Ben exited the building. "Sonny, you seem to have more ideas about what's going on here than Ben and his police colleagues do. I'd question the value of their being here if it wasn't some comfort knowing back-up is at hand if we need it."

"I know it looks that way, Troy, but I doubt that is the case. I can't speak for the others in their group, but I'm sure – in fact, I know – Ben has a theory."

"Is that because you know Ben so well? I didn't hear him say anything to suggest he had any thoughts on the subject." The sarcastic edge to Troy's voice wasn't lost on me.

Oh dear, how thick can I be? Ben has been offside for a few days, and now Troy's claws are showing. Do I find myself in the middle of a male 'rutting season'? These few days of R&R at my beach place is not aligning with expectations. I'm beginning to look forward to being home again, on my own and working a case. But for now, I have to set Troy straight.

"I understand why you think that. Perhaps it is because I know Ben so well, I know differently. We have worked together on many occasions over many years, and I know how to read him. Well, it's more like I'm learning how to read him. You heard him ask a lot of questions as though he had no idea about anything, including what was going on. Did you hear him argue with, or question anything I told him?" Troy shrugged and then shook his head. "No, you didn't. That's because everything I told him coincides with his own thinking. Don't sell Ben short, Troy. He is an astute operator and a damned good detective." A contrite Troy took himself off to the fridge for a couple of beers.

Our late dinner was a sombre affair, prepared by the light of a single candle and eaten by the light of the many LEDs on the various appliances in the living area. Sitting in the dark reminiscing about old times soon loses its appeal. It resulted in an early night for both of us. We agreed there were others on the island now who could sit up all night watching for boats behaving strangely at odd hours, while we slept peacefully. Unable to turn on a light to be able to read in bed, I wondered how long I would remain awake. The answer to that was, no time at all.

*****

This morning saw me out of bed at my usual time and wondering how to fill in my day. Restless, I roamed the living area as I waited for my first morning coffee. Did anything happen last night? Would Ben tell me if it did? By the time my coffee was ready, I rued not keeping watch last night. Troy appeared in the kitchen. Between stretching and yawning, he mumbled, "Anything happen last night?"

"Isn't that today's question? I have nothing to report. Do you?" Even to my ears, I sounded terse. "Apologies … frustration levels a little high at the moment. Can't stand sitting around doing nothing."

"I know how you feel … not about doing nothing so much, as the onset of cabin fever. I'm not used to staying indoors for so long and with no prospect of any immediate change in the situation."

We decided to risk taking our breakfast and coffees out onto the back deck. Before venturing outside, I slipped my Glock into the waistband of my shorts. Can't be too careful, I told myself. Breakfast happened in silence, but conversation flowed once it finished and after I asked Troy what he was likely to do after his return to England.

"Good question, and I'm beginning to wonder when that

might be. My contract with the new mine should have ended a month ago. I should be back at the university and immersed in winter by now. There is always some extra little thing they want done before I go, and it always takes the university a while to approve the extension to my contract. So, I sit around writing reports and twiddling my thumbs for a day or two until everything is in place and I can deal with their latest task. I'm hopeful of leaving soon. It's not about wanting to leave Australia. I have nothing of any consequence left to do here ... and I don't enjoy the summer heat out at the mine site. Why don't you take a break and come back to England with me for a while? Even just a couple of weeks would do you good."

"If only... But I have a business to run and I am in the middle of a case, which is in limbo until I return from here."

Our extended breakfast on the deck ended when Ben arrived. He checked my mug. "Looks like time for fresh coffee. Yes thanks, I will have one with you." He looked hard at Troy as he finished speaking. Troy took the hint.

"Don't get up, Sonny. I'll make them." It sounded pleasant enough, but the look Troy gave Ben said he was not happy.

As Troy left us, I turned my attention to Ben. "I hope you've come to report on last night."

"What about last night? Did something happen?" He looked surprised.

"That's what I presumed you came to tell me."

"I see. It seems we both will be disappointed. Nothing happened as far as I know. They monitored the bay all night, and reported no boating activity, strange or otherwise. It seems our friends had a night off after their time at the beach yesterday. There is some talk of maybe flying the spotter plane across the bay again today. For credibility, it would take the reverse flight path this time. I'll let you know if they decide to go ahead with it."

Troy arrived with the coffees. Ben had nothing more to report so, for the short while it took to empty our mugs, we engaged in speculation about that camp's associated activities. With nothing more to say or do, Ben left us with a parting instruction. "Stay inside and don't turn on any lights again tonight. Stay safe."

"Not what we needed to hear," Troy hissed, "but I suppose he is right and that's how it has to be for now."

While we both found things to do, the day dragged on. After lunch, we spent most of the afternoon reading our books. Mine was a great read, but I fell asleep anyway. Dusk was well established by the time I woke. I decided to check on Troy. Still bleary-eyed, he met me at the door to his room. "If you're thinking of monitoring the bay tonight, I'll be up for it. I feel as though I've slept for a month."

Of course we were going to monitor the bay tonight, and we both would be on watch.

Chapter 13

Something happening so soon after recent activities seemed un-likely. Nevertheless, I intended monitoring the bay all night if necessary. It is better to know what is happening than having others tell me. And, I can sleep tomorrow.

It was eleven o'clock and conversation died a natural death about an hour earlier. Troy broke the silence. "Do you plan to go to bed tonight, or stay out here on the deck?"

"I plan to monitor the bay until three or four o'clock. There's no need for you to keep me company. I don't think anything will happen so soon, but I want to see if there is a pattern to their activities."

"It might be worth filling that thermos with coffee and making up a few snacks to sustain us." Soon, we were back on the deck, both showered and with enough rations to sustain us for a day, let alone the night.

If confident something would happen, I might feel more enthusiastic about sitting in the dark for hours. At about one o'clock, Troy's head dropped forward onto his chest as he dozed off. I nudged him. "Go to bed. Nothing is going to happen. There's too much moonlight tonight."

"Funny how the sky cleared. The clouds looked menacing when I woke up this evening."

"Yeah. That's the direction the storms come from but it must have rolled over the top this time." Although I remained uncertain abandoning our surveillance was wise, I went off to bed more than half convinced we wouldn't miss anything. Nevertheless, I expected to have trouble falling asleep. That wasn't the case. I was asleep within moments.

Startled, I woke and searched the darkness of my room. A noise that shouldn't be there woke me. It took a moment for intelligent thought to return. Then, I was out of bed in a flash.

Those clouds we saw earlier hadn't gone away. They were coming through now in the form of a high-powered squall.

After checking everything in the shed and the boat were secure, I came upstairs and checked all the windows and doors. The wind howled, while quite a light show happened over the bay. I pulled on a jacket and went to sit on the deck to watch Mother Nature at work. Mesmerised by the lightning, and with everything else drowned out by the thunder, I almost missed seeing the boat pounding its way towards the entrance to the bay. Any vessel waiting to rendezvous with the boat was in danger. Its captain would be foolhardy to risk the conditions out there. Even the waves in the bay were at a dangerous height. It would be worse in the open sea outside the bay.

The torrential rain blown almost horizontal by the wind made it difficult to keep the lenses of my night glasses clear as I followed the boat's passage. I was about to put the glasses down and give my eyes a few moments rest when something caught my attention. "What the…?" I yelped as I struggled to keep the glasses glued to my eyes and adjust the focus at the same time. There it was again. This time I had a fix on its position. I trained the glasses on the area from where it originated.

A few moments later, there was another flash. This time I had the glasses trained on it. There's another boat. It was in the bay, tucked in behind the western arm of the entrance and bouncing around. I watched the boat from the campsite alter its course to head for the boat signalling to it. While it was impossible to see much of the waiting boat, it was a large yacht. In spite of the towering waves, I could tell it sat well down in the water. "A heavy load on board perhaps," I wondered aloud.

They can't intend transhipping anything in these conditions, but why else would the rendezvous take place? Spellbound by the potential disaster, I had to watch. At first, the driving rain and bouncing boats made it impossible to discern what was happening. Then, thanks to a fortuitous streak of lightning, I watched fascinated as a drum transferred from the yacht disappeared into the belly of the campsite boat. "Bloody hell. They're either maniacs, or there is quite rare and valuable oil in those drums," I told the universe.

Transhipment of cargo lasted about an hour. I kept the glasses trained on the scene the whole time, not wanting to miss the moment if one or both of the vessels went down. And then it ended and the operation was over. Both vessels were still afloat. Mission accomplished, the campsite's boat carved a risky arc through the waves and headed back to the camp. The other vessel travelled a short distance along the coast to a small, narrow inlet. In those sheltered waters, it managed to turn around and emerge pointed in the right direction to head out into the open sea.

Again, I hid behind the garden bed's shrubbery as the camp-site's boat laboured its way past. Then, I took my laptop to my room and, relying on the backlit keyboard, typed up a record of tonight's vigil. By the time I finished and settled down to sleep, it was approaching five o'clock. The last thing I remember before sleep arrived was hoping Troy slept in until late this morning.

My eyes flew open a few minutes before eight o'clock. I stumbled out to the kitchen. No sign of Troy. It seemed too dark. The clock confirmed it was eight o'clock. One quick look outside explained the situation. A leaden sky greeted me. The wind had abated and it wasn't raining. As I scanned the world outside, I saw a shower coming towards me. Behind it, things looked a little lighter and brighter. Perhaps today wouldn't be as dreary as I first thought. Now, if we could just go outside…

As the coffee machine did its thing, I pondered whether to breakfast alone or to wait for Troy. I needed caffeine now, and was filling my mug when a voice startled me. "I'll have one of those too, thanks." A bleary-eyed Troy leant against the front of the fridge. "I feel as though I've slept forever. Whatever we do today should not involve any more sleeping. Why is it so dark? What time is it anyway?"

"It is late enough to be light." I pointed to the clock. "With the cottage closed up the way it is and a miserable day outside, I suspect it is going to remain dark for some time… especially, as we can't turn on lights if we are to convince people there is no one here." Troy groaned. "Here, get this into you. It might help improve your outlook." He grimaced as I handed him his coffee.

Ben bounded up the back stairs around mid-morning. "Good to see everyone so bright and chirpy. What's with the long faces? The weather is clearing. It could turn out to be a nice day." I scowled at him, but it went unnoticed.

"It might be a nice day for those who can be out and about to enjoy it. As there appears to be no remedy for our predicament, it won't matter to us what the day is like." Ben raised his eyebrows in mock surprise at my bitchiness. I ignored it and continued. "Was there a purpose to your visit, or did you come to gloat about your pleasant life?" He ignored the question. Troy's scowl seemed to have become permanently affixed. Sniping at Ben was getting us nowhere. I made the effort to amend my demeanour in the hope of prising loose some information.

By way of an invitation, I waved a coffee mug at Ben and gave him my sweetest smile. He accepted the invitation. With cordial relations re-established, while making coffees, I got down to business. "Do you have anything interesting to report this morning? Locked away as we are, any updates from your end of things would brighten our day." It did the trick. Once we settled with our coffees, Ben opened up.

"I suppose I came to tell you there is nothing to report today. Conditions were so bad last night, they stood down those rostered to monitor the bay. No boats could go out in that weather."

"Yeah, the storm was nasty and hung around for a while."

"It was disappointing. The police boat was on standby to intercept any operation but, when the weather turned foul, they wouldn't risk going out in it. The only thing to do now is wait until the next time there is activity in or around the bay. No one is willing to guess at how long it might be before their next operation. By the way, everyone was impressed with your sketch of the campsite; most helpful."

Ben didn't stay long. After making sympathetic noises about our situation, and explaining yet again it is for our own safety, he headed back to the police's camp at North Bay. I saw Troy physically relax as Ben went down the back stairs. This situation is ridiculous. I'll be glad to go back to Millhaven and put Troy on a plane to wherever he's going. That thought shocked me. I like Troy – a lot – but the stress of our present situation coupled with the tension between Troy and Ben is likely to bring out the worst in me before long. I don't want to upset either of them, but I do have to live and work in the same town as Ben, and depend on him for help on occasions. Troy has been special since we worked together on Crete but our relationship is becoming strained. The sooner he is back in the UK, the sooner he will return to being 'special'. In hindsight, spending a few days here at the beach was not such a great idea.

Troy announced he was going to his room to check his emails. I decided to do the same. As I waited for my computer to boot up, I thought about Ben's visit. It could be construed as doing the right thing and keeping me informed, but I'm a sceptic by nature. A phone call would save his long trek from North Bay, and the information he shared could be delivered just as well over the phone. Are his visits designed to keep an eye on whatever might be happening here? Such thoughts might be unfair, but I believe they are close to the mark.

Why hadn't I told Ben boats were out risking everything in the appalling conditions last night? No doubt it had something to do with my dark side coming to the fore, but it was more than that. If the mob from the campsite followed their previous routine, they would make a run across to that secluded inlet on the mainland tonight. A vague idea roamed around in the back of my mind. It could stay there for the present. I needed to see how the weather panned out before giving it much serious thought.

The weather didn't moderate during the day. While better than last night, white caps still covered the bay. My gut told me they would do a run to the mainland tonight, and it continued to say so all day. By five o'clock, I had decided. It didn't include him, but I shared my plan with Troy. An argument followed.

"You are not going to that campsite on your own. If you insist on going, I'm coming with you."

"Troy, I need to do this, and it could be risky if that mob doesn't leave the camp tonight. Whatever happens, it means sitting up on that hillside in the dark for hours. I won't know what they are doing until at least three o'clock, but I need to be in position up on the hill before dark. It's too risky climbing up there after dark."

"What you haven't told me is why you need to be there to know what's happening when we could sit here watching for boats out on the bay."

"I want to look inside the second big tent at the campsite … and maybe the smallest one too. I think whatever happens in that big tent is fundamental to their operation."

"You are ignoring several important factors. The first and most important: this is a police operation. You called them in, and now you want to meddle and risk stuffing up everything. No! Don't interrupt. I'm not finished. The second important factor is your assumption the campsite mob will follow your perceived 'previous pattern' of behaviour. There is no evidence they adhere to a routine. After monitoring their activities a bit longer, we might discern some pattern. If you are correct and theirs is a tightly choreographed operation, then tomorrow would be a better day to look at the campsite."

"Why is tomorrow better?"

"Those from the campsite have demonstrated they are dangerous. You need to stop and think about that before charging in. If you believe their operation follows some set pattern, look at the complete picture. The day after their trip to recluse Sammy's property, they went across to that beach on the mainland. Why won't they go across to that beach again tomorrow?"

"It wasn't part of their operation. They went to visit friends and let their hair down for a while. It was a social outing and not part of their 'business' operations."

"I think you are misinterpreting their trip to the beach. Perhaps it was a social outing for most of the blokes. What was the bloke who went off on his own up to?"

"Maybe he arranged an assignation with a 'friendly' lady; went to visit a personal friend; had a private matter to deal with. I don't know. Maybe he had to attend to something private and separate from their operation."

"Come on, Sonny. Think about it. Think about the 'administration' aspect of such an operation. There has to be person or persons who run the land-based side of things. Perhaps the lone player went to report on the recent operation, or receive their new instructions." I started shaking my head. "No Sonny, save your argument. I'm not finished yet. Another possibility is the individual went to deal with money matters. The mob might be messing about with drums of oil, but we both know the real game probably is drugs. I admit I haven't figured out how the oil is involved. Can you produce recreational drugs from oil?"

I took a deep breath before answering. Calm enough for a civil response, I opened my mouth … and snapped it closed again. The archaeologist was giving the investigator a lesson. Damn! Troy was right about what the 'lone player' went to do on his own. This is not the Troy I remember from Crete, or when running for our lives on Sicily. Having my errors and shortcoming as an investigator pointed out to me came as a shock. Nevertheless, Troy's take on the operation made more sense than mine. "Okay, I bow to your wisdom. We shall monitor the bay from here tonight."

"Good. Now there is one other thing intriguing me. Why are you so keen to see inside the smallest tent when you don't seem interested in the contents of the other 'accommodation' tents? Maybe the small tent is where the leader of the gang hangs out."

"I don't think so. When they went to the beach, they left one bloke at the campsite to keep an eye on things. He went fishing but, before he left the camp, he went to that small tent. At the door, he looked inside as if he were checking on something. It seemed he checked whatever was in the tent was okay to be left alone and unmonitored while he was gone. I don't know what's in that tent, but I want to find out."

"Is this something we should share with Ben? Come to think of it, there is quite a bit we haven't shared with him."

"There might be one or two things we haven't shared, but they are speculation. Without evidence to back up our thinking, Ben will ignore it. I want to avoid him doubting our value in this investigation. If that happens, he will stop sharing their information with us. You're going to ask me why we should remain involved. I'll try to explain. Apart from the fact that my boat is still sitting partially submerged in the mangroves, and you were shot, my gut tells me what's happening here is involved with incidents in Millhaven. I can't tell you more because I haven't worked out how or why it is. Just accept I've learnt to trust my gut instinct and to run with it."

"Okay; we will sit on the deck and monitor the bay for boating activity tonight and, if we hear they are heading to the beach again tomorrow, we'll investigate the campsite."

"That's my thinking, but it depends on when and if certain things occur. In the meantime, we'll continue being nice to Ben in the hope he will keep us informed of what their sources are telling them."

With nothing else to do until dark, we went to spend time in our rooms. I spent the time adding Troy's thoughts on the operation to my notes about that campsite and its associated activities. While the weather had improved, the heavy cloud cover and strong wind remained. We would need warm food in us, and to rug up before settling on the deck tonight.

As dusk closed in, I rustled up a pasta dish. It was light enough to work in the kitchen without lights, but we dined in darkness. Rather than subject ourselves to the wind before necessary, we remained inside struggling to make conversation in the darkness until after midnight. Then it was time to face the elements, but not before filling the thermos with hot coffee and loading our pockets with muesli bars. In the time we spent entertaining ourselves indoors, a few light showers occurred. We ventured onto the deck as another scud whipped across from the bay.

Once settled on the deck, a comfortable silence descended over us. It lasted until after two o'clock. The sound of a boat making its way along the bay reminded us why we were sitting in the wind and the occasional misty showers. Fair sized waves breaking to whitecaps still covered the bay. The boat's progress was slow and laboured. It finally came into view, passed by and, as anticipated, headed towards the mainland. We kept our binoculars trained on the boat until it disappeared into that narrow inlet on Sammy's property.

The boat's arrival reignited conversation … and further speculation. We filled in more than an hour and a half with murmured discussion until the boat exited the inlet. The rest of the morning played out much as on the previous occasion. After the boat went past on its way back to the campsite, Troy went to his room to sleep, and I went to my room to type up my notes, and then to sleep.

Habits are hard to break. I woke at my usual time and headed to the kitchen while Troy slumbered on. About half an hour later, I dropped something and woke him. "I think we should get breakfast and anything else we want to do out of the way first thing this morning. It's likely Ben will arrive during the morning to tell us what they observed last night. If I'm right, it's important we both remain ignorant of, but interested in, anything he tells us."

Troy's frown as he considered my comments created deep furrows between his eyebrows. I explained before he questioned me. "Pretending we know nothing about what happened last night will provide us with an opportunity to check on the veracity and completeness of the information Ben shares with us. I know it sounds a bit strange, but I've worked with Ben for years and I know he has a tendency to withhold vital information on occasions."

"Why would he withhold information about what happened last night? What would be the benefit in doing that?"

"I've been known to ask myself that same question. Some-times I think it's because of protocols which I don't understand, but perhaps he makes decisions about what we should know based on obscure criteria beyond my comprehension."

After breakfast, I dug out an old chess set and set it on the coffee table in the lounge area. It is so long since I've played, I'm not sure I remember how the various pieces move. Neither of us was interested in chess, but it was one way of filling in a few hours of another boring day. I was just beginning to get the hang of the game when Ben arrived.

"Must be nice to have time for such intellectual pursuits," he quipped as he strode into the living area. "You might be interested in hearing about last night's activities, and I needed some exercise, so here I am." His report was brief: that boat was out and about again last night, went over to somewhere on the mainland, spent about an hour and a half there before returning. Don't know what it was all about. There's nothing in the area it visited. It disappeared into a little creek or something, so we couldn't see what it did. The thinking is, it has illegal nets strung across the creek and they went to check the nets."

Troy looked at me, and I returned his hard look, in a bid to remind him of how to behave. He played it beautifully. With his brow furrowed, he said, "I don't understand. Is this business of having nets up the creek important and why is it illegal to fish that way?"

If it wasn't a genuine enquiry on Troy's part, he is a damned fine actor. In any case, it gave Ben an opportunity to air his knowledge on Queensland's fishing rules and regulations. Then it was my turn to ask a question. "So Ben, what's the current thinking in your camp, and what's your next move?"

"I think it's fair to say everything remains uncertain in terms of what the mob is up to. As for what happens next, I suppose it depends on what happens at the campsite. Monitoring the bay will continue and, if the weather settles down again, it's likely they will have the police boat on standby ready for the next occasion something looks like happening in open water out front of the bay. It's a bit hard to plan anything in advance. The best we can do is to respond when they make their next move."

Did I believe him? Perhaps, but some of Ben's information is questionable. The annoying thing is, I can't be sure. I contented myself with smiling sweetly and asking him to call me if any-thing happened. He couldn't be more effusive in his promise to do so. That was unlike Ben and suggested I was unlikely to receive a call should the boat be on the move again.

With his report delivered and the raisin toast and coffee he shared with us dispatched, Ben took his leave. Troy and I sat in silence for a few moments after Ben's departure before Troy voiced an observation. "The meeting was cordial, but me thinks the truth was not in him."

I smiled and said, "Not entirely anyway."

"Do we believe the bit about checking nets strung across the creek?"

"Not for one moment."

Chapter 14

About an hour later, Ben called. "The boat from the campsite is on the move. Not sure where it's going, but it seems to be heading for that mainland beach again." Damn! Now I am going to have to tell Troy he was right.

After Ben left, in case we heard the boat was on the move again, we repacked our backpacks in readiness. I allowed a few minutes after Ben's call before taking my binoculars out to the deck to check the bay. "Yes Troy, the boat is heading to the mainland, and it's heading for that beach again. When they disappear from sight, we'll launch my boat." Twenty minutes later, we skimmed across much gentler waves on our way to check out the campsite.

Again, we landed two bays away from the site and set off on foot. The hike to our vantage point above the campsite seemed easier today. With the binoculars glued to my eyes, I watched a replay of our previous visit. Again, only one man stayed behind. He wandered in and out of the small tent a few times, allowing me a good look at him. "I'm sure that's the same bloke they left behind last time," I whispered to Troy.

Copying the previous occasion, he perched on the crate outside the small tent and lit a cigarette. Then, after burying the butt in the sand with his foot, he went to the entrance of the small tent and peered inside. With a nod of his head, he turned on his heel and strode towards the same accommodation tent as last time. Loaded up with his fishing gear, he looked into the small tent once more on his way to the dinghy on the beach at the far end of the bay. A few minutes later he was heading south-east across the water, to harass the local fish population.

"Come on, Troy. This is our chance to check it out. We don't know how long we have, so look sharpish." I pointed out what appeared to be the easiest track down onto the beach. "See that

135

bush growing on the side of the path we're taking, break off a small branch as we go past it. I'll show you why when we're on the beach."

The climb down wasn't difficult. Soon, we stood on the sand armed with our branches. "We don't want to leave footprints all over the beach. Drag the branch along behind you on the sand. Just check occasionally to make sure it's blurring your footprints. There are already plenty of prints on the sand, but we don't want any eagle-eyed bloke noticing some strange ones added to the mix. I'll check the small tent first, and then I'll look in the large tent over there."

"How sure are you there's no one else around? I notice we are still whispering."

"…Not sure at all. So, be as quiet as possible and keep your eyes open." I didn't mention my heart already playing jungle drums on my ribs or my breathing having become short and shallow. I did try for my best reassuring smile, but it didn't remove the doubt from his handsome features. "I'm going to look in the small tent. You might prefer to keep a look out." My suggestion received enthusiastic support.

On my way to the tent, I checked several times the branch was doing its job of blurring my footprints. Before lifting the tent flap to look inside, I scanned the campsite. No change, and Troy showed no increased level of anxiety. A quick peep inside; it was dark in there. I couldn't see anything apart from a darker lump towards the rear of the tent. No one rushed to investigate. In one careful movement, I pulled one of the flaps back to let in some light… And gasped.

The dark lump towards the rear of the tent was a body; a man. I signalled Troy I was going in, and stepped inside. The tent did not have a built-in floor. A blue tarpaulin spread as a makeshift floor now had a liberal build-up of sand on it. While there were footprints, the tent did not appear subject to heavy traffic. Sweeping my branch behind me, I picked my way carefully towards the body. Was he dead? He must be or the sound of my heart beating would rouse him.

He was lying in a semi-prone position facing away from me. I wasn't sure I wanted to go closer. The man's clothes were filthy, and his trousers showed he had urinated in situ. Almost as filthy was the man himself. All visible skin was caked with sand, and his hair was matted and probably loaded with sand. Stop wasting time, I chided myself. If you're going to look at him, do it and get out of here.

An alarming sight caught my attention as I took my first tentative steps towards him. On top of the small crate beside the side wall of the tent were a couple of medical-looking trays. One contained a couple of hypodermics and a crude rubber tourniquet device. The other tray contained forceps and swabs. "This is not looking good," I whispered and swallowed hard. Those instruments are meant for the man on the floor.

It didn't take much to work out the body on the floor was unlikely to spring up and threatened me. He was either heavily sedated, or dead. Caution abandoned, I strode over to the body. There wasn't a flicker of movement. With a cautious hand gently on his shoulder, I rolled him slightly towards me to see his face.

"Jesus…! What the hell have they done to you?" In my shock, I let go of the man and he rolled back onto his side to face away from me again.

Troy heard my exclamation and raced to the tent's entrance. "What is it? What happened? Talk to me, Sonny." I tried to, but my throat had clamped shut and my vocal chords taken leave.

As I stood up, I gestured for Troy to go away. Then I bounded across the blue tarpaulin and out through the doorway to join him in the fresh air. "That's Frank Hensley in there. He is not in good shape."

"Frank Hensley…? Who is he? Is he important?"

"Too complicated to explain right now, and we need to work fast. Troy, race back to where we left our boat and bring it around to the bay next to this one. Keep your phone on. I might need to call you. Don't just stand there. Move! Be as fast as you can." I saw him hesitate, but I was flicking through my phone's contacts list. Troy thought better of asking more questions and started back towards the hill. By the time he started his climb, I was bellowing into my phone.

"Ben … Ben … Where the hell are you? For God's sake, answer your phone. Ben, Ben … Thank Christ! Where are you? Doesn't matter. You and the rest of your blokes need to bring your boat around to the campsite bay now. This is urgent. I'm not going to waste time explaining over the phone. Just get here – quickly – please."

As I ended the call, I heard him ask, "Christ, what have you gotten yourself into this time?" His question went unanswered as I slipped the phone into my pocket and started towards a jumble of rocks at the base of the hillside.

While not the best hiding place, the rocks did shield me from sight. As I tried to make myself comfortable behind the rocks, I heard a boat. I couldn't tell from which direction it came, so I stuck my head up to better hear the sound. It's my boat. Troy was bringing the boat around as I asked. Unless I changed his instructions, he would pull into the adjacent bay and stay there until I gave him further instructions. I was mulling over what that might be when my phone rang: Ben.

"We are about two bays away from the campsite. Where are you?"

"I'm at the campsite. I think Troy just bought my boat around to the bay next to this one. How did you manage to get here so quickly?"

"We thought we might take advantage of the mob's mainland trip to ride past the campsite. I take it you want us to come ashore; whereabouts?"

Where do I want them to come ashore? Best I go down and stand on the beach and wave them in. I relayed my intention to Ben almost at the same time as I saw their boat coming into the bay. Time to apprise Troy of what was going on. Another quick phone call.

The police's boat nosed up onto the sand and I threw my weight against it to stop it running up too far. Blokes seem to leap off every available inch of gunwale. Ben was first off over the nose and was yelling at me before he hit the sand.

"What's the situation? Where do you want us?"

"The small tent immediately behind the first big one; you need to rescue the bloke who is in there." Ben cut me off before I could finish what I wanted to say.

"Why would we want to rescue this bloke?"

"It's Frank Hensley … And he is not in good condition." As I spoke, Ben and I were pounding up the beach towards a small tent with a gaggle of police on our heels. "He will need immediate medical evacuation once you get him away from here. The air-sea rescue chopper will be quicker than by boat to take him to the mainland and the paramedics can treat him on the way to hospital. He's in here." I pull the tent flap aside. A gaggle of police rushed past me into the tent. I moved a short distance away. Moments later, Troy lumbered up to join me.

For the next couple of minutes, everything was a blur. The blue tarpaulin off the floor was folded to use as a blanket lift. Hensley was rolled onto the tarpaulin, and four burly policemen grabbed one corner each and carried him to their boat. Another officer picked up the trays of instruments on the crate. Ben lifted the crate to see if anything was underneath. The other end was open. The trays of instruments went into the crate and the whole lot joined Hensley in the boat.

While inside the tent was a hive of activity, I noticed one officer standing by the crate where our fisherman friend sat to smoke cigarettes. He was barking into his phone and gesticulating with his free hand. As the crate with the instruments exited the tent, he ended his call and came over to talk to Ben. "The chopper will take off in ten minutes. I've told them to come to our camp. I'll leave a couple of men here to report on what's going on, but the rest of us will escort the bloke in the boat back to North Bay."

Ben and the officer exchanged a few words, before the officer raced down the beach to join his boat idling in the shallows waitingfor him. I told the two officers left behind about our vantage point high up on the hillside and they began searching for their own lookout places. Ben, two other officers, and Troy and I remained on the beach. There seemed an understanding amongst the others that they would return to North Bay in my boat. Ben explained, "With Hensley laid out on the floor of our boat, there was no room for us to go back with them. There's plenty of room in your boat, so you can take us back."

I wasn't inclined to argue, so the five of us trudged down the beach towards my boat. As people scrambled on board, Ben's phone rang. "We need to move fast," he said as soon as the call ended. "The campsite's boat looks ready to leave the beach to return here. We need to get away and be out of sight before they are out on the bay."

"Oooh, that could be interesting. The bloke who went fishing might also know the others are about to return, and will race back to be here before they arrive. I suspect he is supposed to watch over the camp and keep an eye on Hensley, and not leave the campsite while the others are away. I doubt he'd want the others knowing he was away for most of the time. If we leave now, we run the risk of alerting him to what's happened here. And that might not be in our best interest." Ben assumed authority.

"Everyone stop — no, not you Troy. You take the boat around to the previous bay. Anchor in close so it's out of sight as much as possible. Hide yourself amongst the rocks until you're told what to do next. You two blokes, hide yourselves close by. We want to nab the fisherman when he comes ashore. Sonny, that applies to you too. Move yourself."

As Troy disappeared, the four of us at the campsite spread out in different directions. I headed for the jumble of rocks at the base of the hillside where I hid after finding Hensley. It was a surprise when Ben bounded in beside me. There wasn't much room behind the rocks and I doubted they were the best place to hide anyway, but we squatted down, squashed up together, and waited. As unobtrusively as I could, I checked my Glock remained tucked in my waistband at the small of my back. Ben gave me a disapproving look, but said nothing.

"This is not the most comfortable position I've ever been in. I hope something happens soon," Ben moaned.

"Shhh; I think I hear a boat approaching. Yeah … it's the dinghy returning."

Without throttling back, the fisherman ran the dinghy up onto the beach at the far end of the bay. Through a gap between the rocks, I watched him jump out almost before the boat stopped. He grabbed his fishing gear and ran – as much as that's possible through soft sand – to the accommodation tent I saw him enter earlier.

As soon as he disappeared inside, Ben stood up and yelled, "Now…" Then he was scrambling out from behind the rocks. As he ran, he pointed towards the accommodation tent. The other two officers materialised from their hiding places, and all three arrived at the tent together … as the fisherman attempted to exit it.

A brief but fierce struggle ensued, before the man was prone on the sand and handcuffed. While the man was being handcuffed, Ben yelled over his shoulder at me. "The boat; tell Troy to bring the boat around to the beach now." I didn't need him to tell me. I was talking to Troy before Ben finished bellowing instructions.

Moments later, I heard the boat start and, no more than a minute later, Troy brought it around to the campsite. The bloke in handcuffs was not inclined to co-operate. Ben and the two officers between them dragged and carried him to the water before heaving him up and over the side to land in the bottom of the boat. Troy kept the motor idling after he arrived. I scrambled in beside him. Troy eased the boat away from the beach as the three coppers scrambled in to join us.

"Get us away from here before the other boat arrives," Ben yelled above the roar of the motor. "I don't fancy having to take on all of them."

Troy needed no encouragement. He had the throttle wide open and was heading north towards home. I took over the wheel. There are a couple of major hazards and several sandbars to cause problems for the uninitiated. After all my time spent here, I knew these waters well … but I pulled the cover off the sounder and switched it on. This was no time to make a mistake. At Windy Point, I swung out wide to avoid the two huge submerged rocks a short distance out from the Point.

As I did so, I scanned the water across to the mainland. Something was not right. Where was the other boat? It should be at least halfway across the bay by now. Further thought on the situation was interrupted by Ben again yelling instructions. "Take us up to the bay where the police are camped." I intended to, but I simply nodded in response. I felt the boat rock as someone on board moved about. Then Ben was leaning in close to avoid having to yell. "You and Troy will need to stay at our camp until this is sorted out. It's not safe for you to go back to your own cottage with the campsite mob still on the loose. After this morning, there's no point in hiding. They will know you are here." Again, that was my intention, but I didn't bother telling him so.

Our arrival at the police camp at North Bay was something akin to a choreographed and well-rehearsed performance. As we eased up to the beach, the three coppers on board jumped out. Blokes from the camp swarmed down to the boat. They hauled the fisherman out and carted him off to one of the buildings. I jumped down onto the sand as several burly blokes dragged my boat further up the beach – with a confused-looking Troy still on board. Further frantic activity followed Ben's brief discussion with the officer in charge. Troy, Ben and I found ourselves abandoned on the beach as the others ran to launch their boat.

"Ben, if their intention is to intercept that other mob's boat, they're in for a disappointment."

"Why do you think that?"

"Take a look at the bay. There is no boat coming over from the mainland. I don't know what's happened, but the mob is not on their way back to the campsite. And, before you ask, no, they have not made it back already. I checked the bay a couple of times on the way here. Their boat was never on the bay."

For such a big bloke, Ben was quick across the sand to where the coppers were piling into their boat. He had another brief word with the officer in charge. It was as if someone pressed the PAUSE button. All activity around the cop's boat came to a standstill. They stood waiting for their next instruction. It was a while coming. The officer in charge was engaged in an animated phone conversation.

Troy tapped me on the arm. "What's happening? I thought they were about to tear off and round up everyone from the campsite."

"They would like to, but first they need to work out where the boat and the mob on board have gone. It didn't come across the bay as we were given to understand it would."

"Then, it must still be at the beach over there."

"Hmm … maybe, but I think they took cover in some inlet or creek; somewhere out of sight and not so public as the beach. I suspect the bloke on the phone over there is marshalling his resources in a bid to locate the boat and its crew."

"Where does that leave us?"

"Here, for the moment, but I'm not sure what our next move might be."

We sat on the sand under a tree to watch the tableau playing out around the police's boat. The officer in charge shouted and waved his arms about, but I couldn't hear what he said. Then they sprang into action again. Those already in the boat jumped out. They all jogged up the beach and disappeared into one of the buildings. Moments later, they emerged carrying backpacks and other paraphernalia. They launched the police's boat. Everyone except Ben clambered on board, and the boat sped off towards the mainland.

Ben sauntered over and flopped down on the sand beside us. "It's probably safe enough to go back to your cottage now. I'll go with you. Give me a hand to launch the boat please, Troy."

Troy hesitated, looked hard at me and then back at Ben. "Hang on a minute. What makes you think it's safe now? While I'm sure we both are happy to go back to the cottage, I want to know what's going on and how safe we are – now that everyone else has buggered off and left us here on our own."

"You won't be on your own. I'll be with you. There's…"

"Stop it, you two. Let's get this boat in the water so we can go back to my cottage. And Ben, when we get there, I do want to know what is happening, and I want to know every minute detail."

After exchanging sullen looks, we were on our way home. Top priority on our return was a late lunch and coffee. On my instruction, nothing about what the police were doing was discussed until we sat down to lunch. Then Ben tried fobbing me off with a few sketchy details. It resulted in his encountering the sharp edge of my tongue. As I sat down to eat, I felt tired and cranky. "This is not a good time to mess with me," I assured Ben.

"You might feel inclined to play the superior cop, but it's our lives and our safety involved. Telling me it 'should be safe enough now' does not cut it. I have an expensive boat sitting damaged amongst the mangroves in a bay further around the island and I still can't be sure it is safe to inspect it or do anything about salvaging it. So, I'll have the truth and all the details when we try this again." That did the trick.

Ben gave me a belligerent look and prepared to answer … and then reconsidered. "Okay. I can't give you an exact situation report because we don't know what it is yet. It does look as though the boat somehow got wind of what was happening here and aborted its trip to the campsite. The thinking is, it returned to the beach, or slipped into somewhere close to it. I hope to hear more soon. That's all I can tell you for now."

"Unless I'm reading this wrong, you didn't stay behind to enjoy our company. You're our guardian; our 'protection detail', if you prefer." Ben gave a wry grin and shrugged. No further comment required.

"I guarantee you, Ben, we are capable of looking after ourselves. Now that's sorted out, let's devote some thought to why events turned out as they did."

Chapter 15

After lunch, I fetched a scribble block and pencil from beside the phone and returned to the table. I think better with a writing implement in my hand. "Ben, I think your comment about the mob being warned something was amiss at the campsite is crucial. Their boat wasn't sighted at any time during Hensley's rescue or the fisherman's apprehension. Two possible ways they were warned: another person of whom we were unaware kept a lookout and warned the mob, or the fisherman warned them somehow."

"Both those are possible and, for now, I don't have any alternatives to offer. Let's explore your thinking further."

"Of the two possibilities, the latter is less likely. For the fisherman to warn the boat, he would need a radio or phone. You and your colleagues took him by surprise. He had no warning, and no time to use either device before he was in custody." I paused, not to wait for Ben to comment, but to review my thoughts. No one interrupted, so I continued. "Nobody mentioned finding a phone on the man…"

"No, he had nothing on him except a cheap older style watch."

"Even if he had a phone or radio in his tent, he didn't have opportunity to use it. Therefore, should we pursue the notion another lookout was somewhere close by, close enough to see what was happening?"

"It's a sound theory, but I don't buy it. I'm sure a lookout's instructions would include not to show himself at any cost. That's why we didn't see anyone else, but I still don't like it as a possible scenario."

"Given all that happened, any such lookout would be stranded alone here. He still had the fisherman's dinghy to get off the island but, under normal circumstances, the police would guard the campsite, making a getaway impossible for quite some time. Why isn't the campsite being guarded?"

"Not enough men; more will arrive around dusk this evening. Some will be deployed at the campsite, but it might not prove the best use of manpower."

"If no one attempts to return to the campsite, they will be sitting twiddling their thumbs."

"No, there is an inventory of the site to do before arrangements are made to deal with those oil drums and anything else found here."

"There are three of us, all capable of looking after ourselves. It's unlikely there is more than one of that mob, if any, left on the island. Perhaps we should spend what's left of today exploring the campsite. We could take a look at my boat as well." I expected Ben to argue. Instead, he scraped his chair back from the table and stood up.

"Why are we still sitting here? Let's go look at the campsite." After agreeing to check on my boat on the way back, twenty minutes later, I turned the boat away from the beach and headed for the campsite.

The fisherman's tent was our first port of call. Ben led the way in. I followed. Troy lingered at the entrance. I realised he wasn't following me. "What's wrong, Troy? Did you hear something?"

"No. All of us in the one tent would be like sitting ducks if someone is lurking about outside."

"Good thinking; keep your eyes and ears open while Sonny and I search the place." There was no sarcasm in Ben's comment, just Ben taking charge of operations.

We surveyed the interior of the tent. It contained four camp beds, one at each corner of the tent. Contents spilled out of duffel bags strewn about the floor. The occupants of three bunks used small wooden packing cases as bedside tables/lockers. "Not exactly *home sweet home* is it?" Ben commented.

"Not exactly, but it looks like long term accommodation." A pile of fishing gear was dumped in one corner. "This looks like our friend's bunk over here," I said as I went down on my haunches beside the bed. It had a packing case as a bedside table.

The packing case stood on its end. Its other end provided a flat surface, while its interior provided cabinet space. On top, a soft porn magazine was open at the centrefold. The locker held two girlie magazines, a towelling hat, tube of zinc cream, and… "Bingo! A wallet…," I chirped, as I waved the wallet in the air, and was almost bowled over as Ben rushed to snatch it from my hand.

"Not a lot of cash, but there are a credit card and a driver's licence. At least we have a name for the bloke now."

"You have a name, but maybe not the man's real name. If this operation is as big and bad as we think, it's possible those involved use false names."

"You are such a ray of sunshine. Much as it pains me, I admit you might be right." Ben slipped the wallet into a plastic bag which appeared from one of his pockets.

For the next half hour, we went through the occupants' belongings, and found nothing of significance. Ben suggested we move onto the next tent, but the day was slipping away. We agreed to head back to my cottage, but I wasn't quite ready to leave. "I want a quick look in that big tent over there. I think whatever goes on in there is fundamental to this whole operation."

To humour me, the other two traipsed after me to the large tent at the terminus of the tracks leading down to the beach. At the sight of the padlocks securing the flaps across the entrance to the tent, I felt vindicated. What went on in there was important. So important, access to the tent was restricted. "I don't suppose you have a pair of bolt cutters back at the cottage," Ben asked.

"As a matter of fact, I do have a heavy duty pair. Perhaps we might bring them with us when we return."

As planned, on the way back to my cottage, we detoured to where my other boat remained stranded in the mangroves. The situation was not as bad as I imagined. The mangroves held it mostly high and dry. At low tide, all the boat was out of water.

The bullet hole in the side of the hull was obvious. Water entered the hull through the hole when the tide rose high enough.

We drifted up beside the boat and I scrambled aboard while the men held both boats together. At worst, there had been no more than about a hundred millimetres of water sloshing about in the bottom of the boat. I examined the bullet hole. "It looks like it was a 410 shell," I shouted at Ben. "I don't know where it ended up… Hang on, I've found it embedded in the cooler I keep the extra life jackets in. It hasn't done the life jackets much good."

The old hard plastic cooler on the floor in front of the passenger's seat absorbed the impact and prevented the shell from puncturing the other side of the hull as well. Troy craned his neck to inspect the damage. "How bad is it? Is it salvageable?"

"Apart from a bullet hole in one side, it's good news. With a temporary repair to the hole, it could be towed back to the cottage. Then, repairing the fibreglass won't require much." I'm sure I heard Troy's sigh of relief above the sound of the waves.

"Are you thinking of towing it back now?" Ben asked.

"No, I don't have anything to make a temporary repair. It can wait until tomorrow."

With my spirits lifted, we continued back to the cottage. I asked Ben if he wanted to be taken to the police camp at North Bay. "I'll stay with you two. There's no point in going back to North Bay now everyone is over on the mainland somewhere. I wonder if the reinforcements arrived." We hadn't noticed any activity on the bay, so Ben was left wondering.

Dusk was becoming night by the time we were ready to head indoors. Ben showed no interest in leaving us, so I raised the subject. "Ben, it's almost dark. Shouldn't you be on your way back to North Bay while there's still light?"

"As I said earlier, there is no point. No one is there. My allocated task is to watch over you two. So, I will be staying here at the cottage with you."

Great…! That makes things awkward. The cottage has only two bedrooms. The one Troy occupies has two beds, but I don't think either man would take kindly to sharing the room. "Ben, I don't have a spare bed. Unless you are planning on staying up 24/7, it's difficult for you to stay here." Troy didn't offer the spare bed in his room.

"I do plan on sleeping, and I don't think the lack of a spare bed will interfere with that. The sofa in the lounge converts to a bed of sorts. I'm happy to sleep there."

While discussing Ben's sleeping arrangements, I bustled about in the kitchen sorting out dinner. Culinary pursuits were interrupted by the sound of an approaching boat. The others heard it as well. Ben's handgun appeared in his hand. Troy raced over, picked up one of the rifles and loaded it.

"What are you two doing?"

"Get your Glock. We are about to receive visitors. They waited until dark to come calling, and they will be looking for retribution," Ben's voice was little more than a whisper as he switched off the lights.

"Turn the lights back on, Ben. That is not the campsite's boat coming to wreak revenge on us. That's the thump of a diesel engine. It's probably a trawler."

"It sounds as though it's coming into this bay," Troy whispered. "Shouldn't we wait until we see who is on board before we put away the weapons?" As Troy spoke, we heard an outboard motor come to life. "They're coming ashore. Ben, what should we do?"

The floodlights mounted on the fascia of the cottage lit up the beach and out a short way from shore. Robbie Stanton came ashore in his trawler's dinghy. I raced down to help him pull the dinghy up onto the sand.

"Good to see you again, Robbie. It must be at least two years since the last time."

"...or a touch longer," the laconic red-headed fisherman replied. "What's with the posse up there on your deck?"

"Come on up and ask them yourself. What brings you here anyway?"

"I took a handful of blokes and an inflatable to a creek near Wilsons Beach. I was supposed to bring a whole herd of them back here, but they've shifted their focus to Wilsons Beach. They drove there instead. Noticed you moving about out on the bay this afternoon, and thought I should check you were all right. Isn't that your boat stuck high and dry in the mangroves back along the coast?"

"Yeah, long story; I'll tell you about it over dinner. By the way, how are your fibre glassing skills these days? I've a small job for you if you're interested."

"If it's a small job, why aren't you doing it yourself?"

"Because I want a proper, neat job, and not the sort of mess I make. Why are we standing here? I was about to prepare dinner when you arrived. Come on up and eat with us."

"Your friends don't look too welcoming."

"They are a bit twitchy at the moment, but safe enough."

With dinner so late happening, we settled for nothing more than steak and salad. After coffee and a nightcap on the deck, Ben and Troy helped Robbie launch his dinghy. He elected to sleep on his trawler anchored a short distance out from the beach. Ben managed to turn the sofa into a bed while I fetched the necessary bedclothes for him. Everyone was in bed soon after ten o'clock. Nobody even suggested monitoring the bay tonight.

*****

Today dawned clear and bright, a more familiar day for this island. The salvage operation took up much of the morning. Straight after breakfast, Robbie suggested he and I take his trawler to my boat. After applying a temporary patch, he towed it back to my place. Conditions couldn't be better for the tow home: sunny with lightest of breeze, and the sea glassed out.

Troy had the trailer submerged ready to load the boat when we arrived. After some tricky manoeuvring – I didn't want to start the motor until I flushed it – the boat was on its trailer on the beach. After a coffee, Robbie announced, "I'll take the trawler back to my place to collect the stuff I need to repair the hole. It might take me until after lunch to do a couple of other things while I'm there."

"Our original plan for today," Ben reminded us, "was to take a pair of bolt cutters back to the campsite. Is that still the plan?"

"I put the bolt cutters in the boat last night. So, let's go."

Moments after we came ashore at the campsite, Ben dealt with the padlocks on the big tent. With the padlocks removed, we threw back the flaps ... and were confronted by the reason for the tracks: a small forklift parked just inside the tent. Attached to its forks was a custom-built platform resembling an overgrown pallet. While only one oil drum fits on a standard pallet, this platform carried two drums side by side.

The forklift blocked our access, so we surveyed as much as possible from the entrance. A number of oil drums occupied one end of the tent. The other end caught our attention. Benches and other equipment there screamed 'chemical laboratory'. For a closer look, we had to climb onto and scramble across the platform on the forklift before jumping off the other side.

Ben used his phone to photograph the lab set-up. I counted a dozen oil drums at the other end. All except two were opened with their lids left loosely in situ. Ben had his phone to his ear and was carrying on an agitated conversation. This was now Ben's crime scene. I had seen all I needed.

Something more intriguing encouraged me to leave Ben alone in the tent. Outside, Troy. poked about among the rocks at the base of the hillside. I went to the fisherman's tent. No phone found yesterday niggled me.

Again, I went through everything near the bed beside the fishing gear. No phone materialised. Disappointment mixed with frustration set in after I repeated the process for the rest of the tent without finding any phones. It was hard to accept none of the four people who occupied this tent owned a mobile phone.

Maybe phones were banned in camp. Why would phone calls be a problem? Perhaps they feared a phone being tracked and its location discovered, or was it simply a lack of trust. If a phone was available, might someone share with the outside world details of the camp's operations? Without a phone or radio for contact, how would the fisherman know when the rest of the mob was returning? I didn't accept the notion of a prearranged time for leaving Wilsons Beach. My next thought was to check the dinghy. Unlikely, but I decided to investigate.

The fisherman's actions suggested he was breaking the rules by going fishing. It appeared he sneaked away from camp to do a spot of fishing and then hurried back to camp before the others returned. With Hensley sedated and out cold for a long period, the fisherman felt it safe to go off and leave him, but didn't want his absence discovered by the others. I mentally debated this as I plodded to the dinghy still pulled up high on the beach. Why would anyone leave a phone in the boat to be subjected to the blazing sun and rain?

It was about a three metre aluminium hull equipped with a fifteen horsepower motor. As well as all the required safety equipment, a landing net, gaff and a couple of heavy weight hand lines occupied the side pockets. At some time, the nose section was closed off, creating a secure storage compartment. A stubborn latch yielded to brute force. The compartment was quite shallow, with the anchor well taking up most of the nose section.

My rummage in the compartment produced a heap of rubbish: short pieces of rope, an outdated book of tide tables, an unapproved old style lifejacket, a pair of cheap, badly scratched sunglasses, and a bottle of sun cream which had popped its cap. Everything in the compartment looked undisturbed for some time. One last blind scrabble around in the corner of the compartment behind the wheel produced something more interesting.

I withdrew a small polystyrene box. It sparkled with cleanliness compared to everything else in there. The brand name stamped into the lid of the box screamed 'fishing gear'. As I wriggled the lid off, I expected it contained lures. I caught my breath; no fishing gear in this there! A mobile phone nestled in the shallow box. With a whoop of victory, and without closing the compartment, I jumped out of the boat and attempted to jog across the sand to where Ben continued in the lab tent.

Almost out of breath and brandishing the box in the air, I

burst into the tent … and banged my shin on the platform on the front of the forklift. I found I still had enough breath left for a few expletives as I rubbed my shin before resuming my original mission. "Look what I found." I said and smirked at Ben who came to investigate the fuss.

"You've found a box of some sort. Congratulations. Were you expecting your find to excite me?"

Supercilious sod! I thought, but kept it to myself. "Not the box perhaps, but its contents might interest you."

Ben climbed onto the forklift's platform and towered over me as I waved the box in front of him. With a dramatic flourish, I prised off the lid and thrust the open box at him. "Christ, how did we miss that? Where was it?"

With evidence bags over his hands as gloves, Ben picked up the phone and turned it on. "The mob called the fisherman to see if it was safe to return." I said triumphantly. "No answer meant not safe to return."

We waited a few moments for it to go through its powering up routine. "Damn. There's not much charge left in it." Ben grabbed the box and inspected it. "You didn't happen to find a charger, did you?"

Okay, once more the detective has me feeling inadequate. Without a word, I turned on my heel and plodded across the sand to the dinghy. My gut told me no charger was in that compartment, but I had to look. I had to redeem myself as an investigator. This time, I pulled everything out, examining each item as I went. Then, with one last sweep of my hand across the compartment, I confirmed my gut's message: there was no charger! Searching every pocket and nook and cranny of the boat achieved the same result.

Stuck for ideas, I wandered up to the fisherman's tent. Instinct drew me back to the tent, and I know better than to ignore instinct. I sat on the bunk I assumed was the fisherman's and waited for inspiration to descend. For a while, it appeared nothing would happen.

"Can't sit here all day feeling sorry for myself," I told the tent. As I heaved myself to my feet, my eyes strayed to the jumble of fishing gear. "I haven't searched all that."

How did the fisherman charge his mobile phone? While fridges and freezers in the kitchen had their own discrete power supplies, a gas lantern hung from the centre pole in the accommodation tent. I saw no other generator on site. As I searched the fishing gear, I pondered the power question.

The last item to search was a black plastic tackle box. It opened out to reveal a three-tiered tray arrangement which concertinaed back into the box when closed. The three shallow trays contained the usual hooks, sinkers and the likes, but nothing else of interest. So, I turned my attention to the jumble of stuff in the main part of the box.

It contained a pair of non-slip gloves, special pliers for removing hooks from fish, a knife in a plastic scabbard, and a small sharpening stone in its plastic case. One other item spread across the bottom of the box was almost invisible, its colour almost the same as that of the box. I found my charger. In a more sedate manner this time, I went in search of Ben, and almost ran into him as he emerged from the laboratory tent. "Here is the charger you wanted. But, I have no idea where you are going to find a power outlet to use it."

"There is a small petrol fuelled generator in the laboratory. I imagine it powered the electrical equipment in there. Nothing suggested it fed power out to the rest of the campsite. Unless the fisherman was one of the 'chemist' members of the gang, I can't imagine he had access to the generator in the lab. So, the question remains. How did anyone charge this phone?" I had no ideas to offer.

"Don't worry about it, Sonny. Soon, it will no longer be our problem. A couple of officers are on their way over from Wilsons Beach. Their job is to keep everyone other than coppers away from the campsite. And, your mate Robbie hasn't been repairing your boat. He went to the mainland to ferry a forensic team across to here. They will arrive late this afternoon. That's it. Apart from repairs to your boat, we have nothing more to do on this island." I breathed a sigh of relief.

Chapter 16

The following morning, Robbie repaired my boat. After lunch he took me aside. "I'm going home tomorrow. It's unlikely the cops will require my services again, not now they're focused on the mainland. Whatever your plans, I'd give that repair a couple of days to cure properly before taking the boat out again."

"I thought you might stay on for a few days. That forensic crew you brought over will need someone to take them back to the mainland."

"The prawning season remains closed for several weeks yet. This is when I undertake my annual maintenance of the trawler and its gear. For a week or two, the trawler will still be serviceable if required. After that, the engine will be out for a complete overhaul."

Robbie didn't hang around after lunch, opting instead to return to North Bay to tidy and clean up there before leaving in the morning. For some reason, I assumed Ben would go back to the mainland with him. By the end of the afternoon, I realised that wasn't the case. Ben showed no sign of leaving. I raised the matter over dinner. "Ben, have you made arrangements to go back with Robbie tomorrow?" I noticed Troy take a renewed interest in proceedings.

"Nah, too awkward to organise at the other end. I'll hang around and go back with you, whenever that is, unless our mob over at Wilsons Beach need me to give them a hand. If that happens, I'll ask you to take be across. Anyway, when you leave here, you could drop me at Wilsons Beach so I can catch up on the investigation's progress." I saw a scowl flit across Troy's face.

"Well, we are stuck here for at least the next two days while we wait for the fibreglass repair to cure. After that, I'm inclined to head for Millhaven. I do have a case on hold while I'm away." Nobody argued. I hadn't intended they should.

For the next couple of days Ben had his phone glued to his ear. While I assumed many of the calls were to the officer in charge of operations on the mainland and the forensic team, he also has the Millhaven police precinct to run. I broke the news to the other two at dinner.

"Well guys, the two days are up, and it's high tide around mid-morning tomorrow. I'm planning on leaving Riposte Island on that tide. So, if there are things you need to do beforehand, tonight is a good time. Straight after dinner, I'll close the shed, except for the tractor's bay, and start packing up. I hate leaving everything until the last minute. Ben, you need to work out whether you're going ashore at Wilsons Beach or not." I suspect it prompted a further flurry of phone calls.

Troy disappeared off to his room, presumably to pack for tomorrow, while Ben took himself out onto the deck to make his calls. For the first time in days, I felt I had time and space to myself. "That's what comes of living alone," I told the dishwasher as I stacked it. "I like having time alone." My phone interrupted my conversation with the dishwasher.

"Emily, good to hear from you … or is it? How are things in your new lab?" I tried for light and friendly but, the moment I saw the caller ID, a frisson of excitement ran through me, accompanied by a slight tightening of my stomach. This will not be a social call. Emily does not call me about nothing when I am away from Millhaven.

"The new lab has settled down well. This call is about some work in that lab. Gina Burtell…"

"Why would a minerals testing laboratory be involved with Gina Burtell?"

"I did tell you before you left, the new lab isn't about testing mineral samples. It's about a whole different world. I'll explain again when you're back here." I felt stupid as recollection of that previous conversation flooded back. I apologised and she continued. "Okay, just accept I had something to do in relation to Gina Burtell. There is a lot of stuff that doesn't make sense about the woman. I'm not sure she even exists. I'm following up on her in between other work, but thought I should alert you to some anomalies. While I haven't sorted it out, I think I can say the 'Gina Burtell' tag is a recent invention. What I can't tell you yet, is who the woman is who adopted the tag."

Our conversation was short, but it left my mind in turmoil. Not the least of the questions pulsing through my mind was why Emily was working on anything to do with Burtell. But, I had things to do. Nevertheless, that question remained with me as I stowed the small boat and various bit of gear in the shed before locking it in readiness for our departure. For one moment, I thought of asking Ben about it. I dismissed that idea in the same instant. I suspected he would deny knowledge of it, regardless of whether he did or not.

Preparations for our departure kept me busy until about ten o'clock when we all turned in for the night. That's when restlessness, tinged with a hint of anxiety, set in. While I was busy, Burtell occupied only a tiny portion of my mind. Once I was in bed in my darkened room, she took over my entire thought processes.

The operation we uncovered here on Riposte Island had connections with Frank Hensley. He remained in a medically induced coma and couldn't be interviewed. If the man was involved in the operation here, was his security services business also a part of the operation? Did the Millhaven police suspect such a connection, and that brought Ben Richards to Riposte? Again, too many questions, and no answers. As I tried to sleep, a memory slammed in from left field.

Burtell 'disappeared' around the same time as Hensley came to see me. It's also when two of his patrol officers were murdered and Hensley experienced a couple of worrying encounters. The time of Burtell's vanishing act was too precise to be coincidental. I need to talk to Ben about what the Millhaven police suspected or knew about all this before his arrival on Riposte Island.

*****

During breakfast, I tried to figure out how to ask Ben about the Millhaven case. If he went ashore at Wilsons Beach, it had to be before we left the island. A complication was that I didn't want Troy to be a part of the conversation. Our departure time was ten o'clock. About half an hour beforehand, I suggested an early morning tea.

As we sat down with our coffees, Troy's phone rang. After a few words, he asked his caller to hang on while he found the relevant file. He went to his room and settled down in there to deal with the call. This was the best opportunity I would have. Ben still wasn't sure where he wanted to go ashore, so I tackled the subject head-on while I had the chance.

"Ben, what's the truth behind your hurried trip up here?"

"It's your fault I'm here. You rang me about funny goings-on in this part of the world, so I spoke to Wickham's lead detective about it. He became very excited, and I realised you might find yourself in a whole mess of trouble again ... and I was right."

"So, you want me to believe you came all the way up here to look out for me? And there was nothing else behind it?"

"Yes... and the fact the Wickham bloke invited me to help out. As I knew so much about what happened, he thought it would be useful to have me on board."

"You knew so much about it...? What did you know?"

"Only as much as you told me over the phone. But, it was more than he knew, and he didn't know that was all I knew." He gave me one of his wide-eyed, innocent smiles.

"It had nothing to do with the Millhaven case?" I saw a flicker of confusion cross his face. I explained. "...The case involving Hensley, the case Sam is working?"

"No. I didn't know there was a connection until we rescued Hensley from the campsite. This is an interesting conversation, but is there something you're not telling me?"

"No, there's nothing," I lied glibly. "Now we are returning to Millhaven, I was thinking about my Hensley case and what to do about it. That is, what to do about it, after I speak to Hensley's son, Xander."

"You might have to wait a while for that. I imagine he is

by his father's side at the hospital. As I understand it, Hensley senior looks like being there for a while yet."

Troy emerged from his room, and it was time to go. The usual flurry of loading the last stuff into the boat and locking up ensued. One last check on the repair and we were heading for the mainland. As we pulled away from the beach, Ben's phone rang. It was a short conversation. I noticed the frown lurking around his forehead deepen as the call ended. He appeared troubled.

"Throttle back for a minute please, Sonny. We have something to discuss before we go much further." The impact of his words on my stomach was immediate. A tight ball developed as I throttled back. Troy, in the rear passenger seat, made to move towards us. Ben waved him back to his seat.

"What's going on, Ben? After recent events, I'm not comfortable being stuck out here in the middle of Regents Bay. We're like sitting ducks."

Why had we stopped out here? A troubling new thought arrived. Was Ben somehow involved in the campsite mob's operation? Had he been tasked with ending our intrusion; out here in the bay and away from prying eyes? Is there anyone I can trust? Where is my Glock? Bugger! It's in my bag in the cabin. No chance of retrieving it easily. Then, rational thinking finally kicked in. Stop it, I told myself. You know Ben. He would never be involved in this. You trust him ... trusted him with your life on several occasions. In the few moments it took my mind to conjure up such rubbish doubts, Ben had spent the time searching for the right words to explain why we were now bobbing about in the middle of Regents Bay.

"I need to go ashore at Wilsons Beach. That's what that call I received was about." I nodded. No problem there. "But, I think you should come ashore with me. The officer in charge has an activity he needs me to undertake separate from the rest of his men. To pull it off, I need your help."

"Can't he allocate another officer to assist you?"

"He says the reason he needs me for this job is because he can't spare anyone … at least, no one capable of undertaking the task. Troy is the problem. You and I working together is nothing new, but Troy cannot come ashore with us, or be involved in any way."

"He is capable of handling the boat. He could take it back to the boat ramp and load it back onto its trailer. There are two options after that. If one of the cabins is vacant in the caravan park adjacent to the boat ramp, he could stay there until we need to be collected from Wilsons Beach. The other option is for him to take my car and the boat back to Millhaven, and then do whatever he needs to after that."

"Go with the second option. Once this is over, we can return to Millhaven in my vehicle." Ben was right. That was the best course of action. I nodded my agreement. "Good. Perhaps we should share the good news with him…?"

Ben assumed command and beckoned Troy to join us. His delivery of the 'good news' was blunt. "Troy, you will have to take charge of this boat. Sonny and I need to go ashore at Wilsons Beach. After putting us ashore, you will take the boat to the boat ramp, load it on the trailer, and head back to Millhaven. Do you have any concerns about that?" I saw Troy stiffen, so I jumped in to avoid a scene.

"It's police business, Troy, and it relates to the case I was working before we came up here. Somehow, it seems tied in with the operation at the campsite. I think Ben's and my involvement will be by way of information sharing, but it could take a day or two. On the off chance our involvement could take longer, it is best if you are back at Millhaven and can deal with whatever you need to do before heading back to the UK. As soon as possible, we will return to Millhaven in Ben's vehicle. I'll give you all the keys you need for my car, the house and shed. Make yourself at home, and I'll keep in touch." It was clear Troy wasn't happy. I felt bad about abandoning my friend and guest this way, and hoped my profuse apologies were sufficient to keep our friendship intact.

"I'll probably only overnight in Millhaven. The call I received before we left the island was to do with my mine site contract. They have one more little thing they want done, and the university has approved the extension to my contract. They want me back at the mine site as soon as possible and are trying to organise a flight for me for some time tomorrow. If I have all your keys, what do I do with them if you're still not back when I leave?"

"Lock everything including the front door, leave the keys on the desk in my office, and pull the front door closed behind you. There is a spare key I can use. Troy, if you are concerned about any of that, speak up."

"No, you know I can handle the boat and trailer. I am a bit concerned about you though." Troy gave Ben a meaningful look as he finished speaking.

Ben rose to the occasion and, between us, managed to reassure Troy he had no cause for concern. I wished I believed it. I started the motor and pointed the nose towards Wilsons Beach.

No welcoming party rushed to meet us. With one bag each, we stood on the beach and watched Troy head back out onto Regents Bay. Then, Ben pulled out his phone and wandered a short distance away to make his call. A few moments later, he strode back to me. "It seems we are on foot. We walk up the beach to the Esplanade, and then turn left. There is a large two-storey building on the right-hand side about two hundred metres along the Esplanade. Apparently we can't miss it. We need to check-in there."

"That's the Surf Lifesavers' clubhouse building. It appears your colleagues commandeered it for the duration of this operation. I'm not sure I feel inclined to dormitory accommodation." My inclination was to call Troy to return and collect me.

"I'm assured we will not be there long – whatever that means."

We tried looking as nonchalant as possible as we hoofed it along the Esplanade. The clubhouse looked deserted. I resisted mentioning it. When we were about halfway to the clubhouse, a bloke walking his dog – at this hour of the day? – appeared from nowhere. He walked towards us and stopped about a couple of metres ahead of us. Then, an interesting pantomime played out. All parties did the 'cordial good-morning thing' before the dog-walker went into his performance.

Swivelling from the waist in a 180 degree arc, he waved his free arm around as if pointing out points of interest to the new-comers. His commentary didn't fit his actions. Without once breaking out of character he announced in a quiet voice, "Keep going to the intersection up ahead. Then turn right and follow the lane running around behind this block. When you come to the two yellow-lidded rubbish bins beside the lane, follow the track past them to the rear of the clubhouse. Someone will let you in." Ben and I thanked him before all parties continued in their original directions.

A few minutes later, the backdoor to the ground floor of the clubhouse opened in response to Ben's knock. We followed the young female constable upstairs to an incident room. A bloke I now recognised as the Officer in Charge (OIC) greeted us and ushered us to a desk and several chairs in the corner. He launched straight into a briefing of sorts. Ben saw me wriggle forward on my chair to ask a question. He shot me a look: don't do it.

Our briefing was superficial. There was a load of answers I wanted. I found myself being dismissed, albeit in a polite but effective way. The same young female officer was told to show me around … just me, not Ben. 'Sexist sod' was on the tip of my tongue, but I smiled and accompanied the young woman.

No coffee making facilities in the incident room so, after be-ing shown around, I enquired about coffee and what to do about lunch. She led me to an area downstairs where an urn boiled noisily amidst an array of coffee and tea making ingredients and stacks of disposable cups. "Help yourself to coffee and tea when-ever you want. Lunch is brought in, but it's whatever's going on the day." As she showed me the coffee-making arrangements, I noticed three sets of double bunks over against the far wall.

So, six people sleep here in those uncomfortable looking bunks. More officers than that were involved in the operation. Where do the others sleep? Nadia, the policewoman, saw me looking at the beds. "They're not great, but they're okay."

"There doesn't appear to be enough beds for the number of people I thought involved."

"There are beds in the back room upstairs. The senior officers bunk down there. The bunks down here are for those manning the incident room. That house with the two yellow-lidded bins behind it is where most of our crew sleep, and meals for everyone are prepared there."

"I was surprised by the cloak and dagger routine we went through to reach the building's backdoor. I don't know about the locals here, but in Millhaven, in spite of such covert moves, everyone within kilometres would know the police were here."

"If the locals are aware, there's no evidence of it. To avoid curiosity, that house we're occupying is rented to a company for training and team bonding activities. Only a couple of the Surf Lifesavers' executive knows the clubhouse is in use. Club members are away for some carnival this coming weekend, and won't be using this building for at least the next two weeks."

This is good information gained over a cup of coffee with Nadia. I saw her check her watch a couple of times and realised she was anxious to return to work upstairs. It was now or never for my remaining critical question. "Nadia, it sounds like there's a lot more officers involved now than there were on the island, but I've only seen three or four people so far. I know you don't solve a case sitting indoors, but how are they moving about to undertake their investigation without arousing the interest of the locals?"

"There are about twenty involved now, including those of us who work upstairs. A few are on night duty, and sleep during the day. We wear civvies to maintain the pretence of being company employees and not police. The blokes go out in twos and threes, sometimes carrying bits of equipment associated with some outdoor activity as part of a team bonding exercise, including paddling surf skis or doing a spot of fishing. Lunch will arrive soon, but I have a few things upstairs to do before then. Make yourself comfortable down here, or come back upstairs, but I have to leave you for now."

On the pretext of inspecting the double bunks, I sauntered over and made a show of testing the mattress on one until Nadia climbed the stairs and disappeared into the incident room. I planted my backside on the bunk, pulled out of my notebook, and recorded Nadia's key points. After finding nothing of interest on the ground floor, I climbed the stairs, unsure what my reception might be when I arrived up there.

No sign of Ben or the OIC, so I wandered across to the chair I recently vacated and sat down to watch those working in the incident room. Nadia worked on a chart spread out on a table-top. It was at the wrong angle and too far away for me to read. More of the helpless female routine required. Nadia spoke on a mobile phone as I sauntered towards her. Minding my manners, I stopped just a couple of paces away from her. It was close enough for me to read her chart on the table.

Well, that is interesting. I wonder if Ben saw this. I did not need her to see me eying off her chart. So, as she ended her call, I directed my gaze to a young man working on a computer. I realised what I saw on his screen replicated Nadia's chart. Phones ringing and two-way radios filled the place with constant background noise. I wanted to see what everyone else in the incident room was working on, but that would be difficult.

Nadia sensed my presence and turned to face me. "Apologies for interrupting; I guess there are toilets downstairs. Are there any up here?"

"I should have pointed them out. Up here, they are on your left at the end of that short corridor over there. Downstairs, they are further along from the bunks, towards the back wall."

As I thanked her, Ben and the OIC came out of a backroom. They were heading for the OIC's desk, so I joined them there. The OIC glared across the room at Nadia. Out the corner of my eye, I saw her respond with a slight shake of her head. Okay, that's interesting too. Is it only me they don't want to see anything up here, or does it apply to Ben as well? The OIC cut short any further thought on the matter.

"Lunch is on its way over. I suggest you eat downstairs before you head off." I raised my eyebrows at Ben. The OIC responded. "Ben will be in charge of your operation. He has the details."

I changed my assessment in quick succession from 'sexist sod' to 'supercilious sod', to 'arsehole'. Ben was in for an earful when we were out of earshot of the incident room.

Chapter 17

Lunch was simple but adequate. We didn't linger over its dispatch before leaving the clubhouse. After leaving by the backdoor, we wandered a short distance through a mix of new and old week-enders before emerging onto the Esplanade some distance from the clubhouse. A short distance further along, a couple of trees amid a scattering of small rocks provided a shady spot to sit and talk away from prying ears.

"I notice the OIC's gender bias is alive and well." Ben's eyebrows created two deep furrows between them as they drew together in puzzlement. "He has appointed you in charge of our 'special operation' while making sure the female in the team is sidelined and knows nothing – even to the extent of having her sleep with the ranks, and removed from the senior officers. Didn't he trust his self-control? Did he think I might present too much temptation if I were to sleep in that upstairs backroom?" I had not intended such vitriol, but it reflected my anger at our treatment since our arrival at Wilsons Beach.

"Perhaps you're being a bit unfair. I haven't seen inside that backroom, but I think it is quite small. It's possible his intention wasn't to ostracise you so much as to acknowledge my seniority. After all, he and I are equal in rank and position, but this is his operation."

"If you say so. Am I permitted details of our *special* operation?"

"Well, that is difficult."

"Why? If I'm a part of the job, shouldn't I know about it and its expected outcomes?"

"If you calm down, I'll tell you as much as I know." I motioned for him to continue. "We are to make like tourists spending a couple of days at Wilsons Beach, taking in the sand, sea air and points of interest. No, don't look like that. While we are being tourists, we are to observe anyone moving about around the place, and report only to the OIC."

"So, our arrival is supposed to appear unrelated to the cops, who are supposed to look like a business firm's staff members? Who dreamt up this wild scheme, and who is it supposed to fool? It seems based on the premise the locals are semi-comatose and don't know what day it is, let alone what is going on in the middle of their community. Do you buy the story?"

"Not exactly…"

"Good. Because if you do, I'm out of here – even if I have to pay one of those semi-comatose locals to drive me into town." I took a couple of deep breaths before continuing. "Let's agree one thing: you are not so gullible and I'm not so stupid as to believe that crap." Ben nodded. "Right; now that's sorted, what did you find out about the cops' progress with the investigation?"

"Not a lot. I asked for a situation report and received rubbish: investigation progressing well; now focussed on the mainland; nature of the terrain hampering searches; all available manpower deployed to this area. No, I found out nothing. Add the important 'special operation' we're to undertake, and things smell rotten around here."

The truth at last! "Is this a case of 'keeping your potential enemies close'?" Ben didn't grasp my meaning. "Does the OIC – Truman, is that his name? – want you where he can keep an eye on you, but to neutralise you so you can't interfere in his investigation? I don't think he is too concerned about me, but is he trying to separate us in case our working together poses some sort of risk?"

"What risk might we pose? Ooh, I see. Two heads being better than one…? I agree with your comment about his trying to neutralise me. I felt it from the start, but decided to play along to find out what was happening. I have to continue. Short of going home, I don't think there is much else I can do."

"…Without running the risk of unpleasant consequences?" I murmured. Now where did that come from? I knew it came from my gut instinct sending me warning messages. "I have a couple of ideas. Let's walk while I outline them for you."

We ambled along the grassy headland running along the seaward side of the Esplanade. "I saw a chart spread out on a table in the incident room. Nadia worked on it, but another bloke replicated it on a computer. It looked like a map of where everyone was deployed. Lots of different colours involved, but I couldn't see the legend to understand how it worked. When you and the OIC returned to the incident room, Truman was not pleased to see me come back to his desk after talking to Nadia at the table where she worked. He glared at Nadia and she gave him a little shake of her head. I think she was telling him I hadn't seen the chart, or that I didn't know what it was. I want a copy of that chart."

"Okay. Are there any ideas about how to achieve that?"

"No, but I think it involves your camping in that back room with Truman for the time being."

"While you camp with the others in that house with the two rubbish bins…?"

"Hmm, maybe … I'll let you know about that one. The afternoon is slipping away. Might you think of a reason to return to the clubhouse while I continue to wander around doing the 'tourist thing' a bit longer? Truman might be more inclined to take you into his confidence if he sees we are not joined at the hip. You might even comment on needing a break from 'that female'." That triggered one of Ben's throaty chuckles.

Within moments, Ben was on his way back to the clubhouse. I crossed the Esplanade to wander along the front of the houses. When I could no longer see Ben – and he couldn't see me! – I hurried to a cluster of houses we wandered through earlier on leaving the clubhouse. Up ahead, I could see my target: a sign in the front yard of a small older style bungalow. The bungalow was for rent.

I obeyed the For Rent sign and enquired at the house next door. The woman there told me the bungalow had been her parents' home and was now available for short-term rental, and came fully fitted out with everything I might need. After a quick inspection, I rented the place for a week. There was no way I'd stay for that long, but it seemed a wise move. Just as I thought we were done, the woman suggested I might take a look in the shed. I couldn't think why, but went along with her suggestion.

The shed housed and ancient small soft-top Suzuki 4x4 and a slightly younger off-road motorbike. Despite their age, both looked in reasonable condition. The landlord assured me they were in sound running order and both vehicles could be included in the rental for an extra fifty dollars for the week. Even half reliable, they were better than no vehicles at all. I paid the extra dollars in cash. She handed over the keys, and I took possession of my abode for the immediate future. Two tasks demanded my attention before the day was over: collect my bag from the clubhouse, and obtain enough provisions for at least a couple of days.

After some thought, retrieving my bag seemed the easier to accomplish. On my walk to the clubhouse, I worked on a plausible reason for collecting my bag from the incident room so early in the afternoon. Most people wouldn't worry about it until later in the evening when they were sorting out their sleeping arrangements. When I reached the clubhouse, I still didn't have a plan. Play it by ear, I told myself as I tried the backdoor. It was unlocked. I let myself in … and almost let out a whoop of joy. Thank you, Ben! My bag was on the floor beside the stairs to the incident room.

On my way back to the bungalow, I pondered what prompted Ben to bring my bag downstairs and leave it where he knew I wouldn't miss it. It would remain a mystery until later. Now it was time to try the first of the vehicles. It started without hesitation. "That's a good sign," I told it. "Now, let's see what you can do."

I reversed the Suzuki out of the shed and drove at a sedate pace through the built up area before taking it out onto the Esplanade and to the general store. It seems the store closes early. When I arrived, the storekeeper appeared in the throes of closing up for the day. I raced in without as much as a hello to the woman. From a refrigerated display case, I grabbed milk, butter substitute, tomatoes … and then went in search of a trolley. The woman's sour look was noted.

The longer I spent in the store, the more I realised I needed. Added to the trolley in quick succession were bread, raisin loaf, cereal, cold meat, eggs, fruit, coffee (instant for want of facilities for anything better), and a couple of tins of baked beans. Thinking my shopping done, I started for the checkout … and then realised there were other necessities to add to the trolley. I went in search of toiletries, and added them to my shopping. At last, I was done and wheeled my trolley to the checkout. The woman peered over the counter at my trolley.

"Might have been worthwhile staying later after all," she announced and accompanied it with an audible sniff. Unsure how to take her comment, I gave her a weak smile as I grabbed the trolley now loaded with bags of groceries and trundled it to the Suzuki. By the time the bags were in the car and the trolley returned, she had half closed the store's front door. She grabbed the empty trolley, hauled it inside and slammed closed the other half of the door. The bolts were driven home as I made my way back to the vehicle. The Wilsons Beach general store was closed for the day. I wondered how long I was likely to be here and, therefore, how often I might have to encounter the sour-faced storekeeper.

With all the immediate tasks taken care of, I wandered about in the bungalow wondering what to do with myself. Would I see Ben again today? It seemed unlikely. I settled for writing up today's notes before calling Troy. He didn't answer. My stomach tightened and I wondered how long to leave it before trying again. Problem solved. A few minutes later, he called me.

"Sorry I missed your call, I was in the shower." He sounded his usual cheerful self. After assuring me he had no problems getting back to Millhaven or letting himself into the house. He told me he was waiting for confirmation of a flight to the mine site tomorrow. Wait-listed for the morning flight, he thought it likely he would end up on the evening one instead. In return, I had little news to share, except that I was still at Wilsons Beach, didn't quite know what was going on or how long I would be here, and I would keep in touch with him.

While I wasn't looking, dusk settled over the place. Too early to eat and, with nothing else to do, I took myself for a stroll. I was surprised at how dark it was outside. Night was not far away. My stroll took me through the houses in my neighbourhood before cutting through to the Esplanade. Was I being too cautious? I wasn't sure but, in my mind, it was safer if no one knew of my present abode.

Unlike my earlier stroll with Ben, tonight I headed north past the clubhouse and the general store to the Esplanade's abrupt end. A jumble of rocks stretching down beyond the low tide line walled off this end of the bay. The sealed surface of the Esplanade terminated about three metres from the rocks. Beyond the clubhouse, the Esplanade gradually increased in elevation. About fifty metres from the end of the Esplanade, I moved to stand at the edge of the escarpment and peered down its sheer face to the beach some six metres below.

It was too dark to see much below, but the moonless dark night showed signs of changing. A heavy cloud bank that rolled in late this afternoon was lifting to reveal occasional glimpses of a thin sliver of a new moon. Cool night air fresh off the bay in my face had a mellowing effect. I felt myself relaxing and looked around for somewhere to sit. While little seemed to happen today, there was much to mull over.

To my left, and a couple of metres back from the edge of the headland, was a small clump of low bushes. I sat cross-legged on the grass in front of them to survey my surroundings. The last of the clouds rolled on to reveal the tiny moon in all its splendour. While only shedding a soft light over the place, it was a welcome companion. I nestled my back into the soft foliage of the bushes and let my mind wander back over today.

I wasn't too far into replaying events when something caught my attention. It was something I sensed rather than saw. A scan of the beach below found nothing, yet something had disrupted my reverie. My eyes wandered out to scan the bay. There it was! In the semidarkness, it took me a moment to work out what I saw. As I continued to watch, my view of happenings below sharpened until I could make out most of the details.

A small inflatable made its way to shore without a sound. Four paddlers brought it silently into the shallows. I did a double-take and checked again. Yes, I was right. It was paddled to shore. Now, that's a sight you don't see too often around here. In this part of the world, even the smallest dinghies have outboard motors. Why would this group of six people be intent on a covert landing on this beach? Maybe they're police officers returning from searching the area for the campsite boat.

In no time, it became obvious that wasn't the case. As the inflatable reached the shallows, two paddlers and two others jumped out to guide it onto the beach as the remaining two in the boat continued with their paddles. Then, everyone was out of the boat, and with three on either side, they carried the boat across the sand. I was almost convinced it was the police officers returning until I realised where the group was headed.

Over the years, a patch of scrub developed in the corner of the beach formed by the junction of the headland and the rock wall. Carrying their boat, the group disappeared into the scrub to emerge about a minute later minus the boat. A little voice in my ear screamed 'definitely not cops'. Okay, that's an obvious conclusion but, if they're not cops, who are they and what are they up to? As I toyed with the question, the gang of six, hugging the foot of the escarpment, made their way along to the path leading from the beach up onto the Esplanade. "Definitely up to no good," I murmured to no one but the bushes behind me.

Would they come this way? I wriggled myself further back into the bushes, but there was no need. Once on the Esplanade, the men travelled south the short distance to an intersection with a street running away at right angles. They stepped out at a good pace and soon disappeared down the side street. I continued to sit and wonder who they were and where they were going. I couldn't shake the idea they were police officers returning for the night.

At last, my feet and my brain synchronised. I was on my feet, crossing the Esplanade and making my way along the front fences of houses. At the intersection, I peered along the side street. No sign of anybody on the street. A stroll across the intersection, and I was jogging towards the clubhouse. Whoever they were had a head start on me. So, where shadows were deepest and houses unoccupied, I change from jogging to a gallop.

Approaching the clubhouse, I slowed to a stroll to allow myself time to think about what to do. The clubhouse appeared to be in darkness. Even I might have been lulled into believing it was unoccupied. A five metres wide strip of ground covered in long grass ran along the northern side wall of the clubhouse. I cut through this neglected area, stumbling over unknown objects concealed in the grass on more than one occasion. At the rear corner of the building, I peered around to check if anyone was about in the area. No one moved.

After a few seconds, I checked again; still no one about. I was off and running. Ignoring the track to the house, I ran in a straight line from the clubhouse between the two houses behind it and out to the edge of the backstreet. Another check for others out and about, and I was hugging the back fences of the houses as I moved towards the two rubbish bins up ahead, their yellow lids beacons in the pale moonlight.

Deep shadow from an overhanging tree at the corner of the fence prior to my target provided an excellent vantage point from which to watch for any cops coming or going from their accommodation. No activity in the area. I maintained my vigil for about twenty minutes. Two upstairs lights went off in the house. Within a few minutes, one light upstairs and one downstairs still remained on. The downstairs light went out and, a minute or so later, the house was bathed in darkness. If anyone was coming back there tonight, no one left a light on for them.

Still harbouring concerns about my occupation of the bungalow, I took a circuitous route through the neighbourhood to my front door. I felt tired and in need of a shower. Revived by a long, hot shower, I was interested in food, but nothing more exotic than a toasted sandwich. As I sat eating it in my tiny sitting room, I thought about Ben and how difficult it would be for him to obtain a copy of that chart I saw. Was there some way I might help. The next thing I remember, it was midnight. Massaging and stretching stiff parts of me I scrambled out of the chair and went to bed.

*****

When I climbed out of bed this morning, several bits of me reminded me about my snoozing in the lounge chair. Over a raisin toast and coffee breakfast, my mind returned to Ben and that chart. Thinking of Ben brought another problem to mind. When we parted company yesterday, we made no arrangements about meeting today. As far as he knew, I spent the night in the house where all the other police officers were billeted. It would be awkward if he went to the house this morning looking for me. I could call him, but something suggested that might not be wise. Nadia told me breakfast was delivered to the clubhouse around seven o'clock every morning. It wouldn't look odd if I arrived there soon after seven o'clock to meet Ben.

A few minutes after seven o'clock, I made my way to the house with the two yellow lidded rubbish bins, and followed a woman pushing a cart wafting the aroma of breakfast along the path to the clubhouse. She used her key to open the backdoor. I followed her in, and wasn't sure whether to feel relieved or not when nobody else was around. The woman unloaded the breakfast, and left without as much as a 'good morning' to me. Heavy footsteps came down the stairs as I stood there wondering what to do next.

"...Morning, Sonny, did you sleep well?" Ben sounded chirpy enough, but the dark circles under his eyes suggested he had not. While he tucked into breakfast, I helped myself to another cup of coffee and told him I'd already eaten. Nadia and the other young bloke from the incident room came downstairs while we fussed at the breakfast bar. We sat alone at one of the small round tables.

My concern was the other two might feel inclined to join us. I asked Ben if he had things to do upstairs before we began our day. He nodded. In a voice I hoped loud enough for the other two to hear, I announced, "I'm going for a jog along the Esplanade to get the blood flowing before we throw ourselves into the day. I'll meet you in about an hour's time." Then, added in not much above a murmur, "Meet me under those trees where we sat yesterday." Ben studied my face as I spoke.

He nodded and appeared to consider my suggestion, before saying, "Yeah, an hour will give me time to do everything I need to here before we start work."

As announced, I left via the track from the backdoor, and wandered some distance along the backstreet before cutting across to the Esplanade. The road ran in a gentle curve away from the beach and around behind the first row of houses. The curve meant our meeting place was out of sight from the clubhouse. A jog was the last thing I felt like but, to maintain the pretence, I jogged as far as our meeting place, and sat down to wait. That was enough physical exertion for my stiff body so early this morning.

Chapter 18

Ben was surprised to find me waiting for him. "Couldn't have been much of a jog. You didn't even raise a sweat." I didn't think it merited a reply. He eased himself down onto a rock beside me and appeared to study the bay. Then without taking his eyes off the sea, he asked, "How was your accommodation?"

"It's fine; very comfortable." Ben gave me a sideways glance.

"Really...? I didn't expect you to enjoy being in the house with all the other coppers, and I didn't expect them to make you feel welcome. Did you notice any comings and goings last night?"

"I've no idea what happened at that house last night. I wasn't there."

"You don't expect me to believe you prowled around Wilsons Bay all night?"

"No. It wasn't an early night, but I slept well ... just not in that house." He swivelled around to face me. I continued before he could ask. "I have a small bungalow south of the clubhouse. It's clean, comfortable and comes with a couple of vehicles. You should visit some time." Ben's face lit up. What had I said to cause that?

"You don't happen to have a computer in that heavy bag of yours, do you?" So that's what caused the excitement.

"I have a laptop in my bag and, yes, it is fully charged. Why do you ask?" Ben's phone played its tune interrupting our conversation.

One look at the caller ID and the phone was to his ear, and he was moving away from me. Before he was out of earshot, I heard him address the caller: 'Sam'. What situation has developed in Millhaven to require Detective Sam Keller to call her boss, I wondered as I pulled out my phone. Sam and Ben probably communicate about routine police matters on a regular basis, but Ben's face suggested this was not a routine call.

That's when I discovered my phone was turned off. I turned it off last night before my stroll. When it came to life again, I saw I had missed two calls, both from Emily. The little voice in my head told me this was not good. Forget about Ben's call. Why is Emily calling me? A text message from Emily arrived around the same time as her calls. It asked me to call her urgently. I complied with her request.

Emily answered on the first ring. "There you are at last. I called last night because I thought you might be interested in something that's happened here." I apologised and encouraged her to share her news.

"It relates to the Hensley case you worked on before leaving town. Remember the two security officers who were supposed to be on duty the night the other two were murdered...?"

"They were supposed to be camping for a couple of days, but no one knew where. Everyone assumed the swap was one of those unofficial mutual arrangements."

"Well, mystery solved. The police found someone who had a rough idea of where the blokes went camping. It took some searching but, the day before yesterday, police found a campsite ... and two decomposing bodies. Those bodies were identified yesterday as the two security officers. Your Hensley case now has four murders associated with it."

While I didn't doubt Emily was correct, I had to confirm it. "Definitely murder...?"

"No doubt, Sonny. It's estimated sometime on the day before the other two were killed."

Ben's call ended, he walked back to me. To avoid a barrage of questions from Ben, I ended my call to Emily. As I slipped my phone back into my pocket, Ben resumed his seat on the rock. I rekindled conversation.

"You look concerned. Something needing your input at Millhaven?" A part of me hoped he would suggest we return to Millhaven today. While I knew whatever was happening here was associated with my Hensley case, I longed to be home and working alone again.

"Eh...? Oh, the call...? It was Sam. They had a bit of a break through on a case. While you're not involved anymore, you might be interested. This morning, they got the forensics back on two bodies they found at a bush campsite a couple of days ago. They were too far gone for visual identification, but forensics identified them as two of Hensley's security patrol officers. It adds yet another dimension to this whole Hensley thing."

Good old Emily, I thought as I attempted my best surprised look in response to Ben's information. I felt sure Emily withheld the results until this morning, with the intention of sharing them with me first last night. "Do they require you back at the precinct? If you need to return to Millhaven, I'm happy to leave whenever you're ready."

"I'll let you know. I need to think about it. Sam's capable of running the investigation without me, but the case has the potential to become huge. What was your call about?"

"Nothing important; I called Emily. She is checking messages and mail for me. I thought I should find out if anything would bite me if I didn't deal with it soon."

"And...?"

"No, everything can wait until I get back." I couldn't tell him anything he didn't already know, and it was better he was unaware I knew about those murders.

"I'll give it more thought during the day, and speak to Sam again later, but maybe we should consider returning to Millhaven tomorrow."

That's progress. Now to return to our original conversation. "You asked about my computer earlier. Did you want to do something?"

"Perhaps you might show me your bungalow. We could fire up your computer while we are there."

We walked some distance south along the Esplanade before cutting through the houses to the back street, and then winding our way through the built up area. "This is it? I was beginning to think we'd never get here," Ben quipped. "What's with the covert approach?"

"Not sure I want anyone knowing where I'm living. I'll tell you about it once we've looked at what you want on my computer." As soon as we were inside, I booted up the machine and invited Ben to sit down.

He hesitated. "Can you get your emails on this machine?" I nodded. "Good, I'll send you one to open now." I watched as he sent the email from his phone, and then vacated the chair so I could take over.

The computer announced the arrival of a number of new emails. I watched them scrolling up the screen to end with Ben's. The others were was of little consequence. Curiosity consumed me. I open Ben's email, and then its attachment. "That's the chart I saw! How did you manage to photograph that?"

"It's a long story. Does this place run to coffee of any sort? Maybe we should get comfortable with coffee first." The delay was no longer than it took the kettle to boil and the water poured onto the instant coffee granules. We moved to the lounge chairs, and I urged Ben to get on with the story.

"I was surprised when only Truman and I slept in that back room last night. It wasn't the most comfortable bed, so it wasn't a sound sleep. A bit after one o'clock, I heard Truman get up and leave the room. At first I thought he'd be back in a few minutes. The toilet upstairs is just across the hall from where we slept. When, after longer than I thought necessary, I still hadn't heard the toilet flush, I decided to investigate. There was no sign of Truman upstairs. I went down the first couple of steps to check out downstairs; no movement down there either. Not knowing how long he'd be gone made it a bit risky, but it seemed a good opportunity for a poke around upstairs."

"You managed to photograph that chart, so I assume he was gone a while."

"Yes. I couldn't turn on any lights, so used my phone. I thought I'd drawn a blank. I peered out through the front windows to see if

I could see Truman down below. There was no sign of anyone moving about, so I toyed with the idea looking on the computer the young bloke uses. As I walked past one of the tables, I brushed against it. The map spread out on top moved a little, and I spotted the chart underneath. Rather than risk being caught out of bed and snooping around, as soon as I photographed the chart, I went back to bed. It was well after three o'clock before Truman snuck back into bed. He was still asleep when I went down to breakfast this morning. Well, he was still in bed and I think he was asleep."

"I assume there were no clues as to where he went or what he did last night?"

"No, nothing at all. It's possible he went across to the house where the other officers are billeted, but somehow I don't think so."

"If he wanted to talk to anyone, he had to dig them out of bed. The place was in darkness before ten o'clock." Ben leant forward in his chair and gave me a peculiar look.

"And you know this because…?"

"Let's just say I too have an interesting story about last night." I gave Ben details of my night time walk and the activities I'd observed on the beach.

"After they came up from the beach, they crossed the Esplanade and disappeared down one of the side streets. I wondered if they might be cops coming back from a night time patrol, so I raced back to keep watch on the backstreet as well as that house where they're billeted. Nobody else was in the area except me. So, the bottom line to my story is, I don't know where they went or why. All I'm sure about is that there were six of them. They concealed their inflatable in the scrub before disappearing into the built up area, and I don't know how long they remained at the beach. Having said that, I suppose it's possible they are residents who go fishing at night and, when they return, hide their boat in the scrub to keep it safe."

"You don't believe that any more than I do. We both suspect those six are part of the mob associated with the Riposte Island campsite. The timing doesn't quite suit, but I'm wondering whether Truman's nocturnal jaunt was to meet them somewhere."

We agreed not to jump to conclusions, and returned to studying the chart filling my computer screen. "I think you are right about what this is," Ben mused. "It's a bit like the sort of thing you see in old war movies. Someone in the 'war room' moves objects about on a map of the battlefield to indicate where soldiers and artillery are deployed. I'm almost sure this represents where Truman has various groups of his men searching for the campsite boat and its occupants."

"Over the years, I got to know this area well. If that's the case, he is wasting his resources. Most of those places are a waste of time." We examined and discussed every aspect of the chart without convincing ourselves of its purpose. I stood up, stretched and rubbed my neck. "What's our next move, Ben? I know we won't waste time on the harebrained task Truman assigned us, and we can't hang around Wilsons Beach forever."

"We have two options: sort out what's going on here by tomorrow, or give up and go back to Millhaven. I say we give it all we've got tonight, but be prepared for disappointment. Then, regardless of the outcome, go home tomorrow." I agreed with his suggestion, but I knew if we did 'sort it out tonight', it was unlikely we'd head back to Millhaven tomorrow.

It was time to plan our strategy. After much discussion, we agreed Ben would remain based at the clubhouse, and would return there for dinner tonight. Over dinner, he would tell Truman we planned to wander around the southern end of the built-up area tonight checking on which houses were occupied. Ben would claim we observed activity there today and intended investigating it. That worked for me, but it didn't address our main issue: how to be out and about in the wee hours of the morning. I voiced my concern.

"I could ask Truman if they have any camping gear we might borrow to make our cover of being tourists more convincing. I'll explain how anyone curious about the tourists in town might become interested in where we disappear to every night.

Camping would make our story more convincing."

"I just remembered something. Come out to the shed." He dragged the heavy shed doors open for me. "I think I remember seeing something like a tent bundled up on those shelves along the back wall." Our search produced just about everything an enthusiastic camper might require.

"Okay, so I'll tell Truman we hired camping gear from a local and are setting up in that camping area at the southern end of the bay. The camping ground is far enough removed from the rest of the place to make Truman and anyone else involved feel safe to continue their nocturnal activities."

We loaded the camping gear into the Suzuki, took it to the camping ground and set it up. Like real tourists we spent the morning photographing everything that stood still long enough. Over lunch of sandwiches and coffee at the bungalow, we planned our activities through to tomorrow morning. One thing we agreed up front was for the Suzuki to remain in the shed, except in case of emergency.

After a short afternoon nap to prepare us for the long night ahead, Ben returned to the clubhouse to spin Truman the yarn about us hiring camping gear. Ben wasn't gone long before he returned with his bag and reported Truman appeared happy about us camping. If the story was to have credibility, as dusk closed in, we needed to be in the tent with a lantern lit.

Soon after five o'clock, we loaded necessary bits of equipment, a thermos of coffee, bottled water, more sandwiches, fruit and muesli bars into our backpacks and sauntered along the Esplanade to our camp. As night dropped its heavy curtain over Wilsons Beach, we were sitting by a fire in an outdoor fireplace, eating sandwiches and chatting like tourists at the end of the day. Around nine o'clock, we extinguished the fire and moved into the tent. About half an hour later, we turned off the lantern and prepared for our long night's surveillance.

"It's ten o'clock. Time for me to go," Ben announced, scrambling to his feet and picking up his backpack, before disappearing into the night. A few minutes later, I picked up my bag and left the tent. In a patch of low shrubbery a few metres from the tent, I sat down to watch for about half an hour. We were the only campers. No one visited the camping ground or our tent while I kept watch. Then, it was my time to move out.

As I coaxed the stiff bits of me into action, my phone vibrated: Ben. "I decided to check out the patch of scrub where they hide their boat. I'm in there now. The track in is clear, and I can see where they stash the inflatable. It's not here now. I'm about to leave here and take up my position on the headland. Are you on the move yet?"

"I was about to move out when you called. No visitors here tonight. Keep in touch if anything happens." After letting the adjustment on my cap out one hole, I pulled it down hard over my ears. It wasn't the comfortable way to wear a cap, but it did help hold the dreaded Bluetooth device in my ear. I rarely use the gadget because it doesn't seem to want to stay in my ear, but tonight it's essential. I can't have it drop out and lose it in the dark. Ben seems to have no trouble with his device. I must have different shaped ears, I thought as I cut through the houses to the backstreet and headed north towards the clubhouse.

A quick check on my bungalow as I passed, and then I was on high alert as I approached those two yellow-lidded rubbish bins beside the street. It was the same as last night. I saw the last of the lights in the house go out. A quick check there was no one on the track by the house, and I crossed the track to the same vantage point I'd used to watch the place last night. Talk about déjà vu; tonight was no different from its predecessor. No one came or went from the house, and the track to the clubhouse remained devoid of traffic.

After the appropriate time spent watching that location, I moved further north along the backstreet to where I could see any movement along that side street the inflatable crew used last night. I hadn't worked out how to hang about on an unlit street at this hour of the night without attracting attention. Light shadow along the fences bordering the street was interspersed by random patches of much deeper shadow. My best hope was to find a suitable vantage point in one of those darker shadows.

Luck was on my side. In a particularly dark patch created by overhanging trees on the western side of the street, I tripped over a low stump. This remnant of a tree removed sometime in the past measured about thirty centimetres across. It wasn't the most comfortable seat I've ever had, but it was more than I hoped for tonight. I sat on the stump. "Bloody useless thing…," I muttered as I shoved the Bluetooth device back in my ear after partially dislodging it when I tripped. I risked a call to Ben. "I'm in position."

"Nothing happening here yet." It was our last conversation for over an hour.

My phone vibrated when I was deep in thought about Emily's new lab and why she hadn't been able to tell me about it. "Inflatable coming ashore now," Ben said. After what seemed like a long wait, he called again. "The boat's in the scrub again and they are about to head up the path to the Esplanade."

Action at last. I rubbed my face to make sure I was wide awake. Less than five minutes later, dark figures moved across the intersection with the side street. Glued to the fence line, I moved as fast as possible towards the intersection, and peered along the side street. I saw the last two of the group stride up the path and disappear into a house. I hurried across to the other side of the backstreet and moved back a couple of houses from the intersection.

Pressing the microphone boom in close to my face, I whispered to Ben, "Six people crossed the intersection. I managed to see the last two enter a house on the northern side of the side street. The house is the third one along from the intersection. It has a freshly painted paling fence which stands out stark white amongst the others in the area."

"Stay where you are, I'll join you. Any sign of activity at the house?"

"Not a light on in the place, but it looks like there's a large shed or something similar at the rear of the house. I couldn't see any lights on in it, but a glow from there suggested the shed was lit up."

I moved up to the intersection in time to see Ben approaching along the side street. He came to stand beside me in the shadows. "That's the house they went to," I said, pointing in the darkness. "The one with the white fence along there on the opposite side of the street. How do you want to play this?" Ben motioned me to follow him back a short distance from the intersection.

"We still need to whisper, but I think it's safe enough to talk here. I didn't expect the inflatable to arrive again tonight, so hadn't planned this part of the operation. It's almost midnight. We should maintain a watching brief. Since the inflatable wasn't in the scrub when I checked out the area earlier, it safe to assume that, sometime before daylight, those six will retrieve their boat and paddle away again. If Truman is involved in some way – and, if he too follows last night's pattern – that house might be where he goes in the wee hours of the morning. For me, it's vital to know if that is the case." As useless as it was in the dark, I nodded my agreement.

Sitting in the dark in silence waiting for something to happen isn't a riveting way to spend an evening. Ben for company didn't improve it, but it did ensure I didn't fall asleep. Sometime later, I yawned and stretched as I looked up the backstreet towards the clubhouse. I caught my breath. "Ben, I think something moved near those two rubbish bins."

"Move!" he hissed at me. Ben was on the move, and I stuck to his heels. We were in a patch of dark shadow. In a quick relocation, we moved to the corner of the fence we stood beside. At that point, some of the fence palings were missing. We dived between the rails, and found ourselves under big old mango tree in the corner of the owner's yard. The tree's lower branches arched down in graceful curves, hiding us in the dense blackness created by its canopy.

While it seemed longer, a minute or so later, a figure hurried past. It moved confidently along the centre of the backstreet towards the intersection. Ben, much taller than I, moved to the fence to watch the man's progress. "He's turned onto the side street. I'll bet he's heading to that same house." As he finished speaking, Ben dived through the fence, whispering to me as he did so. "Come on, hurry up. We need to see where Truman goes."

"Truman…?" I grunted as I followed him through the fence. Ben didn't respond, and I didn't need him to. If Ben said it was Truman, then it was Truman. I was no more than a pace or two behind him, but Ben reached the intersection first and took a cautious look along the side street.

"Ah ha, I was right. He seems in a hurry. Truman rushed up the path of the house with the white fence, but didn't go in. He detoured along the side of the house, and disappeared around the back. I think you were right. The action, whatever it is, happens in the building at the rear of the house. I'm going for a better look at what's going on. Stay here and keep watch."

There are times when I wouldn't dream of defying Ben. This isn't one of them. "Not bloody likely…," I hissed at him.

Already on the move, he didn't hear, or maybe chose to ignore me. Either way, I was not going to remain behind when the action was at that house. We arrived at the white fence together.

Chapter 19

"I thought I told you…" Ben snarled.

"Yeah, you did, but you never expected me to comply, so stop fussing."

"Stay here! And this time I mean it. I'm going to have a little look at what's going on in that backyard, but I need you here as a lookout. Truman was missing about an hour and a half last night. It's possible he won't stay long again tonight. Move a couple of houses further along the street and keep watch from there. If anything happens, call me. My phone vibrating will alert me something is amiss."

It wasn't what I wanted to do. I didn't want to be a couple of houses further up the street. I need to know what is happening in that shed, and I need to know first-hand. Some second-hand version from Ben always leaves me wondering what he neglected to tell me, and why. Pretending to obey Ben's directive, I started walking away from the white fence. My intention was to go no further than the fence out front of the neighbouring house. "That should be far enough for now," I murmured … and checked no one was around to hear me.

Glancing back, I caught sight of Ben picking his way along beside the house. He didn't follow Truman's route down the eastern side, choosing instead to make his way down the opposite side. Risky, I thought as I watched him disappear from view. Truman's familiarity with the place was obvious in his choice of paths to the shed. He wouldn't have gone that way if there were hazards to negotiate along there. Ben had no such knowledge about his route. Regardless, he didn't encounter any delays and, when he was out of sight, I made a move. I started back towards the white fence, intending to follow in Ben's footsteps.

The gate sagged open on its hinges. About a metre from the gate, I stopped in front of a tall bushy shrub to listen for any sounds from the house. Nothing; so I started towards the gate again ... then froze. A sound like a soft whisper drifted to me. I stood rooted to the spot. Then I heard soft footsteps coming my way. Their owner was in a hurry. Indecision abandoned in favour of action, I dropped to the grass and tucked myself in close to the base of the fence.

At the gate, the footsteps hesitated for a heartbeat before racing out through the gate and down the street away from me. I was on my feet and running, my rubber-soled boots almost silent as I crossed the street and set off in the same direction as those footsteps. As I ran, my brain tried rationalising what happened.

It all started with that soft sound: probably the front door of the house opening and closing. Then someone, trying to make as little sound as possible, came to the gate. Now, that person galloped along the side street towards the Esplanade. That's when I realised the person was a woman ... and she was desperate to escape.

Although focused on overhauling her, I screeched to a standstill. As she neared the intersection with the back street, she slowed and hesitated; only a momentary hesitation. She crossed the road in front of me and headed along the backstreet. I watched her from the corner for a moment before taking off after her. Unlike the side street, there were no street lights here. Most of its length was blanketed in shadow. The woman seemed unfamiliar with the street. She no longer ran, but alternated between jogging and walking fast. I heard her laboured breathing as I caught up to her. She was not fit; not used to such physical activity.

When a metre or so behind her, I called to her in a whisper. "I'm a friend. I can help you." It spooked her. She started running again. I kept pace and continued trying to reassure her. "Let me help you. Come with me to somewhere safe." She hesitated. I thought I'd won her over, but no. The woman ran again. Exhausted, she stumbled a couple of times before landing in a heap on the road.

On my haunches beside her, I kept up a stream of what I hoped was reassuring dialogue as I tried to help her up. "I'm a friend. Come with me to my place. I can hide you and keep you safe. You will be okay there. They won't find you." I pondered the accuracy of my spiel. Frightened, she wriggled away from me on her backside, and shook her head. At last, she spoke to me.

In a voice tinged with a foreign accent, she rasped out, "Go away. Leave me alone. You cannot save me. Don't be here with me. When they come, they will kill you too."

"*If* they come…"

"No, *when* ... They will search for me until they find me. I cannot be allowed to escape. I know they will kill me, but that is better… It will be a good thing. Please, go; do not be here with me."

"See that house just up ahead with the two rubbish bins, it is full of policemen. I can take you there. You will be safe there."

"No…!" She recoiled in horror at my suggestion and shuffled further away. "No. No policemen."

"Okay. Okay, no policemen … Come to my house with me. Come on, come with me." I extended my hand and leant over to her to help her up.

With unexpected speed and force, a foot flew up towards my face. I managed to turn my face away, but received an almighty kick to the side of my head. I gasped and toppled forward as everything swam before me. She was either fitter than I thought or had remarkable powers of recovery. While I sprawled face-down on the road struggling to remain in the real world, she was on her feet and racing away along the street. In a blurred semi-conscious way, I watched her run past the police house and on down the street to disappear among the houses.

I sat up and shook my head to clear the fog residing there. My brain wasn't sending clear messages to any part of my body. It was a few moments before I trusted my legs to support me. I eased myself upright on jelly-like legs … and almost toppled over again. On wobbly legs, I staggered past the house with the rubbish bins and towards the houses in my neighbourhood. By the time I reached the second house, my legs almost remembered how to walk properly.

No sign of the woman. I searched as I moved along the street, until I found myself in front of my bungalow. The side of my face felt tight and stiff from the swelling and dried blood where her boot had opened it up. I decided to go inside and check the damage she inflicted. Her shoe broke the skin, but caused no worse damage. Just as well; there wasn't much flesh covering the point of impact. I cleaned it up and applied a Band-Aid I dug out of the bathroom cabinet.

With my face repaired as much as possible – it would be colourful by tomorrow, or was that today now? – my thoughts returned to tonight's operation and how I hadn't stuck to the plan. I should let Ben know about my adventures, but it could be tricky. I don't know what his situation is at the moment. A phone call could compromise the operation ... even his life. I dropped down into a lounge chair to think about it.

It took a few moments for my memory to kick in. His phone was set to vibrate and wouldn't ring. I checked my phone. Ben hadn't tried to call me. Is that a good thing, or not? Does it mean he is engrossed in what he is doing and everything is okay, or has something happened and he can't call me? The latter possibility had me on my feet again. I must return to my back-up duties.

On the doorstep, I checked the front door was locked. A commotion broke out close by. I dived in and waited behind a shrub growing halfway between the front door and the gate. Whatever was happening, it was coming towards me. I parted some of the foliage for a clear view of the street. A scream rent the air as I peered out. No sign of movement, but feet – more than one pair – pounded towards me from somewhere across the street.

The woman stumbled as she emerged from between two houses. Regaining her feet, she rushed onto the street, and then hesitated as she worked out which way to go. I was about to call out to her, to call her over to the bungalow. The sound of other feet, heavy feet, made me hesitate. She was almost level with my gate when they caught her. For a few moments, she kicked and screamed, and fought with all she had. I clenched my teeth tight to prevent me screaming at them to stop. Then she was silent. The drama staged before me left a woman's crumpled and lifeless body in the middle of the road. Bile burned the back of my throat.

Act One might have ended, but the show rolled on. A large chunky figure leaned over the body and then, grabbing it by the ankles, dragged the woman off the road and onto the grassy verge on the other side. His mate, taller and lankier than the first figure, came to his assistance and helped sling the woman's body like a side of beef over the chunky bloke's shoulder. Then they were gone, off between the houses to the Esplanade. The show was over. It lasted such a short time, it was almost surreal. I was stunned; couldn't move or think. Dead bodies are not something I am unfamiliar with, but watching the actual murder was something else. A seething mass of anger and sorrow, I was frozen in an emotional cocoon. I struggled to drag myself out of that world.

Okay, the woman is dead, I told myself. You can't hide behind this shrub all night. They've gone. You've got to make contact with Ben. He needs to know what happened. My instincts came to life. After checking my Glock and shoving it into the deep pocket of my cargo pants, I moved out from behind my shrub and, with all my senses straining on high alert, hit the backstreet. I saw no one, heard nothing, and reached the intersection with the side street without incident.

My thought as I neared the intersection was not to stop, but to reach the white fence as soon as possible. At the corner of the intersection, a little voice in my head screamed STOP! I did as I was told. Hugging the fence where the shadows were deepest, I inched to the intersection, peered around the corner for any sign of movement, and then inched my way around onto the verge beside the side street. On the opposite side of the street to the white fence, I moved from shadow to shadow until passed that fence. Then, one last check for any sign of movement, and I galloped across the street to the front of the house adjacent to the white fence.

This wasn't quite where Ben told me to keep watch, but it would do for now. While I waited for my breathing and pulse rate to normalise, I focused all my senses on the place behind the white fence. No sounds, no movement, nothing to suggest anyone was at the property. From my position, I couldn't see its backyard, and trees blocked any glow from the shed. I needed a better vantage point. Somewhere allowing a view of that shed.

There was nothing for it, I crossed the street again and moved back a couple of houses towards the intersection. Yes, there it was. The glow from lights in the shed was still there. What about Ben? Was he maintaining his watching brief, or had something I don't want to think about happened? I don't know how long it took me to decide what to do next. It involved crossing the street again and taking up a position in front of the house adjacent to the white fence.

If I continue crisscrossing the street, I'm bound to catch somebody's attention. Stop mucking about, Sonny. Do what you have to do, I chided myself. Crouched down in shadows created by overhanging shrubs, I pulled out my phone and used my cap to shield the screen. Taking my cap off reminded me I hadn't put that Bluetooth thing back in my ear when I left the bungalow. I corrected the oversight, and hit Ben's number. It started dialling straight away, and continued dialling as the ball in my stomach grew tighter and tighter.

Common sense made an appearance. What did I expect to happen? Ben wasn't going to answer is phone and say, "What's happening, Sonny?" His phone vibrating in his pocket would only serve as a warning. I killed the call. A cryptic text message might serve my purpose better. After reading over what I'd typed, I hit SEND, and watched the screen until sure it had gone. Right, where does that leave us? I've sent Ben a text, but has he read it? My next thought did nothing to reassure me: was Ben still in possession of his phone? That gave rise to another question: was he in a position to do anything about the message I sent him, even to read it?

Bugger; all this not knowing stuff is driving me insane. This is not how I work. I need to know what's going on, and I need to be the one finding out about it. Come on, Sonny, get your arse into gear. Go in there and find out what's happening in that shed. Sometimes a stern talking to works wonders. I felt much better for this one. Leaving the shadow of the shrubs, I began inching my way along the white fence. Again, a sound halted my progress. Once more I found myself on the ground in deepest shadow and pressed hard up against the fence.

Ever so soft, the footsteps drew closer until they reached the gate. I held my breath. Please don't look this way, I prayed. A figure slipped out through the gate. A huge wave of relief flooded through me. The man-mountain standing just outside the gate whispering my name was Ben. Those shaky legs were back as I tried to scramble to my feet. Can't let Ben see me like this. A firm hand on the top rail of the fence gave me the support needed to create the impression of being more together than I felt.

Ben was beside me hissing in my ear. "What's going on? I thought you were in trouble, or something was about to happen. Why did you call me back here?"

"It's not about to happen. It has happened. I thought it important enough to warrant telling you about it – now and not later." Ben always manages to stiffen my backbone with some comment at just the right moment. This time, it had me snapping at him. He grabbed me by the arm and pulled me with him as he started crossing the road. After a few steps, he realised I wasn't resisting and let go of my arm.

"Back to the bungalow," he whispered as he led the way around the intersection and onto the back street. Staying deep within the shadows, we jogged back to my place, slowing only once on the way to check for activity at the house with two rubbish bins. Without switching on lights, we went through and sat in the kitchen. Ben opened the conversation.

"Did you spend the whole time back there at that house, or have you been tearing around the place?"

"I wouldn't call it 'tearing around the place', but no, I didn't spend the whole time back there on the side street. An incident happened at the house, and I ended up back here at the bungalow for a few minutes. You need to know about that incident."

It took a few minutes to relate details of the escape and murder of the young woman. Ben studied some indeterminate spot on the tabletop as I spoke. When I finished, he was silent for a moment. Then, in the pale glow from the various LEDs in the kitchen, I saw him looking at me with his head on one side. "Is that her handiwork on the side of your face? It will be colourful tomorrow. Approximately how long ago did they take the body away? You are sure she was dead?"

"Yes, I am sure." Don't snap, I told myself. After all, you are not sure. I couldn't check her before they carted her away. How long ago was that? After some rapid mental calculations, I gave him my best guess.

"Come on, we've wasted enough time. Move yourself."

"I'd love to. Where are we going … and do I want to go there?"

"I'll tell you on the way. Let's go." He already had the front door open. I followed him out, locked the door, and sprinted to catch him. We ran flat out towards the northern end of the Esplanade. My legs felt the strain of running on the hard road, but I couldn't slow down. Ben might be a big bloke, but he moves fast and can maintain top speed over long distances … and talk while he is about it. I was not about to let him think me any less fit than he is. It came as a much needed relief when he veered off the Esplanade and onto the path leading to the beach.

The steep path required a reduction in speed. A further reduction was required at the bottom of the path where we branched off to jog along the base of the escarpment. At some point during the jog along the sand, an idle thought about the time passed through my mind. I had lost track of time, but I felt certain it wouldn't be much longer before the sky began its preamble to dawn.

We headed for the patch of scrub where they hide the inflatable. I kept a sharp eye out for anything on the bay or up above. "Oowah …" I barrelled into a stationary Ben. "What? What's happened? Why did you stop?"

"Ssshh … wait here." With that, Ben was running in short light steps towards the scrub.

Wait here…! Alone, out in the open and fully exposed against the escarpment…? I don't think so! Ben disappeared into the scrub. Mimicking his style, I started towards the scrub, and met Ben coming out again as I was about to enter it. "Boat's not there," he said as he rushed past me and started back the way we came.

"They'll have to come back for the others – unless they have already gone …" My initial thought was that the men had taken the woman's body away somewhere. But that might not be the case. Perhaps they all left together, along with the body. Ben read my thoughts.

"They'll have to come back for the others. It will need to be soon, if they want to do it under the cover of darkness. We need to be up top somewhere to keep a look out for the boat's return."

Up on the headland, our previous vantage point offered no cover in the lightening conditions. Low, bushy scrub filled the few metres between the end of the Esplanade and the rock wall end of the bay. Disturbing a few birds by our intrusion, we fought our way into the scrub and sat on the ground.

The gravelly surface didn't make a comfortable seat but, by craning my neck and parting the foliage a little, I could see the beach below. By turning my head the other way, I had a view of this end of the Esplanade and the path down to the beach. Disturbed biting midges and other crawling insects were determined to make our stay as uncomfortable as possible.

As I fidgeted to find a more comfortable position and swat something feasting on my arm, a noise from the Esplanade made me freeze. A look through the foliage, and I was nudging Ben in the ribs. He gave a gentle nod as he too peered through the greenery. All previous discomfort forgotten, we both sat motionless for a couple of minutes.

Four men strolled across the Esplanade and down the path to the beach. Their swagger, banter and giggles suggested they had imbibed well. When they reached the end of the path, I turned my head to see the beach. The inflatable was coming ashore. As it reached the shallows, the men on the beach waded out to about knee deep to grab the boat and climb aboard. "That's interesting," I murmured as I watched four of the crew pick up paddles and begin moving the boat out into deeper water.

"What's interesting?"

"The first time I saw that inflatable come ashore, there was no outboard motor. They paddled it. When there were only two coming ashore in it this time, they used the outboard. Then, once the whole crew was on board, they reverted to paddles."

"Food for thought," Ben agreed. "...Talk about it later. Right now, we need to get out of here. It's too light to be skulking about. You never know who might be out and about, or watching our friends depart." With Ben in the lead and on all fours, we crawled to the western extremity of the scrub before emerging and walking briskly to the first street we encountered parallel to the Esplanade.

I wasn't sure whether Ben was heading for my bungalow or our campsite. I hoped it was the bungalow. I was desperate for coffee ... and information about what he observed at that house last night.

Chapter 20

It was just after four o'clock. Back in the bungalow, over coffee and a makeshift breakfast, a review of the night's operation began. Ben led off by asking me to recount events after I arrived at the house with the white fence. When we came to the young woman's demise on the street outside this house, he again asked if I was sure she was dead.

"No, I can't be sure. All I can tell you is what I witnessed from behind the shrub out front. I will be surprised if she is not dead."

"How was she killed?"

"I think they tried to strangle her, but she fought hard. The lanky bloke received an almighty kick to the family jewels. It sent him reeling and he stayed on his knees off to one side for a while."

"So, how did they kill her?"

"With the lanky one unable to assist, the chunky one struggled to hold her down, even with his ample body planted on top of her. I thought he was going to punch her. He brought his arm back to achieve plenty of drive. There was no punch, but the woman ended up still and limp. I think he stabbed her."

"There's enough light now. Let's take a look." On his way out, Ben grabbed a small torch out of his backpack on the floor near the front door. I wasn't sure where we were going, but I trailed along. He led the way onto the street, and looked around. "Exactly where did it happen?"

From out on the street, I couldn't be sure. I had an idea. Crouched down behind the shrub in the front yard again, I gave Ben directions until he was standing on or near the spot. As I came from behind the shrub, I saw him go down on his haunches. Curious about what he found, I rushed out to join him. Without acknowledging my presence he asked, "Have you got any of

197

those ... I don't know what they're called ... Sticks with a piece of cotton wool wrapped around the end?"

"Cotton Buds or Q-Tips ... If that's what you mean, yes, I saw a small packet in the bathroom cabinet."

"Bring them out. Don't touch any of them; just bring the whole packet."

He opened the zip lock packet and shook one tip partially out, much as a smoker might tap a cigarette out of a packet. Careful not to touch the tip, I saw him stroke the bitumen with it. I crouched down beside him. Then I saw it: a dark stain on the bitumen. "No good; it's too dry to pick up a sample. This thing needs to be damp." He waved the offending cotton bud at me.

For a moment, I was at a loss about how to achieve that. It was obvious Ben expected me to fix the problem. That required an uncontaminated supply of distilled water. It was not an item I carried in my bag. I wandered back to the house. Something suggested I'd find what I needed inside. The last place I looked was the bathroom. Ooh, maybe... the small first aid cabinet screwed to the wall might contain something. "Eureka!" I yelped when I came across a small box containing a number of plastic phials. The label on the box's lid claimed they were for irrigating burns or flushing foreign bodies from eyes. It also insisted the phials' contents were sterile.

On my way out to Ben, I realised I needed more than the box of phials. We needed something to cut the top off the phials. Back to the first aid cabinet. Small sharp scissors, tweezers, a couple of gold safety pins, and a plastic spatula, were in an enamel kidney dish at the bottom of the cabinet. I tipped everything except the scissors out of the tray, doused the scissors in a liberal amount from a bottle of isopropyl rubbing alcohol, placed the scissors and two phials in the tray, and was on my way to Ben with my precious cargo.

My offering received Ben's grunt of approval. I snipped off the end of one of the phials, squirted some of the contents onto the cotton bud, and we were in business. Ben stroked the bitumen with the now dampened tip, checked the sample collected, and sealed it in a small plastic bag from his pocket.

"Over here now," he said as he moved to the grassy roadside verge. "This looks like the place where they dragged her to." I agreed, and another sample was collected. This time there was no need for the phial's contents. The grass, still damp with last night's dew, prevented the blood from drying. Ben stood up and looked around. "There's not enough blood here. You said they threw her over one bloke's shoulder. Which way did they go after that?"

We walked back along the street a few metres. "They went between these two houses. I assumed they went out to the Esplanade." A glance along the gap between the houses confirmed it opened out onto the Esplanade. Then, Ben's bulk blocked the view as he walked along it. Weeds and some breed of low spreading grass covered the ground. Neither neighbour appeared to have any interest in mowing this strip of no man's land. Two more samples went into Ben's pocket before we reached the Esplanade.

At the edge of the road, we looked north past the clubhouse and towards the path down to the beach. "I think it unwise to be seen collecting samples out here," Ben murmured. "Time we adjourned to the bungalow again." He almost knocked me over as he turned on his heel and started back.

This time, we sat in the lounge chairs. Ben sat in silence for a while, and I let him be. I knew the signs. He was deep in thought and was likely to ignore me if I tried to interrupt. At last, he sat back and clasped his hands behind his head. "Looks like your assessment was correct. It's likely she was stabbed. Between when they carted her off and when you called me, did anything else happen? Did you see or hear anything?"

A short answer, "No, nothing," but it started me wondering. Had I missed something? I was strung out by what I'd witnessed but, in my heightened state of alertness, I would have noticed anyone moving about. There was nothing else I had for Ben. Besides, I had been patient, but I wanted to know about what happened at the house. "Did Truman stay long at the house?"

"He was still there when I came to find you. I don't think he was having a good time of it. A bit after his arrival, a couple of the others dragged him off to a small room in the back corner. I did not see him emerge from there."

"Is last night's body count likely to be more than one?"

Ben shrugged and then shook his head. "I don't know, but I doubt they would risk that. It's more likely that, if I visited the clubhouse today, I would find the OIC nursing injuries he sustained in an in-house accident: slipped and fell down the stairs in the middle of the night, or something similar I suspect."

"The six blokes who arrived in the inflatable must have met others at the house. Others, besides Truman, I mean. Any idea how many were in the shed?"

"Not an exact count. I saw nine or ten, but I believe there might have been another one or two in there as well."

"And there could have been one or some in the house also. I don't know if the one who was killed was the only woman in the house or not, but I think why she was there is obvious. She was one of the facilities provided; a working girl. So, what happens now?"

"I'm going to make a phone call shortly. I'll know more after that. If things go as I think, sometime soon after breakfast is delivered, I'll visit Truman at the clubhouse."

"Assuming he survived the night and is back there, why go to see him?"

"It would be normal for me to check with him about any new developments in their investigation. Yes, I know there isn't likely to be, given the way he is deploying his men, but I'm not supposed to know that."

"Okay. What will I be doing while you are visiting Truman? I assume I will not be accompanying you."

"You are going to make like a tourist. Wander around on the headland. Be visible. Try to look like a camera-happy tourist taking photos of everything and anything. I'll tell Truman that's what you're doing. He'll be impressed I've managed to escape the annoying female for a few minutes again so he and I can talk police business."

We twiddled our thumbs until eight o'clock. Ben announced he had a phone call to make, and left the bungalow. I watched him through a gap in the drapes until he disappeared among the houses. With no well-defined plans for my morning, I felt I should be doing something but didn't know what. Sitting around indoors so much did not sit well with me. After rummaging through my backpack to ensure I had everything I might need this morning, I paced the floor.

Ben returned about half an hour later. He looked grim, and the firm set of his jaw, told me to tread carefully. Without a word to me, he went straight to the kitchen and hauled fresh coffee mugs out of the cupboard. Conversation was absent until we were seated at the kitchen table with our coffees. I let him run the show.

"Things might become interesting around here later today. I hope you didn't have anything urgent to attend to in Millhaven. We won't be leaving Wilsons Beach yet. In a few minutes, I will head over to the clubhouse. You should take a cautious route to our tent, and then emerge to do your photographer performance along the headland. See if you can fill in half an hour at least. An hour would be better. When you're done, go back to our camp and wait for me there. I don't know how long I'll be. It's possible I might be waiting in the tent when you return."

That told me nothing. I wanted more, but was told the situation was 'too fluid' to say more at the moment. While I searched for a suitable response, a stray thought fluttered in. "Ben, this will sound weird, but humour me. I think you need to be careful around Nadia, the woman who showed me around and was working on that chart. I don't know her rank or anything about her, but she maybe too 'close' to Truman."

"I'll keep a wary eye out for young Nadia and any interaction between her and Truman. Now, get going. I want you visible out there on the headland by the time I'm at the clubhouse." Terrific…! To comply, I jogged through the houses to the camping ground.

After checking no one was around, I dived into our tent. A thorough visual scan showed nothing out of place; nothing disturbed. That's a relief. It had bothered me that anyone curious enough to come looking, would find no one in the tent all night. My concerns allayed, I fitted a telephoto lens to my camera and, with it slung around my neck, set off to parade and be seen on the headland.

I pointed my camera at the sea, rocks, beach, the clubhouse and the general store, taking my time with each 'shot' as I fiddled with focus and changed lenses. A couple of times, as I worked my way from one side of the beach to the other, I sat on the grassy headland and fiddled with my camera, as if checking the 'shots' I'd taken. When I reached the northern end of the Esplanade, I checked the time. So far, my performance accounted for twenty-five minutes. I moved to the edge of the escarpment and went through the rigmarole of taking several shots of the beach below. Still hadn't wasted enough time.

In a bid to find something else to photograph to waste more time, I headed back to the path and went down onto the beach. After strolling along the sand almost to the northern extremity of the beach, I turned and wandered back towards the path, stopping every few metres to look up at the escarpment. When about halfway back to the path, I stopped, grabbed my camera and faffed about trying to find the best angle to use to photograph the sheer face of the escarpment.

That's it; performance over, I told myself. I came back to an empty tent. I was gone for a little over an hour. Sitting around alone in a tent was fast losing its appeal when Ben arrived about twenty minutes later and announced he had a phone call to make; another call not for my ears. He wandered a short distance from the tent to make what appeared to be an intense call. That grim face and set jaw were in place again when he returned.

"You should go back to the bungalow and stay out of sight there for a while. Do you have enough food and whatever else you need to last you a couple of days?"

"Possibly … Uhmm, maybe not quite enough … I'll manage.

What's going on? Will you be spending time at the bungalow, or at least some time there? I'm thinking of supplies, that's all. Perhaps I'll pay the store another visit anyway."

"No, I won't be based at the bungalow. I might manage the odd quick visit, but that would be the extent of it."

"Was Truman there when you called on him this morning?"

"He wasn't about. Your friend, Nadia, said he had a bit of an accident last night and was resting this morning. I expressed my concern for him and went to the back room to check on him. He was dozing. His face sported a couple of bruises and a small cut across his nose. The wildly coloured shirt he had on was partially undone exposing a fair expanse of torso in the midriff area. All the area I could see was adorned with about fist-sized severe contusions. Somehow, Nadia's story – Truman heard a noise downstairs, went to investigate, missed his footing in the dark and fell down the stairs – doesn't tally with his injuries."

"Did you have a chance to talk to him about it?"

"No. I left him resting in peace. He won't have long to enjoy it. You should be aware, in about half an hour's time, things will become a bit hectic around here. Keep your head down and stay alert."

"What does 'hectic' mean? I stand a better chance of staying alert if I know what I'm likely to encounter."

"Nothing I hope, but I can't be sure. I'll let you know when the dust settles and it's safe to come out again."

"No. That's not good enough, Ben. Details please, or I am not going to stay holed up in the bungalow. I will either continue being a 'tourist', or I will start doing my own thing. Which is it to be?"

I braced for the tirade as I watched the red mist come down across Ben's features … then recede just as quickly. He heaved a sigh of resignation and sat down on the tent floor. I followed his example.

"I knew you would be like this; wouldn't just do as I asked for once. Okay, here it is. In less than half an hour now, the place will be overrun by a squad of special officers comprising police from other areas and members of the Federal Police. Those in the clubhouse, along with any of the billets still in that other house, will be taken into custody and quietly removed from here. While a lot of officers are involved, it will be a stealthy operation. The main thrust is scheduled for tonight. The last thing I need is for you stumbling about and getting in the way."

"Stumbling about and getting in the way…! Really! What do you take me for, some rank amateur?"

"We both know better than that, Sonny. Your comment is uncalled for. This will be a dangerous operation. We are not dealing with a small town gang of petty thieves. Please stay safe at the bungalow so I don't have to worry about you, or be distracted by concern about what you are up to. If you are not going to do this, I will have you removed from Wilsons Beach for the duration of the operation."

Okay, I get the message. Argument and refusal do not make for a sound strategy in this instance. My rendition of backing down and agreeing to comply was worthy of an Oscar nomination. Well, maybe not, but it was convincing. Ben oozed relief as he thanked me. "If you want to visit the store, I suggest you hurry and do that now, then come back here before taking the 'tourist' route back to the bungalow. I've a meeting with people along the road into Wilsons Beach, so I'll head off in the other direction. Stay safe. I'll be in touch whenever I can."

No point drawing attention to myself by hurrying. With camera in hand, I strode towards the store, stopping a couple of times to appear to be looking for something to photograph. Madam Storekeeper's eyes lit up as I entered, but I fear she was disappointed by the paltry amount bought today. Then, back to the tent as instructed and to collect a couple of things I wanted, before spending about twenty minutes roaming around to end up back at the bungalow.

With senses on high alert after Ben's comments, my first priority was to check the place for any signs of intruders. In spite of no evidence of any 'visitors' in my absence, instinct kept insisting I also should check the shed. Who am I to argue with instinct? With nothing out of place in the shed, I decided to check both the vehicles. I knew the Suzuki ran okay and the gauge indicated the fuel tank was full, but I hadn't looked at the motorbike. On my way over to it, I checked both for flat tyres; all okay. The bike's fuel tank was about half full. As I'm supposed to be in hiding, I can't even try the bike to see if it starts. With the shed checked, there is nothing for it but to go back inside and try to work out how to occupy myself for however long.

The day dragged on. I kept checking the time, only to discover on each occasion the day had advanced no more than a few minutes. It was frustrating not knowing what was happening outside, particularly around the clubhouse. Cocooned in the bungalow as I was, I felt excluded from the rest of the world. While I didn't expect to see anything happening around here, I did expect to hear sounds of an operation in progress. There was nothing. It's like being trapped in some void or time warp. Perhaps something was happening out there, but I couldn't hear it. I eased one of the side windows open a fraction in the hope of hearing something to suggest an event was in progress. I was disappointed.

I decided catching up on work might be a good idea, and booted up my computer. Emily was doing an excellent job of fielding my messages and emails. What managed to slip through to me required little time or effort. It's probable she doesn't know Troy is back at the mine site, and she is doing her best to ensure nothing interrupts my break away at my beach place. Since my brief stint in hospital after I was attacked while working a recent case, Emily is overprotective; reminding me frequently I should rest and not overdo things. The temptation is to ring her for a chat, but she is at work and does not need the interruption.

As a last resort, I turned to the stack of three ancient magazines on top of a low cupboard in the sitting room and settled back in a lounge chair.

Chapter 21

It was dark when I rejoined the real world. I was still in the lounge chair, but the magazine I was reading was on the floor, and most of me was stiff. My watch insisted it was after seven o'clock. If it is telling the truth, I slept for about three hours. I must be ill. I don't do that during the day. After easing myself out of the chair and coaxing bits of me back to life, I staggered to the kitchen to explore what culinary delight I might conjure up for dinner.

Dinner is delayed. Curiosity has the better of me. With the bungalow in darkness, I eased open the backdoor and, after a quick look around, stepped outside. Still nothing anywhere in the area to suggest heightened activity. After a few moments outside, I went back to pondering the contents of the fridge and questioning my tastebuds about what tempted them. For want of inspiration or input from said tastebuds, I settled for sardines on toast eaten in front of a news broadcast on TV.

Later, the smell of the sardine tin in the kitchen bin was more than I could handle. Ignoring instructions about hiding myself away, I gathered up the kitchen bin liner and headed for the front door. I marched out to the rubbish bin. While at the bin, I surveyed the house. The blinds on all the windows worked well, but a soft glow still emanated from inside.

The rubbish bin's lid heavy coating of grime transferred to my hands. It combined with some oil from the sardines can to produce in a tacky mess on both my hands. I left the front door open when I came out. Rather than transfer the mess from my hands to the door, I walked through to the kitchen to wash my hands before closing the door. As I reached for a towel to dry them, a sound, outside and out of place, caught my attention.

There it was again; louder this time. That sound was not unlike one I heard last night. I remembered the front door was open and, still drying my hands, rushed to close it. Ben was right. Things were about to become interesting. As I approached the door, a wild-eyed woman rushed in, barrelling into me and knocking me back into the kitchen. The towel fell to the floor as my right hand dived into my pocket.

Exhausted and out of breath, she croaked, "Help me. They're going to kill me."

This can't happen two nights in a row. The woman didn't follow me into the kitchen, but rushed past into the sitting room. I wondered if she intended continuing through and out the back-door. I craned my neck to see through the house. She stood near one of the lounge chairs, swivelling her head from side to side as if searching for a way out. Terror distorted her features. I'd be a lot happier if she did leave.

I hesitated as I weighed up the wisdom of taking her to the backdoor and showing her out. By now, the woman was bent over the back of the lounge chair gasping for breath. I should do something to help her. Help her take whatever her problem is somewhere else. No time to do any more than think about it. As I went to go to her, heavy boots thundered in through the front door. Two men, dressed in dark clothing – and foreign looking, I later recalled – dashed past me and into the sitting room. The woman began screaming in terror. She made my blood run cold.

The scenario playing out before me caused something like suspended animation. I stood anchored to the spot in the kitchen doorway, my right hand still deep in my pants pocket. Then, my brain and whatever else was required, clicked into life again. My hand came out of my pocket holding my Glock with my left hand working its slider before the barrel was out of the pocket. Then came the final act. It was all over in seconds.

One man grabbed the woman; her struggles useless. I think she was dead before she hit the floor. The screaming stopped. The struggle was over. Once she was on the floor, he made sure his work was done. I saw the light glint off a long thin blade. That's when the second man remembered me.

When they rushed into the sitting room, he stopped a little

distance short of the first man. It was as though he was the back-up in case the woman tried to escape. Now the deed was done and the first man was in the process of ensuring a thorough job. A back-up no longer was required. That's when the back-up remembered me.

He came at me. The lethal looking knife in his hand was a clear indication of my intended fate. No thought required. I responded automatically. It was a double tap, my Glock sounding deafening in the tiny building. The noise and the sight of his mate hitting the floor had the other man up in a crouch. His right arm went up, taking his hand and the knife it held back past his ear. That's as far as he got. The knife never left his hand. My Glock spat three times in quick succession. The man pitched forward onto his face on the floor.

In some sort of fugue, I stood and stared at the carnage decorating my floor. The Glock still dangled from my hand. Reflexes kicked in again a moment later as more sounds came towards me. Another two men rushed in through the front door. My Glock came up in an instant. That brought them to a sudden halt with the second bloke banging into the first man. Two pairs of hands shot up in the air. "Don't shoot!" the leader said. "We're part of the good guys."

Maybe so, but I wasn't about to take his word for it. Then he substantiated his claim. "Ben asked us to keep a watching brief along this stretch of road. We were distracted by a commotion out on the Esplanade and went to investigate. When we heard the shots, we raced back here. Are there any live ones left about the place?" I shook my head, and tried to stir my vocal chords into action. They eventually responded.

"No, I don't think so." I pointed to the woman's body. "She raced in yelling for help. Those two were chasing her, and rushed in after her. The one over there near the woman dispatched her while the other one looked on. Then, this one here, decided I should go too. Why would Ben waste two valuable resources on watching this street? Was there a reason to expect something to happen along here tonight?"

The two men exchanged an embarrassed look before one of them shrugged and cleared his throat. "Our instructions were to keep an eye on you; to keep you safe. He said he half expected you to sneak out after dark to do a bit of sleuthing of your own."

"Just shows how wrong he was. I had no intention of going anywhere tonight for fear of interfering with your operation." Not strictly true, but they don't need to know that. "What happens now? I don't much fancy spending the night with three bodies outside my bedroom door."

The two men giggled. "Didn't we say?" One of them asked. "Our instructions were, if anything happened, to take you back to the lifesavers' clubhouse. So, come with us. We'll escort you back."

No, I don't think I'm going to do that. I've seen no IDs. They haven't introduced themselves properly. Apart from mention of Ben's name, there's been nothing to substantiate their claim of being 'part of the good guys'. The second bloke seemed edgy. He kept looking over his shoulder towards the door still standing wide open. This pair looked less convincing by the minute. Time I tested the situation, I think.

"Ah, look, thanks a lot for the offer, but I would much rather stay here. If someone took care of those bodies, I will be okay here. Is that something you can organise; someone to remove them?" The men exchanged a look. That prompted the edgy one to speak.

"Look lady, you're to come with us. No one is coming to remove the bodies at this hour of the night. We've more to do than stand around here listening to this nonsense. So, come on. Let's move it. We haven't got all night." They both took a step back to provide a clear path to the door. The speaker made an angry gesture towards the door. "We are taking you back. So, move yourself."

They shuffled back a further step, smiled falsely and, in unison, made what was supposed to be an inviting sweeping gesture towards the door. When they looked back at me, their jaws dropped. They were confronted by the barrel of my Glock.

"No-o-o; thanks for the offer, Gentlemen, but I don't think I'm going anywhere with you. Now, if you would be so kind as to step over there and go down on the floor, I won't have to disturb the neighbours again tonight by firing this thing. So guys, hands on your heads, please, and move yourselves."

Hands crept up onto heads. The two men exchanged uncertain looks. There was no mistaking the defiant look on both faces when they turned back to me. I raised the Glock and pointed it squarely at the one whom I judged to be the leader. "Whatever you just decided between you, I wouldn't recommend it. I have no qualms about adding two more to the body count on my floor. And, in case you're wondering, spending the night with five bodies wouldn't bother me any more than spending it with three. Now, do I shoot you both, or do you measure your length on the floor in accordance with my polite invitation? It's your choice."

At last I could breathe a little easier. The two men moved towards the open area of floor I indicated. "Face down, thanks Lads," I chirped as they fell to their knees.

Now what do I do, I wondered once they were prone on the floor. The most intelligent thing I could think of was to call Ben. But that was problematic. It would mean juggling the phone with one hand while keeping the Glock pointed at the men. Also, I wasn't sure it was wise for them to overhear my conversation with Ben. I continued wrestling with the problem until the sound of feet thundering in my direction swept it from my mind. Christ, how many more are coming?

With no time to do much else, I stepped back into the kitchen doorway. From there, I could see the men on the floor, but I was hidden from anyone coming to the front door. "Don't move, guys. I haven't gone anywhere, and your chances of being shot remain strong."

"What the hell...? Sonny, where the... Oh, there you are. What are you doing, and why are you threatening to shoot two of my officers?" Ben's confusion was genuine.

"Are you confirming these two blokes are your officers?"

"Yes. Jensen, Knowles, get up off the floor."

"Not so fast thanks, gentlemen. Ben, what were your instructions to these two regarding me tonight?"

"They were to keep watch. If they had the slightest suspicion something was amiss, they were to bring you back to the clubhouse. I can see something I construe as an 'amiss' happened here earlier tonight. So, why are my men on the floor instead of on their way back to the clubhouse with you?"

"They need a lesson in protocol – and manners too. If they identified themselves, maybe even showed some IDs, I might have considered going with them … maybe."

"For God's sake, get up off the floor you two, and get out of here. Get back on the job. We will discuss this again later. Jesus, Sonny, would you mind putting that canon away and trying to behave rationally while we discuss this?" Under the circumstances, I did feel a goose standing there with the Glock still dangling from my hand. I managed a sweet smile as I shoved it back in my pocket.

"Thank you. Now grab what you need and let's go. We'll discuss what happened here when we are back in the safety of the clubhouse. No, don't start asking questions. Just get your gear and let's get out of here."

'Getting my gear' involved nothing more than a quick trip to the bathroom to retrieve my toiletries, grabbing my computer off the kitchen bench and stuffing them both into my backpack. On my way from the bathroom to the kitchen, I stopped to take photos. Ben had turned all three bodies face-up. I snapped off a quick shot of each. Then, ready to go, I scurried to the front door, pulling the backpack onto my shoulders as I went.

As I followed Ben, he called out, "Turn the lights off and lock the door when you leave."

"As if I wouldn't have thought of that," I murmured as I followed him out into the night. Nobody in this bungalow needs lights tonight.

Ben jogged down the path and out onto the street. As he turned onto the street, I saw the weapon in his hand. I copied his example, and reached into my pocket for my Glock as I galloped to catch up to him. Damn it; his long, loping strides had me running to keep up. Why does he have to be so tall … and why am I so unfit?

At the two rubbish bins, we rounded the house, now ablaze with lights, and continued along the path to the backdoor of the clubhouse. Unlocked, Ben pushed it open and continued on with me at his heels. I heard the door slam shut behind us. "Upstairs…!" Ben yelled over his shoulder as he started up the stairs to what had been the incident room.

It still was an incident room, but had become a hive of activity. I counted at least seven people beavering away in the now crowded space. "Dump your stuff in the back room and then come and talk to me." I did as I was told and had my first look at that shoebox-sized room.

Ben sat at Truman's former desk, now pushed further back into the corner to make room for the expanded workforce. I took what was becoming my customary chair in front of the desk and the debrief began. I related tonight's event in as much detail as I could remember. Ben had plenty of questions, most of which I couldn't answer. At my first opportunity I asked the question gnawing at me since before we left the bungalow. "Have you any idea who that woman was; the one occupying space on my floor? She struck me as being a bit too old to be working the same game as the girl murdered last night. Nevertheless, I assume she had some association with the house with the white fence. I feel she is familiar somehow."

"It seems likely she was at that house. I didn't see her while I watched the shed. She might have been in the house, or in the part of the shed I couldn't see into. The forensic guys will take fingerprints and dental details. Maybe they will tell us who she is. Did the two men who chased after her speak at all while they were in the house?"

"Not as such, but I think there was a murmured exchange just as they were about to come through the front door. I don't know what was said, but I think they shared a couple of words.

They looked foreign to me. Maybe I wouldn't have understood even if I did hear what they said."

"They do look foreign. I think we will find they are Colombian nationals, but I'm guessing."

"Do we know anything more about the inflatable they hide in the scrub?"

"Not yet, but we should before the night is over."

"Am I wasting my time asking what has happened to Truman, Nadia and the rest of that crew? You told me Truman looked as though he'd been given a good going over. I can't help but notice he, Nadia and the other young bloke who inhabited this incident room previously are nowhere to be seen tonight."

"As of about six o'clock this evening, the trio is helping with our enquiries. Most of those billeted in the house with the two rubbish bins find themselves in the same situation."

"Okay, I didn't need to be a genius to know something fishy was going on here but, was everyone involved? And involved in what?"

"That's what we are endeavouring to find out. So far, we're sure a number of them were involved in whatever it is. And yes, Truman and your friend Nadia were definite players. By morning, we should have a better handle on the business they're involved in. I might have to go out again soon, but I don't want you leaving this building. You are safe here, and I want you that way when I return. Unless I personally come to collect you and take you out of the place, please stay here in this room. You are free to roam around to see what everyone is doing, just don't interrupt or get in the way. It's possible the situation here will change. The place will empty out leaving only two or three officers on duty, but they will be busy and won't have time to talk to you. My advice – not that I think you will take any no-tice of it – is for you to make yourself comfortable in the back room and catch up on sleep."

Well, that's not going to happen, but I won't bother telling him. Ben looked as though he was anxious to deal with the paperwork building up on his desk. I didn't fancy watching him.

"You have things to do, so I might wander around to see how the place operates." No argument offered, so I began drifting around the room.

There were a number of whiteboards and glass boards with scribbled handwriting all over them and, in some cases, hand drawn maps. I was about halfway around the room, stopping to read each of the boards as I went, when the quietness of the room was shattered by chairs scraping across tiles, the squawk and squelch of two-way radios, and shouted commands. Within moments, a major exodus emptied the room, leaving only me and two others behind. Even Ben was gone. With headsets on and in front of computer screens, the remaining two officers continued at their desks.

*****

My eyes fluttered open soon after first light this morning. Disoriented and confused by the strange surroundings, I spent some time trying to remember where I was and how I came to be here. As recollection dawned, my eyes flicked to the other bed in the room. Empty, and it looked unslept in. If Ben returned to the clubhouse during the night, he didn't go to bed. One other detail worked itself into my mind: the heavy drapes were drawn back to allow daylight into the room. Come to think of it, all the windows in the incident room were the same. Creating the impression the building is deserted is a thing of the past.

Trying not to look like one of the walking dead, I wandered out into the incident room. Four people seated at desks this morning. The two officers from last night were still at their posts. All four were busy at whatever they were doing. Ben's desk remained deserted. Not much I can do up here. I strolled towards the top of the stairs, half expecting to be tackled and dragged back into the incident room.

Nothing happened. I doubt my presence registered with anyone in that room. Sounds drifted up from below. At the top of the stairs, I took a cautious look over the railing. Where the double bunks were yesterday, a meeting was in progress. Ben had the floor and, it looked like heavy stuff being discussed.

About a dozen officers gathered around two long trestle tables. They didn't sit at the tables, but were scattered around them, with Ben alone out front.

As I peered over the railing, Ben threw the meeting open to questions from the floor. A couple of hands shot up. Their questions soon dealt with, the meeting was over. With much scraping of chairs and pounding feet, the attendees headed for the backdoor. One lingered to speak to Ben. He glanced up, and then alerted Ben to my presence above.

Not sure what my reception might be, I smiled and gave a cutesy waved to those below. They both stood, hands on hips, looking up at me. I heard Ben say, loud enough for me to hear I'm sure, "Don't be fooled. That's not what she's like." Bloody cheek! I'm on my best behaviour, and that's how he maligns me to his fellow officer. As the officer walked away, he continued looking up at me and, with a wry smile, shook his head.

That was good enough for me. It appears I haven't transgressed in any way, so I asked, "Is it okay for me to come down?"

"Yeah, you might as well. Breakfast will be here in a few minutes."

We found ourselves alone on the ground floor waiting for breakfast to arrive. I made the most of those few minutes before the aroma of fresh coffee, bacon and tomatoes wafted in through the backdoor. While they wouldn't provide nearly enough time for me to discover everything about last night, I intended extracting as many details as possible from Ben while we waited.

Chapter 22

I started the 'inquisition' as soon as we were alone. "Did the inflatable appear again last night?"

"For a while, I thought it wasn't coming, but it turned up much later than on previous nights. The crew did their usual thing. My officers nabbed them as they came out of the scrub after stashing the boat. There were six, but we don't know if they are the same crew who manned the boat on other occasions."

"I take it they were expected at the house with the white fence? Did their non-arrival put the place on high alert?"

"It appears they expected the blokes at their usual time. After about one o'clock, every few minutes, someone from in the shed wandered out to check the street. It was well after two o'clock when the inflatable came ashore. Our guys paid the shed a visit soon after that." Ben chuckled. "We've been running something akin to a courtesy bus service for most of the night, ferrying prisoners from Wilsons Beach to the lock-up. Those who were billeted in the house with the two rubbish bins were taken straight out of the district to a northern centre for processing. We hoped our night's work would drag in a whole lot more. If that eventuated, the Wickham lock-up wouldn't hold all of them. It necessitated transferring a few more of the prisoners out of Wickham in the early hours of this morning."

As the breakfast trolley made its way to the buffet table, I asked the BIG question. "I know the rest of the details will have to wait until after breakfast but, can you answer me this: does this mean our work – your work – here is done and we are able to return to Millhaven?" He gave me an apologetic look and shook his head.

"Not yet. Since Truman was removed, I'm now running the show. We think we're close to wrapping it up, but it might take another day or two. If you need to return to Millhaven, I can arrange someone to take you into Wickham to catch a bus."

"I'm not sure my work here is finished either. I think my best chance of progressing my open case lies in this area. It suits me to go into Wickham, but I will take the Suzuki. That way, I'll be free to spend as much time as I need in town before returning. In the meantime, what's your next move? You appear to have every one of the local contingent in custody."

"…And a few others as well. The boat from the campsite on Riposte Island was on the move again last night. We received word it travelled through Regents Bay, staying in close to the mainland coastline. They disappeared into a creek a fair distance from here. Our informant provided the GPS reading for the creek. While they were hard at work up that creek, a couple of our officers mounted their own covert exercise. We now have valuable information on the mainland end of the campsite's operation. The officers managed to place a device on the boat. We tracked it to its current location."

"You indicated a few others were arrested…"

"All those in the party who met the boat at the creek on that remote property are also behind bars."

"What about the blokes from the inflatable, weren't they from the campsite's boat? How come they were here when the boat was busy elsewhere?"

"We allowed the boat to leave again after completing the night's business before arresting the land-based mob as they prepared to leave the scene. The campsite boat returned to this area before launching the inflatable. At Wilsons Beach today, the focus is on apprehending the campsite boat and its crew. Part of my task force is following up on the land-based side of the operation."

"I assume this all confirms the operation is about drugs." Ben nodded. "Okay, so what are those oil drums all about? It's obvious, from what you've said, the scale of their operation is huge. Even a major operation wouldn't require so much oil, would it?"

"There are some theories about those drums. We won't

know anything until the results come back, however long that takes. Wickham doesn't have a forensics laboratory. Anything from their cases is sent to their northern neighbouring precinct, which is backlogged with work at the moment. So, I arranged for everything from this case to be flown to Millhaven. The new Millhaven lab should have a quick turnaround."

"The time required depends on the type of tests needed. Some tests take more than twenty-four hours just for part of the test, or so I've learnt in the past. Given you will be busy doing whatever you're doing today, I think I'll rinse out a set of clothes and then take the Suzuki into town. It's lucky that, when I'm out in the boat, I always have a spare set of clothes in my bag in case I get wet or fall in the mud. Nevertheless, more underwear would be handy."

After breakfast, I received grudging approval to return to the bungalow. With my washing draped over the clothes line – no pegs available – I fired up the Suzuki and headed for town, and hoped the Suzuki was still up to the half hour drive involved. Citing my need for underwear as the reason for my trip to town wasn't too far from the truth. I did need said underwear, but it was incidental to my main reason for the trip. Shops hadn't long opened for the day when I hit town, so I dealt with the underwear situation first. Then, I hoped it was an acceptable hour to tackle the real reason I was in Wickham.

Hospital visiting hours didn't start for another half hour. The receptionist was adamant I couldn't see anyone until then. In the ensuing discussion, I mentioned I was there to see Mr Frank Hensley. It occurred to me that perhaps I should have asked if Hensley was still in this hospital before plunging into the verbal tug-of-war with the receptionist. Mention of Hensley's name pulled her up short.

"Oh well, If that's why you're here, you've wasted your time."

"Are you telling me Frank Hensley is no longer a patient here? ... Because I don't believe that's true, is it?"

"He might be a patient, but you can't see him. Only family allowed in."

"What makes you think I'm not family?" Taken aback by the question, she shook her head and blinked a couple of times. I didn't give her a chance to think of an answer. "I am one of those investigating what happened to Mr Hensley, and I need to check something with him."

"Seeing him won't do you any good anyway."

"Is he still in a coma?" Another couple of blinks before she answered with a brief nod. "Okay. Is his son, Xander, with him?" Another nod after consulting her computer. "Good. I assume he is in ICU or isolation somewhere. Is there a nurse on duty with him?" This is worse than playing a late night game of twenty questions. The receptionist seems to be struck dumb. Once again, her only response was a nod.

I kept reminding myself, to stay relaxed, smile and keep my voice friendly, but it was becoming a struggle. "Perhaps you could contact the nurse. She should tell Mr Xander Hensley that Sonny Whittington wishes to speak to him at reception, and it is urgent." She hesitated, unsure about the situation. I pointed to the phone on her desk and gave her a hard look. It worked.

About two minutes later, Xander strode into the reception area. "Sonny… she said it was you, but I thought there was some mistake. What are you doing in Wickham? I tried to contact you – I can't remember how many days ago – to tell you they found Dad."

I saw a sign indicating where coffee was available. "How about we talk over coffee?"

Seated with our coffees at a small table in a pleasant courtyard outside the coffee shop, I eased my way into the reason for my visit. "Before we begin, how is your father progressing?"

"He is still in an induced coma. They tell me he is making good progress, whatever that means. His coma seems lighter than it was. I overheard the doctor telling the nurse they might bring him out of it in another couple of days. But, you still haven't told me what brings you here."

"I've been here all along. Not in Wickham, on a small island off here. With the police taking over the investigation into your father's disappearance, I had to step back for a few days. The timing was good. A friend came to visit before returning to the UK. I have a beach place on the small island I mentioned, so we decided to spend the time on the island. The rest of the story is a long, rambling tale that includes my friend's being shot. Then another friend, the officer in charge of this investigation, and I discovered your father and managed to move him off the island. Since then, I have been involved in the ongoing investigation into the mob responsible for what happened to your father."

"So, you have been working the case the whole time…?"

"Yes, I suppose that's true, but don't worry, I'm not charging you for all that. My account won't knock your socks off when it arrives."

"I wasn't thinking about that. The nurse said you had something urgent to speak to me about."

"I would like you to look at some photos. They're not pleasant, but I wonder if you recognise any of the people in them. Do you feel up to it?"

"I was a soldier remember. I've probably seen worse than your photos."

The first photo I showed him was of the girl killed on the first night, the one who slugged me. It wasn't a good photo, taken without her knowledge while I talked to her on the back street. Xander studied it, enlarging it for a better look before shaking his head. "No. I can't say I've ever seen her before. She looks young … and dead. What a waste!"

After signifying my agreement, I flicked to the next photo, the bloke who murdered the woman in my house. "The next two photos I show you might mean nothing to you. Take a good look though in case something about them strikes a chord with you."

At each photo, Xander shook his head. Then, taking my phone from me, he flicked back to the photo of the first man, the one of the murderer. He studied it for some time. "I don't know why, but there is something about this photo. I can't say I know the face, but … maybe … yeah, it could be. I'm sorry. I can't be sure, but there is something familiar about this one. He does trigger a vague response."

"Don't dwell on it. I'm sure the police will work out who he is. I just thought it was worth asking if you recognised him. There is just one more photo to show you. As with the others, it's not a happy snap." I flicked onto the photo of the woman killed in my sitting room, and handed the phone back to Xander. "Anything familiar about this one?"

I heard his intake of breath as I asked the question, and looked up at him. He was shocked, and held the phone away from him. I snatched the phone back. Something about that photo registered with me, and now it shocked Xander. "What is it? I'm sorry if I've upset you. Do you recognise this woman?" He shook his head. I thought he was going to tell me he didn't know her. Then I realised he was shaking his head in disbelief. "What is it, Xander? Who is she?"

"That's Gina Burtell, Dad's wife, or whatever she is. At the risk of stating the obvious, she looks very dead, every bit as dead as the ones in the other photos. What happened? Do you know what happened to her? This will knock Dad for six. I want it kept from him for as long as possible. I don't know what their relationship was like. I suspect it wasn't all it could be, or should be, but that won't make it any easier for him. It could push him over the edge."

"I understand what you're saying, and I'll pass it on to the officer in charge. It might not be much reassurance, but I vouch for the integrity and sensitivity of the officer involved. I don't suppose there is any chance you might be wrong about the identification?"

He shook his head as he handed back my phone. "No, there's no mistake. That's Gina Burtell. I need to know what happened to her. It doesn't matter how bad it is, I want the details." I started to argue on the basis that it wouldn't do him or his father any good at this time. He stopped me. "For Christ's sake, Sonny, I saw worse than this in Afghanistan. You're not talking to some little old lady who will faint."

"I don't doubt you have seen worse, but they were not people close to you. That makes a difference."

"You think losing mates who were standing close to you only seconds before is not like losing someone close to you…?"

I apologised and we ordered fresh coffees. I attempted to mentally compose the conversation I was about to have. After dawdling over stirring my coffee and the first few sips, I took a deep breath and continued. "There is no easy way to say this, so I'll tell it as I know it. Last night, Gina Burtell was being chased by two men when she raced through the front door of a bungalow I've rented for the week. The two men followed her in. Those two men are the ones in the photos I showed you. The one who gave you pause for thought stabbed her to death in my sitting room." I paused for him to digest the details, and because I wasn't sure I had anything else to tell him.

"Those two blokes in the photos looked dead – were dead. What happened to them?"

Don't you just love the hard questions when they come? There was no point in being evasive. He didn't want shielding, he wanted the truth; needed the truth. I took another deep breath and cleared my throat. "They are both dead. I shot them. That's all there is to the story, Xander. I don't know any more than I've told you. What I do need to do is warn you that, as the investigation proceeds, some of what is uncovered might prove uncomfortable, even disturbing for you and your father." I saw him prepare to ask more questions, so I jumped in. "Xander, as unsatisfactory as it might be for you at this time, I don't have any more to add. And I'm not about to embark on speculation. So, don't ask me to."

With downcast eyes, Xander nodded, and took to vigorously stirring his coffee. My heart went out to him. From the outset, I guessed he held no high opinion of Gina Burtell, but his concern for his father was real and deep. "I'm sorry for doing this to you, Xander. It's not a great way to start the day, and I'm sure I've managed to mess up your day no end. Anything I've told you this morning must remain in confidence. It might be unnecessary, but I'm going to say this anyway. Keep a close watch over your father. The investigation is progressing well and is achieving rapid results, but the full extent of the problem remains undefined at this time. I'm not trying to be alarmist, but the last couple of days cause me to be cautious at all times. Perhaps you should be too. On that depressing note, I should leave you to get on with the rest of your day."

We shook hands and I went across to the counter to pay for our coffees. Xander, on his way out of the coffee shop, paused at the door before coming back. He motioned me out to the courtyard again. "Could I see those photos of the two blokes again, please? The first one you showed me, I think." I brought up the photo of the murderer and handed Xander my phone.

He took his time examining the photo before commenting. "I still can't be sure, but I think I have seen this one before. It was the last time I was home. I saw Gina out on the street talking to a man. Nothing unusual in that I suppose, but it seemed like she was giving him a bollocking about something. At first he tried giving as good as he got. Then, it appeared he lost the battle, and took the rest of what she had to say in silence. As I said, I can't be sure this is the same man. I didn't get a close look at him, but something about him looks familiar."

I felt like kissing him, but proffered my thanks instead. He started walking away, then turned to face me. "Please keep me informed if you can. It doesn't matter how much, how little, or how horrible it might be, I want to know." There was nothing to say. So, I nodded my agreement, and he continued on his way, leaving me alone in the courtyard. I sat at one of the tables for a few moments replaying my time with Xander. That is one guy I *would* want in my corner if I got into a scrape.

With nothing else to keep me in Wickham, I nudged the Suzuki into life and headed back to Wilsons Beach. The shed presented no problems, so I put the car away, and went to inspect the bungalow. The place had changed since this morning. Now festooned with crime scene tape, it was clear no one was to enter the bungalow. **I went around to the clothes line. My wash**ing, blown off the line, decorated the grass, but it was dry. After collecting it, I went to the backdoor. More crime scene tape. My hesitation was brief. Ben gave me permission to return, and I intend to do so. With the tape carefully unstuck from one side and now flapping in the breeze, I opened the door and strode inside.

It was a shadow more than a figure, but it was a person. As I opened the door and strode in, I glimpsed a movement and froze. No more than a dark shadow visible for only a fraction of a second, it disappeared from sight into the kitchen. My hand's automatic reaction was to reach into my pants pocket. But there was no heavy weight in the pocket. Deciding it was bad form to stride around Wickham with the Glock in my pocket, I slipped my weapon into my bag when I arrived in town.

With the washing discarded on the floor, I rummaged in my bag until my hand found the required object. Then, with my bag also discarded quietly on the floor and Glock in hand, I inched towards the kitchen doorway. The stealth of my approach allowed me some moments to think about what to do. When about a metre from the kitchen doorway, the issue remained unresolved. Whether instinct or training intervened is unclear, but whatever it was propelled me across the hallway and away from the kitchen.

At the end of the hall and not quite opposite the kitchen doorway, I turned left and followed the wall along one side of the small entrance foyer. Pressed hard against the wall, I continued inching away from the kitchen. I didn't know whether whoever was in the kitchen could see me or not. If they stood on the correct side of the room, they could see this wall – and me. So far, no one showed any interest in me. Is that good or bad? Just keep going, I told myself.

One more step and I will be at the corner. Continuing will take me along the end wall, opposite the kitchen and in full view of anyone hiding there. Positioned not quite across the corner and out from the end wall a short distance was a big old-fashioned two-seater sofa. Like others of its era, it sported a plush velour-like covering in dark tones, and once was heavily padded. Long past its youth, it now is one of those chairs that swallow anyone who sits in them, and requires stamina and determination to escape.

Despite all its shortcomings, the chair has a certain allure. I took three steps in quick succession towards it. Movement caught my eye as I took the third step. I dived down behind the sofa. A resounding 'thunk' sounded loud and close. Scuttling along the floor, I reached the other end of the sofa and peered around it. Movement visible in the kitchen. I wriggled around for a better position. A figure stood in the kitchen doorway. The Glock barked twice, loud and deafening beside my ear. A dark shape occupied the floor in the kitchen doorway. No further movement detected from that direction.

My left hand felt all my pockets. No phone in any of them. I remembered dropping my phone into my bag, the bag lying just inside the backdoor and now some considerable distance away. A few more seconds spent listening for any sounds louder than my pounding heart. Nothing. I squirmed my way back to the other end of the chair, to where I had dived in behind it. Still nothing. Then, I was up on my feet and running for the backdoor. Snagging my bag up from the floor on my way past, I raced on through the backdoor and out into the backyard.

Flattened against the rear wall of the shed, I dragged my phone out of my bag and made a clumsy left-handed job of negotiating my contacts list to find Ben Richards' name. "Come on, come on," I whispered as the dialling continued. And then he answered.

"What…? I'm a bit busy at the moment."

"So am I … trying to stay alive. And, in case you're interested, there's another body for you to deal with."

"Christ, Sonny, it's not safe to be anywhere around you. Where are you?"

Chapter 23

While the backyard was safer than the house, I felt exposed. Against the rear wall of the shed felt a little better. Not knowing how long this might last was not reassuring. My Glock remained in my hand and every sense was on high alert. The middle of the day; the sun had a bite to it.

Feet thundering up the front path focused my attention. While attempting to flatten myself further against the shed, I lifted my Glock. I felt confident I could deal with one. More than one was another matter … and it sounded like more than one coming towards me. Then a familiar voice called out.

"Sonny, where are you?" Ben's voice had an edge to it. I stepped out from behind the shed. "Where's this latest body?" I gestured towards the bungalow. "Any others still in there?"

I shrugged. "Don't know, but I don't think so." After a quick word to one of the two officers with him, that officer went back to the front of the house. Ben, followed by the other officer, strode towards the backdoor. He stopped to inspect the crime scene tape fluttering in the breeze. Expect to hear about that, I told myself as Ben shot me a look before pushing open the door and marching inside.

A short distance behind the other two, I heard Ben bellow, "Where…?"

"In the kitchen…" When I caught up, Ben stood over the body and his colleague was on his haunches beside it. The officer rolled the body over. I snapped it with my phone. This one was young and fairish; not foreign looking at all.

"I'd say dead, Sir," the young officer announced.

"Probably has something to do with the two large holes in his chest." Ben was not a happy chap. "Sonny, I assume this is your handiwork." I nodded. "Why did you shoot him? He might have been one of my blokes. Did you interrogate him at all? Why not hold him at gunpoint until we arrived? Why the hell do you have to shoot everyone? He might have given us information."

That's rich: Ben Richards accusing me of being trigger happy. I kept the thought to myself, and clenched my jaws tight to prevent the response I wanted to deliver. Instead, I gestured with my head towards the old couch in the corner. Because I knew about it, I could see the reason why I shot him. Ben couldn't until he stood directly in front of the chair. Up close, the handle was obvious, while the blade itself was out of sight, buried full length in the headrest of the sofa. "If your guys go around throwing knives at me, there is a strong chance they will be shot."

Ben had a brief exchange with the young officer still standing beside the body. The young officer, phone in hand, went out the backdoor. "Now, Sonny, tell me what happened. No ... first, what's with all the crime scene tape, and how did you come by it?"

"It's not my tape. I assumed your guys were responsible. This morning, you told me I could return here. When I arrived, there was no tape. On my return from town, I found the place looking like a Christmas tree. I had permission to return, so I collected my washing and let myself in the backdoor ... and, yes, I did remove some of the tape."

Explaining what happened after that took little time. I just finished telling Ben when his young officer returned. The two men moved away to talk and then went into the kitchen. A bit miffed at being left out of proceedings, I returned to my washing scattered across the floor, and took it to the bedroom to fold it. The job, not requiring any thought, allowed my mind to wander. It chose to explore why someone who wasn't one of Ben's men would be in here this morning. The bodies from last night were gone. Nothing and no one of interest remained here.

A little voice in my head urged me to review that last thought. If the present body was somehow connected with the activities of the other three, he probably knew of their demise and of the removal of their bodies from the premises. So, why come inside? If Ben's blokes didn't decorate the place with crime scene tape, did he do it … and why?

Something brought him here. Perhaps he intended the tape to prevent others from interrupting his mission. Perhaps he expected spending some time here. But doing what? Did he think one of those earlier bodies dropped something? It must have been something small ... something small maybe hidden in a pocket. Other than the two with knives, none of them carried anything else. Well, I saw nothing else.

It doesn't take long to fold one set of clothes and, with my mind now buzzing with the notion of something dropped somewhere in the bungalow, I went to the sitting room. The front door was open. Ben and his two officers wandered around outside. While they searched for evidence out there, I explored my theory. A scan of the sitting room found nothing out of place since earlier this morning.

Stop for a moment, I told myself. Think about how the situation played out in here last night. I visualised Gina rushing in and continuing into the sitting room, and then the two men racing in after her. Okay; so I'll start in the sitting room. After running my hand over every surface of the bookcase and shifting the few items on it for a thorough search, I moved onto the small cupboard adjacent to it. Nothing found so far, and why would there be anything to find? No one went near the furniture. I moved the unit with the TV. Still nothing.

Anything dropped would be on the floor, not the furniture. On my hands and knees, I searched the floor… except under the lounge chairs. Back on my feet, I shoved the nearest lounge chair out of the way. That uncovered nothing. I checked the chair before pushing it back into position. My theory looked shaky. One last piece of furniture to check before moving to another room.

As I pushed the second lounge chair out of the way, I noticed the cushion looked a little askew. It was so slight, I didn't notice it before. Maybe I bumped the cushion as I moved the chair.

Moving the chair stirred up dust, but produced nothing else. While pushing the chair back into position, I remembered this was where Gina stopped. Gasping for breath, she was leaning over this chair when they caught her. Her body ended up on the floor there behind it. Did Gina dislodge the cushion?

My gut urged a closer look. I yanked the cushion out of the chair. "Ah ha! So that's what you were looking for, eh...?"

"What who was looking for?" Ben asked as he came in the front door.

Excitement played havoc with my vocal chords. My response came out as a cackle. "I was talking to myself. But, maybe I know why the bloke adorning my kitchen floor was here. I think I've found what he was looking for." Ben was beside me in a heartbeat.

"Ooh, you might be right. Have you touched this?" I shook my head. "Good. Let's see whether it's relevant to the case, or if it's something left behind by a previous occupant." In gloved hands, he carried the large brown envelope to the kitchen. With complete disregard, we both stepped around the body on our way to the kitchen table. "Find a tea towel or tablecloth; something to cover the table for me to empty the envelope's contents onto."

My short time here didn't allow me to know where such items were. After opening several drawers, I found a couple of tea towels and a tablecloth. I chose the tablecloth and floated it over the table ready for the big moment. It seemed to take Ben forever to prise open the envelope. As I stood watching and waiting, it occurred to me that this was a large, thick envelope, too big to conceal in a pocket, and she wore a dress. How come it wasn't obvious when Gina came into the house?

At last! Ben upended the envelope and an interesting mix of items tumbled onto the table: a wad of large denomination bank notes, a small notebook, several handwritten pieces of paper, and a couple of keys. Those things fell on top of other items, obscuring them. What looked like credit cards peeped out from underneath. The temptation was to reach over and spread it all out. Ben had his phone out photographing the scene on the table. He did that at every step of the way from when I first showed him the envelope in the chair. I decided I needed a few shots for my case file too.

Ben went to the front door and called out to Williams, one of his officers. On my way back to the lounge chair to photograph where I found the envelope, I heard Ben tell Williams to fetch a large evidence bag from the clubhouse. Back at the kitchen table, Ben had the envelope's contents spread in a single layer. I gasped. "Did all this fit in that one envelope?" Of course it did you fool, I chided myself. Where else did it come from? Ben's look confirmed it was a stupid question.

New items included four credit cards in different names, three passports in different names… and two driver's licences in different names, none of which was Gina Burtell. As I watched Ben further spreading out the items, my phone rang. Emily. I went to the backyard to answer it.

"Apologies if I interrupted something important. How goes the holiday? Stuff coming in over recent days appears to be linked to your Hensley case. At least, it seems so to me. There are a few anomalies for you to consider while you take in the sun, surf and sand. Do you want to hear about them?"

"Yes, I do but, before you begin, there are two things you should know. First, I am not at my beach place anymore. It's a long story for later. The other thing is, Troy returned to Millhaven three days ago. He took the boat and my car, and is probably back at the mine site or on his way to the UK by now."

"Bugger! I had great hopes for the relationship. If you don't have a car, do you need me to bring you back to Millhaven?"

"No, thanks. Ben is here – working. We both are. Might finish in a day or two, and then I will travel back with him. Now, what are these anomalies you wanted to tell me about?"

"Analysis of fingerprints and some other evidence sent here link directly to Gina Burtell. The problem is, it also links to a couple of other foreign sounding names. So far, researching the background of any of those names has drawn a blank. Are we sure this Burtell woman ever existed?" Emily rattled off the various names, and I made mental note of them in the hope I'd remember until I could write them down.

"Oh yes, she did exist. Xander Hensley identified her photo after she ended up dead on the floor of the bungalow I'm renting. I'll send you a photo. Not a pleasant one but, if you have a spare moment, please show it to Jock at Hensley Security Services' office. Ask him if he recognises the woman. I'm sure he will confirm it is Gina Burtell. While I'm certain Xander is on the level, I'd still like to confirm his identification of the woman. Sorry, Emily, I have to go. I'll send the photo now."

Ben scooped the last of the envelope's contents into the large brown paper evidence sack Williams held open for him. The last item left on the table was a memory stick. As he photographed it, Ben asked, "Everything all right?"

I snapped off a couple of shots of the memory stick. "Yeah, just work stuff; nothing urgent. What's your next move?" Ben raised an eyebrow at me, not in response to my reply, but about my photographing the memory stick. He didn't question it, so I didn't enlighten him. Truth is, I don't know why it seemed important to photograph it. As I shoved my phone back into my pocket, the memory stick disappeared into the evidence sack.

Thrusting the bag into Williams' hands, Ben told him to take it to the clubhouse and put it on Ben's desk. Williams, on his way out, did a fancy two-step around the other officer as they passed each other on their way through the front door. "Sir, the…," the new arrival began. "Rennie…? What the hell happened?" he demanded. He glared at me, causing more than a little discomfort. I was about to justify my actions when Ben cut in.

"Taylor, you know this man?"

"Yes, Sir. It's Rennsberg; Tim Rennsberg. We were at the Academy together. The pair of us and another couple of recruits used to knock around together. What happened here?"

"So, he was a police officer. What do you know about him after the Academy?"

"Nothing much, Sir. After we graduated, I lost contact with him and the others, and I didn't hear anything of him after that. I was posted down south. I think his posting was somewhere up this way. I moved around a bit before joining the Feds."

"Thanks Taylor. The man's identity must remain between us for the moment. You must not discuss this with anyone. Is that understood?"

When Ben uses that tone of voice, it's hard to disagree. Taylor was no exception. On their way to the front door, Ben gave Taylor his instructions then, as Taylor went to leave, Ben called him back. "What was it you came to tell me before you saw the body?"

"Oh, sorry, Sir. I forgot. Forensics said they would be about another half hour before they finished what they were doing and were free to come here." Ben, lingering at the front door, looked uncertain about what to do next. Then he returned to where I waited wait at the table.

"There isn't much point in our hanging around here much longer. Let's go to the clubhouse and explore the contents of that envelope. Collect your gear and we'll go."

"Why do I need to take my gear? Won't I come back here afterwards?"

"No, I don't want you staying here. In theory, it should be safe, but I can't be sure of that, and I can't spare anyone to watch the place. So, come on. Move yourself. I want to get stuck into that stuff that's waiting for me on my desk … And I suspect you might be interested too."

He was keen to return to the clubhouse. I almost had to jog to keep up. We grabbed coffees on our way to his desk. I waited, expecting him to tip everything out onto the desk as he did at the bungalow, but that's not what he did. Item by item everything was removed and examined before being set aside. It was like drawing winning raffle tickets. He thrust his hand in the sack and pulled out the first thing he felt.

The first thing out of the bag was a passport. I opened my phone to confirm the photo in the passport was of the woman who ended up dead on my floor. The one whose photograph Xander identified as Gina Burtell. That was not the name in the passport. It was issued under a foreign sounding name. Seeing the name, brought to mind the list of names Emily gave me. I dug out my notebook and scribbled them down from memory. There it was. Amongst Emily's list was the name on this passport.

Should I mention this to Ben now, or wait until we see what else we find? While I dithered about, Ben examined the passport before putting it aside and reaching for the next item. This time, he scrabbled around a bit and withdrew three items; all credit cards. "I'm sure there was more than three," he mumbled before diving into the bag again. He found another two cards, and lined them all up on the desk. All bore different names, none of which was Gina Burtell. "There were some driver's licences as well. I'll see if I can find those." Ben scrabbled around in the bag again. "Gotcha; here they are." He added them to the line-up on the desk.

Yep, all the names Emily gave me were there, plus one I hadn't heard before. Ben brought a magnifying glass out of a drawer to examine the photos on the driver's licences. I galloped around the desk to peer over his shoulder. It took only a quick look at each to know they all carried a photo of the woman we knew as Gina Burtell. "What do you suppose her real name was?"

Ben waved his hand over the cards and licences on the desk. "Take your pick. Your guess is as good as mine. There is one common thing about these names. All foreign-sounding, they all seem to come from the same language group … a bit Spanish-sounding. Sorting that out is a job for the experts. Let's see what else is in here."

The bank account information we found echoed the names on the cards, licences and passports. After counting out the cash bound with a rubber band, Ben let out a low whistle. "The lady was not short of cash. Each of these bank accounts has a significant balance, and this wad of notes holds eight thousand dollars."

"Was this an emergency escape stash?"

"Information we've found so far tends to suggest it might be. But, let's not jump to conclusions until we know more."

My 'emergency escape' suggestion gained credence as we worked through the remainder of the material. The only things left in the sack to examine were the several sheets of paper. My gut kept telling me they were important. I couldn't think why, but I know to heed my gut. On this occasion, listening to my gut didn't do me any good. I might misjudge him, but Ben appeared to go out of his way to ensure I didn't see those pieces of paper.

It came as a surprise when he announced we had finished with the material, and loaded it back into the evidence sack. The memory stick was not amongst it, and we hadn't looked at what was on it. Tempting as it was to inquire about it, instinct warned against it. With everything back in the bag, Ben leaned back and clasped his hands behind his head.

After several seconds, he announced, "There is a strong foreign connection associated with this investigation, not only in this material, but also from the appearance of some of the players. That connection shifts some of the investigation to someone else's desk. I need to make a phone call."

I recognised it as my cue to disappear while he made the call. "Say hello to your brother, Neil, for me." As I pushed my chair back to stand up, Ben demanded to know what I meant by my remark. "Really …? Do you think me so naive? Of course you're going to unload that part of the investigation onto your brother … who just happens to be head of the Federal Police." Before he could respond, I turned on my heel and went downstairs.

Still indignant, I wandered around downstairs. My inclination was to defy Ben, collect my gear and go back to the bungalow, but sheer animal cunning intervened. If I stayed at the clubhouse, there would come a time when Ben wasn't around. Then I could look at those sheets of paper he didn't show me – and maybe the memory stick as well. Besides, it was late. The evening meal would arrive soon. Whatever it is, it will be better than anything in my fridge. I might stay at least until after dinner.

When Ben ventured downstairs, he found me alone at a table in the corner and halfway through my meal. He loaded his plate before joining me. "After dinner, I have a meeting scheduled down here with all my troops. It might be best if you didn't attend. I'll let you know if anything you should be aware of comes out of it."

Is that a golden opportunity I hear knocking? It would be handy to know how long the meeting might last. "Will it be okay if I hang around upstairs while the meeting is on, or would you rather I went for a walk, or back to the bungalow, for an hour or so?"

"Don't go anywhere, just stay upstairs." That's exactly what I wanted to hear. I waited until I saw the first attendees arriving before going upstairs.

When all the scraping of chairs and babble subsided, I guessed the meeting had started. My computer was set up on my side of Ben's desk. If he came up unexpectedly, I will be checking my emails. Making as little noise as possible, I removed the evidence sack from his bottom drawer and fished out the pieces of paper I wanted. Without reading them, I photographed each piece before replacing them in the bag. "Now for the memory stick," I murmured to myself. No amount of scrabbling around in the bag located the stick. "Bastard! He has hidden the thing," I hissed.

As I replaced the evidence sack in the drawer, an idea drifted in from left field. I opened every drawer of the desk. There it was. I recognised it straight away. In a flash, it was in my computer and a copy was downloading. The stick must be full. It took so long to download, I felt my nerves tightening as the seconds ticked by. At last it was done. I replaced the stick where I found it, shut down my computer and breathed a sigh of relief. My computer went into my bag under my bed, and I stretched out on the bed with the half read magazine I took from the bungalow. That's where I was when Ben returned about twenty minutes later.

He said he had calls to make and might work on until late. I didn't press him about his meeting. "I think I'll take a shower and call it a night. Talk to you in the morning."

Chapter 24

Ben's bed looked slept in, but he was already up when I woke up this morning. I went to find him. It was still early, at least an hour until breakfast. Only Ben was in the incident room, making it ideal for a chat. I initiated what I hoped would be an enlightening conversation. "Good morning, Ben. Are you free to discuss a few things? What was Neil's reaction to the stuff we found yesterday?"

"Yeah, tying up loose ends at the moment. Very interested. He has his resources sifting through everything I gave him. It seems our operation ties in with something the Feds have worked on for a while. I should hear more from my brother this morning. If everything goes to plan, we might be on our way to Millhaven tomorrow. Ah, there's the fax machine. I hope they're results from the forensic lab."

The words 'forensic' and 'results' in the same sentence had me on my way to retrieve the documents from the machine. I made a show of ensuring they were in the correct order as I carried the half a dozen pages to his desk. "I think they're all there and in the right order. I'll leave you to read them for a few minutes. I have a call to make."

I plonked the documents on the desk in front of him, was down the stairs and out the backdoor before he opened his mouth. Emily's phone was ringing as I made my way out to the headland. "I saw your signature on some documents faxed through to Ben, so I assume you are up about this morning."

"Haven't been to bed yet, but I'm about to rectify that. You seem excited about something. What can I do for you?"

"Any chance you could send me those results you sent Ben this morning?"

"Check your emails. You received them first."

"We need to talk when I return. In the meantime, enjoy your sleep."

As I waited for my emails to download, I told myself they would be easier to read on a computer, but I will have to make do with my phone for now. There they were, the same documents I took off the fax machine. "I ... did ... not ... see ... that ... coming ..." I told the universe. But there it was, and I didn't dispute the results. Now, how do I get Ben to share this information with me if he doesn't offer me his copies to read? I'm not going to let him know I have copies.

It wasn't a problem. Ben pushed the documents across the desk to me as soon as I sat down. "You might find these interesting." It was good to have a decent sized copy to read.

"Cocaine, eh? Looks like our assumption drugs were at the bottom of all this was correct. This must be a high tech operation they're running. How do you mix cocaine with oil and keep it in suspension? It might still settle out even if emulsified. Is that what these results tell us, or am I misinterpreting the information?"

"That's what the results say. I don't know what process they used. Whatever it was, the campsite laboratory on Riposte Island was where they reversed the process to extract the cocaine. After that, the drums contained nothing but oil."

"The cocaine might explain those foreign looking bodies. Is it possible they are from somewhere in South America, somewhere like Colombia?"

"It's a strong possibility. Anyway, the Feds are looking into that side of things. Some of the names on Gina Burtell's material suggest a connection with the same area. It would be easier to figure out if we knew exactly who she was. It's possible none of the names we found is her real one."

"If the oil and drugs were separated at the campsite, the drugs then needed access to an Australian distribution network. Is that what those trips to the inlet opening onto old Sammy's property were about, handing over to the distribution chain?"

"So it appears. The night before last, when the campsite's boat visited the inlet, we arrested three men with a substantial quantity of the drug in their small van. They are not being cooperative, so we don't know its intended destination. Drums were observed on the campsite boat when it entered the inlet. The drums disappeared before our officers arrived. No drums were evident on the boat when it left the inlet."

"Oil would be much easier to dispose of through 'normal' channels than the drugs. All that's needed is a tame agent with a depot. A legitimate business selling fuels and lubricants adding the drums to its stock wouldn't arouse suspicion. This is part of a huge geographic area involved with various rural industries. There are bound to be plenty of depots supplying farmers and graziers with fuels and lubricants. Finding the 'right' one might present a challenge."

"Someone drew up a list of such enterprises. You're right, there a few."

"Let's assume the drums of oil, now minus the drugs, were transferred from the boat to a vehicle at the same time as the drugs were handed over. It's likely two receiving parties were involved: one for drugs, and one for oil drums. I imagine it takes longer to transfer drums than to hand over the drugs, but only the mob with the drugs was there when your officers arrived. How did the drums get away so fast?"

I had Ben's attention. He sat forward on his chair. With no questions or comments forthcoming, I continued theorising. "Unless the drums disappeared into a hole in the ground at the unloading site, they needed transporting to somewhere else, whether that is on Sammy's property or miles away. A vehicle had to be involved. I imagine transporting several drums of oil even a short distance would require a truck of some sort."

Ben jumped as if I hit a nerve. He yanked open a desk drawer. "Another vehicle … Another vehicle …," he chanted to himself. He flicked through the contents of a folder from the drawer until he reached a particular document. After skimming it, he yelped, "Yes … another vehicle!" His excitement was infectious. I was up off my chair and leaning over his desk to see what he found.

It was a long emailed report. The print was too small for me to read upside down.

"What have you found?" Ben lifted the email. I thought he intended handing it to me. I was disappointed. He simply held it up while he scanned the document below, an official-looking report. I wanted a piece of his excitement. "Come on, Ben. Share. What did you find about another vehicle?"

"I felt something was missing from the report on the take-down on Sammy's property. I asked if they encountered any other vehicles in the vicinity and if they suspected any other persons might be on the property, even at Sammy's house. The supplemental information is interesting. It says no other persons were observed on the property and the home appeared deserted. They passed a truck on the main road a short distance from the turn-off to the property. It is described as *an old farm truck with a cattle crate on the back.*"

"Do they think it came from the property?"

"No, they didn't see where it came from, and dismissed it as unrelated. Trucks like that transporting cattle to the meatworks are common in the area, and often are on the roads at ungodly hours of the morning. It headed towards the main highway. They tell me the local meatworks are off the highway a little south of there. So, nobody associated the truck with the property or the night's operation."

"And, on a country road servicing rural properties, there are no CCTV cameras. I don't imagine they would use a truck with distinctive markings anyway, and a registration number is out of the question."

"I'm not so sure about no markings on the truck. If I were stopped along the road with a load of full oil drums on board, markings indicating I had legitimate reason for transporting them would avoid awkward questions. Hmm …I wonder … I need to make a call." I stood up to leave. "No, before you go, there's something I need to talk to you about."

Something about the way Ben said it, tied my stomach in knots. I flopped down on the chair again. "Okay, what is it?"

"I'm going to need a spare bed from tonight, and not over in the house with the others. I can't fit another bed in that back room, so I wondered if you might let us use your bungalow."

"No, I don't think so. I assume another high ranking officer is about to arrive."

Ben grudgingly gave a half-hearted nod to confirm my assumption.

"He can have my bed in the back room. I'm renting the bungalow, so I'll go back there to sleep."

"That's not going to happen. I'm not having you sleep there on your own. We've been through this."

"Well, here is the bottom line: unless you arrest me, I am going back to the bungalow and, as I'm over eighteen and have broken no laws, there's not much you can do about it." I thought we were doing well up to this point...

"Look, there will be a whole lot of changes this evening. Once they are in place, we should be able to return to Millhaven sometime tomorrow. I'm talking about just for one night."

"What are all these changes?"

"A busload of other officers and their commanding officer will arrive around dinner time this evening. The bus will then take some of the existing officers from here back to Wickham. Only Feds will remain. I will handover this investigation to the Feds. That might take up most of tomorrow morning. After that, we are on our way back to Millhaven."

"I could go into Wickham on the bus with the others tonight, spend the night at a motel, and you could pick me up tomorrow when you are ready to head back home."

"No, that's not going to happen. Why can't you just allow us to use the bungalow tonight?"

"Either I go to Wickham on the bus, or I move back into the bungalow. Those are the only options available to you. Take you pick, but one of them will be in place for tonight. Let me know which you prefer." I flounced out of the room and down the stairs before he could deliver the explosion I knew was imminent.

Well, that was clever, I chided myself. I'm out here on the headland and my bag, including my computer, remains upstairs in the back room. Going back upstairs to collect them isn't an option for the moment. A stroll along the headland took me as far as the camping ground where I sat under a tree for about half an hour. I can't stay here all day, I told myself. Besides, I need of a coffee. I could go back to the bungalow for a cup of the instant variety, but the machine at the clubhouse makes a nicer brew.

As I crossed the Esplanade near the clubhouse, I saw Ben striding along the path from the clubhouse to the house where the officers were billeted. "Now is my chance," I told the universe. I jogged to backdoor, raced up the stairs, collected my gear and was downstairs again in about a minute flat. The coffee in my take-away cup sloshed around a bit as I hurried back to the Esplanade. A brisk walk and I was back in the bungalow's kitchen sipping coffee while my computer booted up.

This was why I needed to come back to the bungalow, not because I didn't want someone else sleeping here. I wanted time and solitude to look at what was on that memory stick I copied, and those forensic results Emily sent me. It wasn't difficult to choose which one to look at first: the memory stick's information. And interesting it was. So interesting, it would take me a while to comprehend some of it.

A stroll along the headland in the cool night air at dusk provided opportunity to ponder the stick's information. A portion of it might relate to offshore bank accounts, but it requires someone wiser than I to sort it out. A large silver four-wheel drive wagon on its way to the clubhouse passed by, the trappings of a hire car visible even in the soft evening light. "Probably the new commanding officer moving in ready to takeover tomorrow," I told the night as I continued back to the bungalow.

I was searching the fridge for inspiration for dinner when a knock on the front door interrupted my culinary pursuit. Ben and his brother, Neil, stood on the doorstep. "We thought you might like to join us for dinner," Ben chirped. The caterers' idea of dinner far surpassed anything I might conjure up. It was an amicable interlude and, when dinner was over, we adjourned to the incident room upstairs. My inclusion in superficial discussion of the investigation to date, was obvious for what it was: an attempt to smooth my ruffled feathers and win me back onside. After about an hour of playing the game, I announced I was going back to the bungalow.

Neil insisted on driving me back. Ben climbed into the back seat. I expected them to drive off again as soon as they dropped me off. That wasn't the case. Ben opened the rear hatch and removed an awkward looking long object. Then Neil drove off, leaving me with a sheepish-looking Ben. "There's only one bed, so I brought my own ... Might need a hand to set it up though." He followed me in. I pointed to the small entrance foyer, and he began wrestling with setting up the camp stretcher … while I closed my computer and took it to the bedroom.

*****

We returned to the clubhouse in time for breakfast this morning. I was surprised to see last night's late bus still parked at the house, and commented on it. Neil explained, "The plane was delayed, the bus arrived after midnight with only half the expected contingent on board. The driver stayed overnight and will return to Wickham this morning to drop some of the previous mob at the airport and collect the remainder of my lot."

That was handy for me. "Ben, you and Neil have a bit to get through this morning. I might hop on the bus and spend the morning in Wickham. Give me a call when you are ready to leave to arrange where to meet."

"We should be finished here by mid-morning." Neil looked at Ben for confirmation before continuing. "Then I'll drive him in to collect his vehicle and you. We might all have coffee or lunch together, depending on the time, before you head out." Today the gods appear to be in my corner.

I grabbed a cab to the hospital as soon as I arrived in Wickham. A different receptionist didn't need persuading to call

Xander to the lobby. "Dad is conscious and doing well," he told me. "He still has some way to go before they release him, but the worst is behind us. I haven't mentioned anything about Gina, but I... it seems as though he does not want to discuss Gina with me."

"Do you think he is able to handle the truth yet?" After thinking about it for a few seconds, Xander nodded. "Okay. I'll play it by ear as we go along, but I will only tell him as much as I think he can handle. I need you there while I talk to him."

Frank gave me a wan smile as I walked towards him. He went to shake hands, but saw the drip sticking out of it and dropped his hand again. "Thanks for coming. Xander tells me I have you to thank for my being here and still alive. That seems like going a long way beyond ..."

"Put it down to luck. I happened to be in the right place at the right time, but you look a lot better than the last time I saw you. Frank, I need to talk to you about a few things, but I need you to stop me if there's any discomfort, or it becomes too hard to handle." After a glance at Xander, he nodded and motioned for me to continue. "Has anyone from the police been to speak to you?" He shook his head.

"If they did, I wasn't in any condition to know about it." He raised his eyebrows in question at Xander, who confirmed no police had been.

"I'm certain someone will come soon. When they do, it's important you act surprised at anything and everything they tell you. It's important they aren't aware you know certain things. They will know it came from me, and that will not be good."

They both assured me of the confidentiality of our discussions this morning. Time to move onto the hard stuff.

"Can you identify the person in this photo?" I showed him the photo of Gina on my phone. A darkness flashed across his features. He didn't flinch, but maintained his hold on the phone and his focus on the image.

"That's Gina. Is she dead?"

"Yes. I'm sorry."

"Are you sure … sure she is dead?" Not the response I expected, but everyone is different.

"Yes, I'm certain. I'm sorry for your…"

"I don't know what I feel, but it isn't loss. Maybe that's a good thing. Something … something was not right there. I can't explain. Something was going on. That's why I came to you."

"I can tell you her name wasn't Gina Burtell. So far, we don't know who she is. We found several possibilities, but none might turn out to be her real name."

"But you are sure she is dead?"

"Yes. She was murdered in front of me after being chased by two men. If it's any comfort, they too are dead. I shot them." He shrugged, indicating his lack of concern for the men.

"What was she mixed up in? It sounds like something major. Was it drugs?" Xander asked.

"The operation we investigated does involve drugs. Frank, there are other concerning things I need to tell you. Two bodies were founded at a bush campsite. They were identified as your two officers who should have been on duty the night their substitutes were murdered behind the warehouse in Millhaven."

"So, I lost four good officers that night?" I nodded and he continued. "Everything that happened to me after that was a part of this operation she was involved with?"

"It appears so, but there is also suggestion that Gina was running another lesser parallel operation on the side; a rogue operation. I don't deal in speculation, so I don't want to discuss it now. Until I returned to Millhaven later today and dig around a bit more, it remains speculation. What I do need to tell you both is that a considerable number of people are in custody as a result of the police investigation over the last few days. There is no way of knowing whether everyone involved locally has been rounded up. I don't want to alarm either of you, but I feel obliged to warn you to keep vigilant. From what I've seen so far, it's a big operation, they have much to lose, and they are ruthless when it comes to defending it."

Both men were stunned, but managed to ask a few questions. When the question stopped, I suggested Xander might walk me down to reception. He looked surprised, but held the door open for me. "I won't be leaving his side," he told me quietly on our way down.

"Xander, if I'm honest, I'm not sure how safe Millhaven will be for Frank in the immediate future. It will depend on how effective the police are at shutting down this major operation. Please wait here for a moment, Xander. I need to make a quick phone call." He looked surprised when I abandoned him near the reception desk and went to a bank of public pay phones. My call was short. The deal arranged with the usual speed and efficiency, I returned to Xander.

"I need to get back to the centre of town, but there is one last thing I've put in place. When I leave, you should tell who-ever is on the reception desk that a friend named Mitch will be asking after you later today. They should call you down to the lobby to meet him when he arrives. He will have a parcel for you and will need somewhere away from prying eyes to hand it over. When you meet him in the lobby, you must call him 'Mitch', and use the following code to identify yourself: *Sonny mentioned you might call.*"

We stood on the pavement outside the reception area finishing up our meeting when a cab arrived. A single occupant alighted. He gave me a salute of recognition and came towards us. "Xander, this is Mitch. He's arrived a little earlier than I expected. Please give him the code, and then the pair of you go somewhere quiet so he can give you your 'gift'. When this is all over – and we are sure it is all over – you might hand that gift on to me to deal with. Oh, there is another cab arriving. I'll try to grab that one. Mitch, I assume the arrangement is for me to visit Ruby when I get back to town?" He smiled and nodded, and I sprinted to the cab. The woman extricated the last of her four children from the rear of the vehicle as I reached it.

"Anywhere in the main street will do," I told the driver as we left the hospital. A quick visit to a newsagent to buy a large envelope, followed by a visit to the bank to fill the envelope, and I was hiking along Wickham's main street on my way to Ruby's massage parlour. After exchanging a few pleasantries, and the envelope, with Ruby, I continued along the street to the large service station complex at the other end of the block.

It was gone eleven o'clock. No call from Ben yet. Should I go into the diner for a coffee while I wait? While I debated the idea, Ben called. He arrived about ten minutes later. "Let's have an early lunch before we hit the road," he suggested. I didn't argue.

Chapter 25

Ben dropped me at home. After a quick shower and fresh clothes, I headed for my city office. Most people were leaving the city for home at the end of the day. It was almost five o'clock and I would be late home tonight.

My desk bore evidence of Emily's meticulous handiwork: message slips clipped in chronological order, and a pad beside them with various notes taken during my absence. I worked my way through the material until soon after six o'clock. My stomach rumbled. Maybe a call to Emily wouldn't interrupt her work. She answered on the first ring.

"How's your day been, and do you feel like eating?"

"I'm finishing up. What do you have in mind? I craved fish and chips all afternoon."

"Okay; fish and chips at my house around seven o'clock."

I placed our evening meal in the oven to keep warm. An almost over ripe tomato and the remnants of a head of lettuce, once the wilted outside leaves were removed, would improve our meal. Emily arrived about half an hour later. Both of us starving, eating took priority over conversation. Then we took our glasses of white wine out onto the deck and caught up on events.

"First, tell me about your new laboratory. In recent times, you seem to know about stuff other than minerals."

"It's a contract arrangement. The forensic lab at the local police precinct churned out suspect results, and the Ralston lab was overloaded. They decided to privatise the Millhaven lab. My mob won the contract. With some government funding, a state of the art forensics lab was established. I manage both the minerals testing and the forensic laboratories, but forensics take up most of my time. Only one of the former lab's staff came across to me. One old bloke was offered a redundancy and was encouraged to take it. The other bloke I rejected as not sufficiently qualified or competent. That left only one young graduate to come across. Recruiting two more staff took time. When I thought staffing was settled, I discovered I needed one more. The upshot of all that is, I now have an excellent staff. I'm busy, but I'm in seventh heaven working in forensics. Studying for the extra degree was worthwhile. And this new arrangement will help in some of your cases. Even if they are not part of police investigations, I now have a beautiful forensics lab in which I might carry out private analyses when required."

We spent the rest of the evening catching up on the police's investigation and, in particular, Sam's progress with the Millhaven end of things. I walked Emily to her car at about ten o'clock before adjourning to my office. One o'clock rolled around before I knew it. It was time to call it a night.

*****

My day started at a frantic pace and continued that way until I stopped for a late lunch. With a sandwich in one hand and a mouse in the other, I scanned recent online editions of the local newspaper. Only one item caught my eye. It wasn't a direct link, but I suspected relevance to my Hensley case. Time to chat with Jock at Hensley Security Services again. I interrupted his lunch, but he was happy to chat while he ate. 'Caution' was the keyword when talking to Jock.

I couldn't say anything to compromise the police investigation, but I could tell him Frank Hensley was on the mend and Xander continued keeping a close watch over him. After a few minutes telling him nothing much about little of the events of recent days, it was time to raise the issue of the newspaper article. "The article said a local business owner reported the disappearance of funds. He claimed funds were siphoned off over a lengthy period. The owner has commissioned a forensic audit."

"Yeah, I remember the article. What's your interest? Do you think there's a Hensley connection?"

"Maybe; it occurred to me, a security courier service, similar to Hensley's, might provide opportunity for cash to end up somewhere other than its intended destination. Do you know if Hensley's couriers serviced the company in question?"

"No, and I wouldn't. Gina took over running the security courier service. She wasn't about to tell me anything about it. I suppose an idle thought along those lines did cross my mind. Nothing I could do about it though. The files relating to the courier service are in the cabinet over there. It's locked. As far as I know, Gina has the only key. I don't know why Frank lets her takeover the way she does. Anyway, unless you have a key or Gina reappears, we can't access those files."

"Well, that doesn't have to be the case." I checked the cabinet. All drawers were locked. "Jock, you might not be comfortable with what happens next. You should look away or, better still, go for a walk." He studied me for a moment before responding.

"If you are going to do what I think you are, I will stay right here. Go for it. Do you need my help to break into it?"

"No help required, thanks Jock. Just photograph every stage of the operation with my phone in case we need it later." Over my years in the Public Service, I broke into numerous filing cabinets when staff lost or forgot their keys. This was one of the easiest models to open. A couple of minutes later, we were peering at the contents of the top drawer.

"Jesus, it's jammed with files. I didn't know we had so many businesses using the service." Jock ran his fingers across the tops of the file pockets as he spoke. "If these are all client files, what's in the second drawer?" He photographed the top drawer before I closed it and opened the second one. "They look the same; different companies though."

"They are in alphabetical order. This second drawer holds files for businesses in the latter half of the alphabet. Let's see if the company referred to in the article is in here. If it has a file, it will be in the top drawer." Sure enough, there was a file. I pulled on gloves before lifting the file out and placing it on the desk.

"Jock, did you notice how some of the files have coloured flags attached, like this one?"

"Not all of them had those 'flags', but a lot did." I skimmed the documents in the file.

"I need to make a phone call. I'll put this file back in the cabinet first, and we'll close the drawers."

"We haven't checked the bottom drawer."

"No, and we won't until after I make this phone call." Disappointed, he wanted to argue, but I was on my way out the backdoor.

Detective Sam Keller answered on the first ring. "… Yeah, back in town and working again. That's why I'm calling. I think I've discovered something of interest to your Hensley investigation. I'm at Hensley's premises now if you want to join me." She was on her way. I printed out the article that triggered my visit to Hensley's ready for her.

Sam concurred with my thinking about the files. "Two different coloured flags were used. Any clues about that?" Both Jock and I shook our heads. "I'll have my guys talk to relevant people at the flagged companies. I'm off to talk to the owner who initiated the forensic audit. I want to know what alerted him to something being amiss." Sam went outside, made phone calls and, soon after, an officer arrived to list the files with flags. While we waited for him to arrive, Sam asked, "What's in the bottom drawer? I hope it's not more flagged files. We've enough of those."

"We can't get it open," Jock volunteered. "Maybe it's for 'special' files." Sam gave him a look and yanked of the handle. The drawer didn't budge.

"Jock, does this place have tools?" I asked

"Like what?"

"Like a pinch bar, a large hammer, and anything else to get us into that drawer."

Armed with a pinch bar and a mallet, I gave the drawer a solid whack in a spot I knew sometimes opened recalcitrant drawers. I didn't think anything happened, but Sam thought otherwise.

"Have another go. I think I saw it move a bit." I declined.

"We need to attack the source of the problem." The cabinet stood about twenty millimetres out from the wall, but it was impossible to see down behind it. "Give me a hand to move it out a bit." It took all three of us to move it a few millimetres out and skew it around a bit. "Hold it. Let's see if there's anything down there before expending any more energy on it." A vague shape visible in the vicinity of the bottom drawer was enough to initiate a further burst of effort.

Mystery solved. The ingenious arrangement was obvious once the back of the cabinet was visible. A seventy millimetre square of the rear panel was removed. A hasp and staple type fitting attached to the back of the bottom drawer protruded through the opening and was padlocked to the cabinet. Sam took a firm old on the handle of the drawer as I jammed the pinch bar into the lock. One solid whack freed the drawer from its tether.

"Bingo!" I yelled as bits of the locking arrangement flew off. The drawer shot open, and retaliated for its rough treatment by cracking Sam on the shin.

"What's all that stuff?" Jock asked as he peered over Sam's shoulder. "Never saw any of that around here before." Whatever it was, it filled the drawer. Sam flicked through some of the material before answering.

"Dunno … but it looks interesting. I think I might be busy for the next day or two." Photos of the busted lock and the open drawer taken, Sam was on her way out of the place. "Sonny, I'll talk to that business owner about what tipped him off. Then I'll make a start on this stuff. Don't touch anything until my blokes arrive to collect the cabinet."

Her car started and I heard it drive out of the building's carpark. Once it went past along the street out front, I succumbed to temptation.

"Should you be doing that? You told Sam we wouldn't touch anything. I don't want to upset the cops."

"It's okay, Jock. I agreed not to touch anything … while

she was here. I can't help it if she thought I meant something else." Everything I looked at was handwritten, involved lots of figures – most prefixed by a dollar sign. To my untrained eye, it resembled some form of accounting system.

My rummage through the material in the bottom drawer was brief. Two officers arrived, loaded the cabinet onto a trolley and wheeled it out to their van. "Efficient chaps; not talkative though…" Jock commented as they drove out, "and they expected me to help load the bloody thing!" Their officious manner didn't impress either of us. "What was all that stuff anyway?"

"Not sure, Jock; I'm not an accountant. I suspect it is evidence of the opportunity being a part of this business gave Gina. Oh God, Gina… Jock, there is something I can't talk about, and you mustn't know about, until the information is released."

"Oh aye, and what might that be?"

"I can't tell you Gina won't be coming back – ever."

"No-o-o, I never heard anything about that. It will come as a complete surprise when I hear it." His grin spoke volumes, but he was decent enough not to ask questions. "Will Frank come out of all this okay? I minds me own business, but I smelled something rotten around here."

That's a good question. I think enough has happened to clear Frank of any involvement, but I won't raise Jock's hopes by speculating. Another poke about, both upstairs and in the office, produced nothing new, so I returned to my office and dealt with other matters arising while I was away.

Sam rang late to ask if I would be home this evening. Ben called around five o'clock to ask what I fancied for dinner. I told him there might be four of us tonight. Then a call to Emily confirmed she would join us for dinner. She walked into my office as I ended the call. "I was on my way here when you called. Thought you might be interested in looking at all our material relevant to the Hensley case." There was a stack of test results from five bodies and a mountain of other material. We called it quits soon after six o'clock and adjourned to my place to wait for dinner.

It was a balmy night, so we opted to eat out on the deck. Afterwards, conversation worked around to recent investigations, both in Millhaven and Wickham. At Ben's prompting, Sam led off with a report on where her investigation was at. Most of it, I already knew, until her final comments relating to her interview with the business owner following our discovery of the filing cabinet.

A sharp-eyed woman in accounts, filling-in for the financial officer while he was on leave, noticed anomalies and took her concerns to the owner. The structure of their accounts section meant a couple of different staff, as well as the financial officer, looked after various aspects of the accounting function. It resulted in none of them ever having opportunity to view the whole operation. The woman filling in for the financial officer, found anomalies on bank statements held in his office. Deposits did not tally with the deposit slips she prepared. She checked back over some time, and found the anomaly was consistent over a long period. The deposit amounts on the bank statements were less than the amounts on the deposit slips she prepared.

"You would expect the owner to ask the bank for copies of the deposit slips they received," Emily mused. "They would confirm the error and he could take the matter directly to the police, instead of messing about with a forensic audit, which will take forever to complete." After a quick glance at Ben for approval, Sam explained.

"He did approach the bank. They send all their archiving to a facility in the capital city. After he requested the return of those documents, they had to be found and scanned before copies were forwarded. In this case, he needed the original documents, not copies. That required approval from high up the line, and more paperwork, before the request was considered. The owner decided the audit might be the more expedient option."

"There hasn't been much time, but is there any response from the other businesses with flagged files?" My concern was, a business unaware of a possible anomaly, would require time to conduct an internal investigation. It might take ages before they found anything."

"One of the business owners my officers spoke to called me this afternoon. He thinks they have a similar anomaly in their records." Sam addressed her next remark to Ben. "We will follow up with other businesses tomorrow, and impress upon them the urgency of the matter."

"I imagine suggesting they were being skimmed might create a degree of urgency," Emily said. It echoed my thought.

"Thank you, Emily. I think that is the first time tonight I've heard this called what it is: skimming. I don't think it's embezzlement. Hensley's were contractors, not staff, so it could be called skimming … or theft. Either way, if those flagged files indicate the businesses targeted, this was a lucrative sideline indeed." Ben appeared deep in thought as he spoke. I felt a whole lot more was going on in his head than he shared. Maybe a comment challenging his words would bring forth something more.

"I still think a contractor ripping off a client amounts to embezzlement. Calling it 'skimming' doesn't give it the gravitas it deserves." My comment brought murmured agreement from two, but only a shrug from Ben. His detective's mind was busy elsewhere. I longed to know where.

The night ended early, and with no revelations from Ben. While I cleaned up afterwards, my mind replayed everything said during the evening. Were there any clues, however veiled, as to Ben's preoccupation? Nothing enlightening found, I went to bed frustrated and tossed and turned for some time before falling into a restless sleep.

*****

This morning found me less than enthusiastic about the day ahead. I had potential new cases waiting for attention, but I couldn't let go of the Hensley case … not yet, and not until I knew the full story. The drive into my city office gave me time to think, and left me in little doubt today would be devoted to the Hensley case. Where to start, was the question on my mind as I let myself into my office. The blinking red light on my phone flashed like a beacon in the darkened office.

Xander left a message at four o'clock this morning: *An unwelcome visitor came a couple of hours ago while I was out of the room for a brief moment. Thanks to you and Mitch for your gift, I winged him and he fled. Have spoken to hospital and police. Arrangements in place for me to fly Dad out of Wickham at first light. You have my number if we need to talk.*

Does this never end? How entrenched in the country is this mob, and what is the scale of their operation? Then a frightening thought hit me. I checked the time; after nine o'clock. First light today would have been soon after five o'clock. "Probably enough time," I told my empty office as I hit Xander's number… and heaved a sigh of relief when he answered. "Xander, are you and Frank okay? You told the police you were flying him to your place. I don't think that was wise."

"As I checked the plane for take-off, I remembered what you said about the Wickham cops. I rang my business partner. We are joint owners of a houseboat on the Hawkesbury River. He met me at a private airfield about two hours out from the city and drove us to the house boat. We have an old vehicle we leave there, and I've just come into the local village to buy provisions. It's likely we will stay on the boat for a while, or at least until I know it's safe to do something else."

It was a relief, but it didn't allay all my concerns. There's nothing like sharing concerns, even at this early hour of the day. I keyed Ben's number.

Chapter 26

"I need to hear Xander's message," Ben demanded as he walked into my office. "The Wickham police were mystified when I rang them for details of this morning's event."

"What about the Feds? Did you try your brother, Neil? If Neil is now in charge of the case, maybe everything goes through him and not the local cops."

"Of course I tried him. He's not answering." That explains the tension I detected in Ben. Is Neil not answering because something has happened to him?

"Who is second in command? Do you have their number, or that of anyone else in Neil's team?"

"Dunno; and no I don't have other numbers."

"Well, I do. I managed to 'see' a couple of numbers while I wandered around the incident room." He was about to chew me out, but changed his mind and held out his hand. I copied them off my phone and gave the scribbled note to him while he tried Neil's number again. No response, so he tried the first of the numbers I gave him. I overheard a one-sided conversation.

"…I'm trying to reach Commander Richards … Where the hell is he? … Yes, that was me trying to reach him … This is urgent … How about you race over to the house with his phone? … Well, give me the number of someone at the house so I can get a message to him … Son, I have run out of patience; identify yourself so I … Great! Well, direct him to his desk so he can answer his phone when I call the moment I end this conversation … Thank you." He murmured a few obscenities as he waited for Neil to answer.

This was an appropriate time to wander over to the coffee machine in what passes for a kitchen in my office. The racket made by the coffee machine eliminated any chance of overhearing

Ben's conversation with his brother. He was ending the call as I strolled back to my desk with two mugs of coffee. Ben's demeanour hadn't changed much as a result of the call, so I waited for him to make the first move. He drank half his coffee before that happened.

"The Feds know nothing about this morning's incident. The local Wickham cop shop currently is under investigation. Their response to my call this morning could be another nail in their coffin. Anyway, that's not the main thrust of my conversation with Neil. When one of his officers tripped on something on the beach last night, he put his hand out to break his fall and punctured it on a shard of glass in the sand. Another officer took him into the hospital to have it sutured. While they were waiting in A&E, the injured officer noticed a bloke staggering towards a vehicle in the car park. Believing him to be drunk or high, they wanted to stop him driving, and gave chase."

"That would be the bloke Xander claims to have winged. Did they get a good look at him? Members of that mob keep oozing out of the very fabric of the place."

"Not only did they get a good look at him, they also got his registration number. The two officers followed him while they waited for information on ownership of the vehicle to come through. By the time that happened, the vehicle, registered to a Millhaven address, was on the highway and heading for Millhaven. As he approached the town, it seems the bloke realised he had a tail and made sure he lost them. The Feds gave me the car owner's address and a description of the bloke. Sam and her team are on their way now to pick him up."

"If this is another foreign looking bloke, he must know Millhaven well to be able to lose a tail here. If he was badly wounded, he did well to drive all the way to Millhaven and then employ evasive measures without having an accident or collapsing behind the wheel."

"Yeah, that's an interesting point. It seems this one is a local and not foreign looking at all. I'm not sure he was the vehicle's owner. The registration information has the registered owner as a local businessman who has strong community involvement. We'll have to wait to find out what Sam's team discover. See you this evening."

About now might be a good time to visit Hensley Security Services and interrupt Jock's day again. He fielded a string of phone calls while I waited. I heard him tell at least two callers to call the police and speak to the lead detective. Then, the calls ended and Jock slumped in his chair. "It's a madhouse this morning. The phone hasn't stopped."

"I'd make you a coffee, but I'm not sure how to do that here. Is there something I can do while you make yourself a cup?" He tapped the side of his nose and produced a thermos flask from under the desk. Having just finished a coffee, I declined his offer of one from his thermos.

"Well now, Lass, what brings you here today? Surely, there can't be any more for you to find here."

"No, I didn't come to poke about. Today, I'm after information; information about whether a local businessman is a client of Hensley's." I gave him the man's name. Jock responded with the name of the man's business. "You know him?"

"Everyone knows him, or knows of him. He's involved in just about everything that happens in Millhaven. But you wanted to know if he is a client. I don't know about the courier service, and we can't check now the cabinet is gone, but he is one of our Security Services' clients. Now I think on it, I don't think he would use the courier service. His business wouldn't handle much cash. Clients' bills would be large. They would pay by cheque, credit card or direct debit. In his line of business, you'd be a bit suspicious of someone wanting to pay cash for bulk fuel or oil."

"Good point…" There wasn't anything else for me at Hensley's, and Jock began asking difficult questions about Frank Hensley and what was going on. Questions I didn't feel inclined to answer. Citing a fictitious impending meeting, I rushed back to my office to spend the rest of the day typing up my case notes and trying to make sense of the Hensley case so far.

There would be four of us for dinner tonight. I left the office early, having promised everyone a baked dinner, and called at the supermarket on the way home. The aroma of roast lamb filled the house by the time Emily arrived first at six o'clock, and just in time to help prepare the vegetables. Then, we filled in time until the others arrived by discussing the case and Emily's latest forensic analyses.

"A few bits came in today, but not much from Wickham. The interesting stuff was from Millhaven. A number of oil samples taken locally arrived from Sam this afternoon. We are trying to catch up on the backlog of work I inherited. It was tempting to leave them until tomorrow morning, but they had me intrigued. Some of them were just oil. A couple were really interesting. They contained slight traces of cocaine. Better still, further analysis matched them to the samples taken from drums on Riposte Island."

"Ooh, that is interesting. Does Sam know about those samples yet?"

"I sent them through as soon as they were done. She should have them by now. Do you think she will mention them tonight?"

"Well, I don't know about the samples … but I do know what they were doing today. If nothing is forthcoming from Sam or Ben, I might have to engineer a situation that invites them to share." Such a contrivance wasn't required.

As soon as we took our coffee through to the sitting room after dinner, conversation turned to the case. Emily left almost straight away. She later confided she felt it best to leave rather than risk compromising her position in the forensics laboratory. Sam reported on her team's investigations today, and ended by sharing the results of those oil samples.

"What happens now?" Nobody mentioned arrests being made. I was curious about why not. Ben explained.

"We have the business owner and his business under surveillance. The wounded bloke was arrested after an ambulance dropped him at the hospital. He collapsed in the street and a bystander called the ambulance. The guy was shot in the upper chest/shoulder area and had lost a lot of blood. Once his injury was identified as a gunshot wound, the medicos called the police. His wound became infected, and he is in a bad way. They admitted him and we have him under guard. He was delirious and babbling … about getting back to work because they would be busy tonight."

"That could mean anything, or nothing. I'm inclined to think your boys might have a busy night ahead." Sam's phone rang as I finished speaking. She took the call out onto the deck, and returned grim-faced.

"I have to go. Activity is stepping up at that fuel depot. My guys think something is about to happen. I need to be there." Ben nodded his approval, and she jogged to her car.

What happened next came as no surprise. Ben announced he should be there too – in case they needed a hand with anything. Within moments, they were gone. The house was silent, and I was at home alone. It will be another frustrating night waiting to hear how things went at the fuel depot.

*****

Today, I heard nothing more about the case until Ben called at about three o'clock to say he was bringing takeaway for dinner and would arrive early. I asked how things panned out after they left my place last night.

"Eh? Oh yeah, last night's operation… It went well. I'll tell you about it later."

He arrived, loaded with carrier bags of food, just before six o'clock. The food went into the oven to keep warm and we took our drinks out onto the deck. Already sliding behind the distant hills, the sun's bite disappeared as the first cool breeze of the day replaced it. We sat in silence sipping our drinks for a while before Ben spoke.

"The population in our lock-up increased by a few last night. A certain local businessman and five others were arrested. Thanks to the information Xander gave you, a certain Wickham police officer is now an ex-officer and behind bars. Meanwhile, in a certain distant southern city, two men showing particular interest in Xander's home are now in custody."

A sombre mood settled over the group as we sat in the sitting room after dinner. It should have been a joyous occasion. The Hensley case and its associated operations were wrapped up, at least at the local level anyway. Emily stirred in her chair and cleared her throat. "It's been an interesting case, almost like watching a magic show."

"I know what you mean," Sam agreed. "Everything about the case seemed to be done with smoke and mirrors. Nothing was real."

Emily agreed. "It was like watching a magician creating one illusion after another. Nothing real; everyone and everything masquerading as something else. Frank, Xander and Jock were the only ones who were what they purported to be. They were real. Everything about the case was an illusion. It was a whole lot of illusions coming together to create the one big illusion that became the Hensley case. Gina Burtell was an illusion. She wasn't Gina Burtell. 'Gina' was a persona she adopted, as was her role as a wife helping her husband run his business. Her interest was in feathering her own nest – made possible by the illusion of the secure courier service she ran. She recruited so many people to take care of so many unsavoury 'jobs' for her. The transport company clients' employees were a convenient distribution network."

"Don't forget, the image of that local businessman as an upstanding pillar of the community also was pure illusion." I received murmured agreement from the others.

"…And those police officers only created the illusion of upholding the law in the Wickham area. Most of them were no more trust-worthy than Gina or that fine upstanding businessman," Sam added in disgust.

"Well, it's over," I said. "One by one, we've peeled back the layers, to uncover the deceit and reveal the truth. Once you know how a magician does it, you shatter the illusion."

"I still don't understand why Gina was killed. She appeared

to be a key player in the organisation's 'business' operation. Have I missed something?" Emily asked.

I explained. "She fell afoul of the mob on two fronts. They were unhappy about the secondary scheme involving the security courier service she was running here in Millhaven. It wasn't so much that she ran it, as the fact she ran it independently *and kept the profits.* They wouldn't object to her paying it into the mob, but keeping it for herself went against their principles. Nevertheless, the main reason she was eliminated were her skimming activities. It appears she also was skimming both product and cash from the mob's drug distribution operation."

Sam added to the explanation. "It's likely Gina realised things were going bad for her. Her so-called visit to family was her failed attempt to disappear before the mob caught up with her." Emily nodded sagely as she digested the information.

"Then why did they abduct Hensley, and I suppose, who instigated it?" Ben cut in as Sam search for an appropriate answer for Emily.

"The 'who' part of your question remains unclear. I believe it was Burtell. Because of his suspicions, Hensley called in Sonny. Although Burtell already had disappeared from Millhaven, she was concerned an investigation might uncover more than she wanted sooner than she needed. She probably organised for the mob or some of her lackeys to do the actual abduction. I suspect they planned to eliminate Hensley and arrange for his death to point to Gina. They had to get the timing right. But, before all that could happen, they already were onto Gina's extracurricular activities in Millhaven. We ruined the mob's plans by rescuing Hensley, and Gina had to pay the price for crossing the mob. At least, that's the way I see it but, like so many details of this case, Now that others are responsible for winding it up, we might never know the whole story."

Emily was deep in thought for a few moments before speaking. "That 'magic show' impacted so many lives. Those shattered illusions and the truth we revealed impacted so many innocent people. But, in spite of the hurt and grief it caused, removing those illusions – whatever and whoever they were – makes this a better place for everyone in the long run. Don't you agree?" she asked.

We did, and raised our coffee mugs in salute. After another hour or so of nothing of consequence, they all left. Out on the deck with a single malt, I spent a quiet time with my thoughts, and coming to terms with all the events over the last however many days.

*****

A couple of days later, Troy Donaldson's chatty email brought news of his return to the UK, and of a major new archaeological dig posting somewhere outside Rome.

Towards the end of the month, Xander flew into Millhaven with his father. I had coffee with them and was impressed by how well Frank looked, and how happy Jock was to have him back. In accordance with our arrangement, Xander handed back the 'gift' I organised for him. Looks like I'll take a trip to Wickham to visit 'Mitch' in the near future. I hope his refund on the return of the 'gift' is reasonable.

Life seemed to settle back into its usual pattern, until about six weeks after I closed my case file. A certain businessman, out on bail while preparing his case, disappeared. Evidence uncovered a few days later showed him boarding an overseas flight under a false passport. Strange how his Australian bank accounts held no more than a few hundred dollars. Records show massive transfers of funds to offshore accounts, to banks renowned for their security and confidentiality.

Tonight, for the first time, dinner was to be at Sam's place. Emily couldn't join us. At the last minute, Sam had to cancel in favour of visiting a murder scene. Ben and I settled for steak and salad on my deck. Life was back to normal … and just the way I like it.

The End

Other Books by the Author

An Ancient Solution
A public Service
Missing!
Connections
A Different Obsession

About the Author

Neive Denis is the creator of the series featuring the Private Investigator, Sonoma Whittington. Neive Denis is the pen name of a writer who was lured from her usual genre to focus on the mystery and excitement that are a part of Sonoma Whittington's world. Neive came into being specifically for this series and, for the moment at least, intends remaining faithful to only stories from Sonny's case files.

This series tells of the intrigue and scrapes – some on occasion life threatening – that are part of the life of Sonoma Whittington, an Australian Private Investigator based in a Central Queensland coastal city. However, Sonny doesn't confine her escapades to Australia, and that provides Neive with an opportunity to weave some of her other areas of interest into Sonny's hair-raising adventures.

See more about Neive Denis and her work at
www.neivedenis.com

or contact her at
contact@neivedenis.com